THE SWEETEST DISCOVERY

LAURA ANN

UNTITLED

"The Sweetest Discovery"

Three Sisters Cafe #4

To my twinners.
I'm in awe every time I look at you
and see what wonderful young women
you are becoming.
Thank you for allowing me along
on the journey. It's been such an honor.

ACKNOWLEDGMENTS

No author works alone. Thank you, Tami.
You make it Christmas every time
I get a new cover. And thank you to my
Beta Team. Truly, your help with my
stories is immeasurable.

NEWSLETTER

You can get a FREE book by joining my
Reading Family!
Every week we share stories, sales
and good old fashioned fun.
Go to lauraannbooks.com to sign up!

PROLOGUE

*M*ichael leaned his shoulder against the wall, a soft smile playing on his lips. He was excited for Maeve. She and Ethan would be very happy together. Anyone with a lick of sense knew that and had known it since they were all kids together.

Ethan's extroverted carefreeness and Maeve's more watchful and reserved personality would keep their relationship balanced. She would pull him down from the clouds and he would push her out of her comfort zone.

As witnessed by this morning's surf lesson, Michael thought with a chuckle.

"Cake?"

Michael nodded as Gavin handed him a plate, then leaned against the wall himself. "Thanks," he murmured, taking a large bite. Geez, his cousin could bake. It paid to be related to the Harrisons. World class food for free. No one could top that.

"What's got that smoke coming out of your ears?" Gavin questioned.

Michael snorted. "Smoke? The wheels aren't turning that hard."

Gavin shrugged. "Something's churning in there. Figuring out your lesson plans for tomorrow?"

Michael chuckled. "Nah. They're set for the year. Though, how to keep the kids engaged is another story. This is the time of year when they start feeling like it'll all last forever and they get antsy."

"I thought that was only the little guys," Gavin said. "In middle school they have sports and other activities. Doesn't that help?"

Michael shook his head. "Nope. They still can't sit still."

"I'm so glad I don't have your job."

"I don't know…putting out fires and teaching literature to tweens and teens carries about the same amount of danger."

Gavin's laughter was heavy and low. He was a large guy and his voice, though usually quiet, had a depth to it that few others could pull off. "I'll stick with the fires."

"And the weight benches." Michael frowned. "Is it my imagination, or are you getting bigger?"

Gavin smirked. "It's the off season," he said. "Gotta do something to keep busy."

Michael nodded. "Understandable. Wildfires are a lot less frequent during the winter and I don't usually hear of too many house or business fires around here."

Gavin shook his head. "Nope. Not too many. Which is a blessing… and a curse." He gave a jerk of his chin. "I'm gonna go get a drink. Want anything?"

"Nah. I'm fine here in my little corner, thanks."

Shaking his head good-naturedly, Gavin weaved through the crowd.

Michael sighed and set himself back into people watching. Slowly, his group of friends was starting to pair off. First Aspen, followed by Mason and Harper. Now it was Ethan and Maeve. What was interesting was how long they'd all known each other, and the last two engagements were the result of people finding love within their group.

He tilted his head, letting his eyes linger on the other women he was friends with. There was Riley, of course. She was close with his cousins. She was peppy and fun and her light blue eyes would attract any man's attention.

Michael blew out a breath. *Nope. Not that one.* She was his friend and he never found himself wanting to push those boundaries.

A flash of red caught his attention and Michael watched Brielle throw her head back and laugh at something Jayden was saying. Brielle was also beautiful, in her own way. Long, wavy hair and brown eyes. She was spunky, said what was on her mind and loved to try and "keep up with the boys," as she put it.

Michael shook his head again. That wasn't for him. He liked his quiet life, and time spent with Brielle was anything but quiet.

He let his eyes wander again. His mother would be so disappointed in his lack of interest. He was one of the oldest of the cousins and now that there were two getting married, she'd be pushing him to find his significant other. But single females seemed to be getting thin on the ground, at least amongst those he was familiar with.

For the umpteenth time, he debated whether he should look to start next fall in a bigger city. There was something to be said for the peaceful familiarity of the small beach town he grew up in. Michael had his students for multiple years and got to be good friends with a few. He enjoyed knowing all the parents and being able to work one-on-one with children in a way that larger schools and areas couldn't handle.

But knowing everyone since birth also makes for a hard social life.

"We're so glad you made it!" Aspen gushed, jerking Michael's attention away from his musing. Aspen was hugging someone at the front door and Michael frowned, unable to figure out who had been missing.

Dark, nearly black, corkscrew curls were pulled up into a bun with a few stray spirals framing an oval face.

Quinn, Michael said to himself. He'd forgotten about her. She was fairly new to Seagull Cove and Michael had yet to be introduced, though they'd attended a couple of events together as a large group. Quinn had opened an antique shop in town, which was a perfect addition to every small coastal city along the Pacific coastline.

He watched her smile shyly and tuck one of the curls behind her ear, only for it to spring right back where it wanted to be.

Michael laughed softly to himself. He couldn't see her eye color from his corner, but they looked much lighter than her hair, creating an interesting contrast. Her skin was a study in porcelain, giving her a slightly paranormal look. She could easily pull off a vampire anytime she wanted with a simple swipe of red lipstick.

She was taller than Aspen and willowy in a way the Italian Harrisons lacked. While no one would ever mistake Quinn for anything but a woman, her curves were much more subtle.

Michael found himself slowing down in his cake consumption as he watched her. Something about the line of her jaw and the tenderness of her smile kept his attention. Her movements were fluid and elegant and when she finally spoke, it seemed that her hands were an active part of the conversation.

There were scores of poems and ballads written about women just like Quinn. Her ethereal beauty was the kind that Medieval men went to war over and Michael could just see some soldier declaring his undying love to her before shipping across seas.

"There's that smoke again."

Michael blinked, finally wrenching his mind out of his too wild imagination. His love of stories and fantasy didn't always serve him well in social situations. "Are you feeling more hydrated now?" Michael asked, hoping no one had noticed his staring.

Gavin huffed. "Yeah. But I'm about ready to blow this joint. The cake's gone and no one will stop talking about dates and dresses." He raised an eyebrow. "Do school teachers ever play hooky?"

Michael cleared his throat, still trying to force his brain into an appropriate line of thought. "Uh, yeah. Sure. I'm done here." His eyes flashed to those dark curls one more time and his curiosity went up yet another notch. Maybe he hadn't quite ruled out all the possibilities in this town.

He'd muse on it for a while, but he was starting to think that a trip to the newest shop in town just might be in his future.

CHAPTER 1

"And yet another lantern," Quinn muttered to herself as she tried to find room on the shelf for her newest addition. While she personally adored a vintage lantern, they weren't selling quite as fast as she was able to acquire them. "Actually…" She continued grumbling. "They're not selling at all."

She sighed, pushed the inventory around until it all fit and headed back to her box of treasures. When she'd left her job as a teacher on the East Coast and moved to Oregon to open an antique shop, she'd had grand dreams of becoming so popular she'd be featured on television shows and travel vlogs around the world.

Reality had been a cruel mistress, and instead, Quinn had found herself barely scraping by after paying the bills every month. It didn't help that her shop was tiny and the sign out front wasn't nearly as eye catching as she wanted it to be. But how could she upgrade if she couldn't make any money?

It takes money to make money.

A grin pulled at Quinn's lips. That had always been one of her grandfather's favorite sayings. She wished he would say it to her again, but he'd passed several years ago, leaving her alone, which was exactly why she'd had no support system when it came to fighting for her position at her last job.

Shaking her head, Quinn forced the dark thoughts out of her head. "It always takes time to build a dream," she reminded herself. She'd only been open for six months. Businesses sometimes took years to get off the ground. "At least you're paying the bills," she continued speaking to the empty store. "You might not be gaining ground, but you're not losing it either."

She glanced at the clock, noting that it was still two hours before closing. Maybe, if she was lucky, there'd be a small burst of customers during the dinner hour. *One can always hope.* She grabbed her duster from behind the front desk and started walking through the shop, slowly shifting the dust around.

She'd learned from hard experience that the dust in a coastal town didn't really go away. Between the sand on the beach and the ocean wind, dust was an everyday part of life here in Seagull Cove.

The bell above the door chimed and Quinn turned, a smile quickly crossing her face. "Welcome," she called out, hurrying to the front. She forced herself to slow a little. *Don't want to frighten them by being overeager.*

Three elderly women walked in and Quinn rubbed her mental hands in glee. They were always the ones to spend the most in a shop like hers. "How can I help you?" Quinn asked, setting the duster on the counter.

"Do you have any doilies?" one of the women asked.

Quinn held back a groan. Doilies. What was it about those lacey little things that grandmas liked so much? *They're cheap.* Quinn smiled at the thought, but tried to present it like it was in response to the question. "Of course. Allow me to show you."

The three women chattered quietly behind her as Quinn led them to a curio cabinet where she had porcelain dishes, crystal knickknacks and, of course, the desired doilies, on display. "Anything visible is for sale," Quinn clarified. "If you want me to reach something that's under another antique, just let me know."

She started to walk away, leaving the women to look at their leisure, but a hand on her arm stopped her.

"Thank you, sweetie," the woman said with a soft smile. The lines around her eyes deepened as her mouth widened. "You know…you remind me a lot of my granddaughter."

Quinn's smile was much more genuine this time. "That's very sweet, thank you."

"Please tell me you don't mean the granddaughter who ran off and married that bozo in Vegas?" one of the other women piped up.

Quinn's smile fell.

"Now you hush," the original speaker scolded. She turned back to Quinn. "You pay her no mind. Just because my granddaughter made a fool of herself, doesn't mean she wasn't beautiful. Just like you."

"The trouble is, she knew she was beautiful." The other woman snickered.

The one speaking to Quinn rolled her eyes. "At least I expect Avery to grow up," she called to her friend. "That's more than can be said for you, Martha."

The woman who was teasing huffed and began looking at the display again.

The first woman patted Quinn's arm. "You're stunning. Don't let anyone tell you otherwise." She lowered her voice and leaned in conspiratorially. "And also don't let anyone use that to their advantage."

Quinn's smile had turned brittle and she hoped the woman couldn't read her discomfort in her eyes. "Thank you," she said tightly. "I'll remember."

After patting her arm one more time, the woman returned to her friends and Quinn walked on stiff legs back to the front of the shop. Stunning. Bah! Who cared? Quinn tucked one of her tightly ringletted curls behind her ear, though she knew from plenty of experience that it wouldn't stay there.

She hated it when people spoke about her looks. She knew some of her features were…unique. But there were plenty of prettier and more sophisticated women out in the world. Why did people have to pick on her?

The curl she'd tucked back sprang out and softly hit the side of Quinn's face. She winced, though the touch hadn't hurt. But it reminded her too much of... Quinn shook her head. *No*, she scolded herself. *I'm not letting Adam have any more brain space. He's taken up too much of my life already.*

Picking her duster back up, Quinn went back to work while keeping an eye on her customers. The next couple of hours went slowly, though she had a few people in and out. Hopefully, patronage would pick up as the tourist season hit in the next couple of months.

The Oregon Coast in the late winter and early spring wasn't exactly a huge draw. *Cold* and *damp* were descriptions that landed on very few people's dream vacation lists. A few diehards came through, but her new friends warned Quinn that the amount of people wouldn't pick up until May or June.

Let's just hope I can wait that long, she thought.

Finally, she turned the sign to "closed" on the door and locked up. After triple checking every entrance to the storefront, Quinn pulled out her bike and headed home. She had a car, but unless it was raining, she used her bike as a way to get in her exercise.

What would have been a seven minute commute in the car was more like twenty minutes on the bike, but it always helped her feel better when she got out and got her body moving.

Punching in the code on her garage, Quinn parked her bike against the wall, closed the garage door and headed inside. Once there, her evening ritual began. She picked up the baseball bat she kept at the garage entrance and walked into the house, checking that all was still locked up tight and that she was indeed alone. Once she felt relatively safe, she put the bat back where it belonged and headed to the kitchen to make dinner.

Flipping on the television to make a little noise, Quinn sat down with her plate and zoned out while she ate. After finishing, she washed her dishes by hand, placed them in the drainer, grabbed a cookie from the cupboard and her current read and settled on the couch.

Fifteen minutes later, she sighed and tossed the book away from her. Most of the time there was something so comforting about having a routine, but other days, she found herself struggling. She didn't used to be so strict in her behavior. She loved to dream and imagine and create...but Adam had stolen more than brain space from Quinn. He'd taken safety and replaced it with fear. He'd taken her whimsy and replaced it with logic. He'd stolen her dreams and replaced them with strategy.

Leaning forward, Quinn put her head in her hands. "No more," she chanted. "No more...please no more..."

* * *

"So your assignment tonight..." Michael trailed off when his class groaned. He smirked. "We're three quarters of the way through the school year," he reminded the group of middle school students. "Did you really think you wouldn't have homework?"

"Maybe we're just hoping that you're running out of material," a boy from the back called.

Everyone snickered at his comment.

Michael smiled in return. "Sorry. I never run out of material." His smile widened when the kids made another fuss. "Read the rest of the story and we'll discuss how the themes carry through the end. Also, come prepared to talk about symbolism. What we started out with might not be how we end."

The bell rang and the kids moved faster than they had for the last fifty minutes. Desks were cleared and sneakers skidded across linoleum with enough speed to make a Kentucky Derby horse jealous.

Michael shook his head with a chuckle, then walked around his desk and plopped into his seat with a sigh. He tried not to sit down while he was teaching because he felt that it helped engage the students when he was up and moving. But each year, the relief he felt when he finally sat down was getting stronger and stronger.

He pushed a hand through his hair. He probably needed a haircut, but he'd been enjoying the slightly longer look. *Because it makes you look younger,* he thought. Michael rolled his eyes at the thought. Okay…so he was pushing thirty. That didn't make him old…did it?

"Probably depends on who you ask," he muttered to himself. Waking up his computer, he pulled up the pages he needed in order to start sorting essay grades. His eyes strayed to the stack of papers he needed to finish reading. The idea of spending his entire evening mired in poorly written papers about Gary Paulsen was far from enticing.

Michael enjoyed teaching. He really did. Fiction, nonfiction, fantasy, contemporary…it didn't matter. He loved literature and he loved sharing it with others, particularly kids. But sometimes…the tedious parts of the job got to him.

Teaching the history of *Moby Dick* was fascinating. Reading teenagers' interpretations was a lesson in patience. Most of the youth he worked with didn't care at all about the tales, which meant their writing efforts were less than stellar. But every once in a while, Michael would come across a student who had the same head for words that he did, and that helped him keep going in his job.

"Not this year," he muttered, pulling the stack of papers over and trying to guess how many he had left. He'd already started the grading process a couple days ago, thank goodness, so he didn't have nearly as many now, but he still wasn't looking forward to slogging through the last of them.

Just as he began reading, his phone buzzed and he glanced at the screen, seeing a text come through.

Need an afternoon sugar high? Aspen has a new flavor…

Michael chuckled. His cousin Jayce was a restless soul. He was a photographer and also helped out at the Gingerbread Inn that Michael's parents ran. But none of that kept Jayce from bouncing around like a kid who'd had too many soft drinks. "You don't need an afternoon pick me up," Michael muttered, even though he was typing a response.

Sounds good to me. What time?

No time like the present.

Michael eyed the clock and his stack of papers. It's not like there was anything happening tonight that would keep him from grading the papers then. His social calendar was embarrassingly sparse, though Michael hated to admit it.

Be there in five.

Grabbing his shoulder bag, he stuffed everything he needed inside and walked out of his classroom, locking the door behind him. It took him almost ten minutes, rather than the predicted five, to arrive at Aspen's shop, The Three Sisters Cafe.

Aspen and her two sisters, Estelle and Maeve, were also Michael's cousins. They were one of the largest families in their small town of Seagull Cove, and featured prominently since their family had owned the Gingerbread Inn for generations.

The picturesque, Queen Anne-style mansion sat grandly on a bluff, overlooking the town and the ocean. It had been built by Michael's great-great grandfather and was now passed down to his own parents.

In fact, the inn was a key component in Michael's parents getting married. When his mother, Grace, had come to help her grandmother one Christmas, Michael's dad, Enoch, had been working as the handyman at the inn. They both claimed it was love at first sight, at least as adults. They had known each other as children, but hadn't been close. Once they were older and met again, apparently sparks had flown.

Michael grinned. Call it sappy, but he kind of enjoyed the story of his parents getting together. It involved a thief and a few other interesting bits that made it a little more like an adventure novel than a romance, so he felt little guilt in enjoying the retelling.

"Michael, my man!" Jayce hollered when Michael got inside, shutting out the cold, winter wind. "What took you so long?" Jayce came over and slapped his cousin's shoulder.

If Michael had been a smaller man, he might have stumbled at the contact, but beneath all his education, he was actually pretty decent sized, thanks to his father. His quiet demeanor and head for books definitely came from his mother, however. "Got stuck talking to Mr. Colson as I headed to my car," Michael explained.

Jayce rolled his eyes. "How long is that guy gonna stick around? He was ancient when we were in school. He's gotta be at least a hundred."

Michael gave his cousin a look. "I think he's only in his seventies. That's hardly ancient."

Jayce shook his head. "Old is as old does."

Michael scowled. "What in the world does that mean?"

"It means that we're aging as we stand here, cuz. Let's get up and get some cake!" Jayce rubbed his hands together and began walking toward the front.

Michael chuckled and shook his head. He wasn't sure whether he should admire his cousin's care-free attitude, or pity him. *Or maybe just pity any woman who ends up with him.*

Michael rubbed the back of his neck as they waited in line. He couldn't help but turn and lean just a little so he could see through the front window to a store halfway down the block. Treasures of Seagull Cove. The store had opened last fall and with it, had brought to town one of the most beautiful women Michael had ever seen.

But despite his empty social calendar, he had yet to meet the beauty face to face. He'd crossed her path a couple of times at gatherings with his friends and cousins, but not so much as a "hello" had ever passed from him to her.

Maybe it's time to change that?

"Oof." Michael wheezed when Jayce slapped his back again. "Dude. Are you trying to kill me?" Michael rotated his shoulder. He was positive it would be sore tomorrow.

"What's got your head in the clouds?" Jayce asked, his eyes on the menu.

"Nothing," Michael said quickly. He wasn't about to tell his loud-mouthed cousin about his interest in the new girl. That was asking for a world of hurt. Michael's mom was already getting bolder in her hints that it was time for him to settle down. Having Jayce blab that Michael had a potential crush would make life unbearable.

"Well, then, come on. It's our turn."

Michael put his focus back on getting a slice of cake and less on a curly-haired woman he barely knew. Maybe tonight while he was grading papers, he could decide whether or not he wanted to try and meet her officially. At least that thought should make his work more palatable...he hoped.

CHAPTER 2

"Another day…another quiet afternoon," Quinn murmured as she went through her usual dusting routine. She dusted every day. Every. Day. Mostly because it was quiet enough that there was nothing else to do. Maybe she needed to take up another hobby? Something she could do while sitting at the front desk waiting for tourists to enter.

She pursed her lips and swept the feather duster over a hurricane lamp. This one was bright blue and absolutely stunning. If she didn't need the money, Quinn would take this one home and add it to her own collection. She loved blue glass. There was something so peaceful about the color and now that she lived by the ocean, she loved it even more.

Her tiny cottage needed some major upgrading, but it had been livable when she'd arrived. Once her collection had been placed just right over the fireplace mantel, Quinn hadn't cared at all that the hardwood needed a new stain and the windows weren't quite able to keep out all the cold. She'd replace things when her business got off the ground, but just seeing what was left of her collection after the… disaster…was enough to help her feel at home.

Her cell phone rang and Quinn pulled it out of her back pocket, accepting the call. "Treasures of Seagull Cove," she said cheerily. "This is Quinn. How can I help you?"

"Is this the lovely young woman I spoke to yesterday?" a voice asked.

"Is this the sweet woman who compared me to her granddaughter?" Quinn teased back.

There was soft laughter on the other side of the line, letting Quinn know the joke had gone over well. "I'm so glad you remember," the woman said. "I don't know that I actually introduced myself, but I'm Agatha McCain."

"Nice to meet you, Agatha," Quinn said politely. She began moving her duster around again. "What can I help you with?"

"Well, I wonder…do you ever retrieve antiques at auction houses?"

Quinn frowned. "At times."

"Would you be interested in doing so on commission?"

The feather duster fell to Quinn's side. "Can I ask exactly what you have in mind, Mrs. McCain?"

"There's a bureau, an antique bureau that I've wanted for years. The owner recently passed away and before I could speak to anyone, it was sent to the auction house, who is taking care of the estate's belongings." Mrs. McCain coughed and Quinn held the phone away from her ear for a moment until the sound calmed down. "Anyway, I'd like to go purchase the piece, but I don't get around very well anymore."

A picture of the woman, slightly hunched and shuffling her feet, came to mind and Quinn nodded. She could see how traveling to pick up furniture might be a difficult thing. "Are you wanting to hire me to go bid on the piece and bring it back to you?"

"That's exactly what I want!" Mrs. McCain exclaimed, her voice eager. "You see, the bureau is said to be part of Sir Francis Drake's ship the *Pelican*. He explored our coastline in the sixteenth century, looking for a northwest passage."

Quinn's eyes widened and she whistled low. "How in the world did the bureau get into someone's estate?"

"I'm not actually sure," Mrs. McCain muttered. "The woman who owned it was an old school chum of mine." She snorted. "Though, she turned into an old, righteous biddy in her old age."

Quinn nearly choked on her laughter. "I take it, you didn't stay friends?"

"Not even close," Mrs. McCain stated emphatically. "She married some rich fisherman and stuck up her nose at the rest of us." Mrs. McCain sighed. "Though, I did try to visit her a time or two. Poor Valerie never had children and I could tell she was lonely."

Quinn nodded along to the story. This was far more interesting than anything she had ever done before. "So, your friend passed away, and now you want her furniture, but you have to buy it at auction."

"Exactly. Do you think you can do that for me? I'm sure it's going to cost an arm and a leg, but with your expertise in antiques, you should be able to know what it's worth and help me get a decent price."

Quinn grimaced. She wasn't really much of a haggler. That's what she enjoyed about having a store. Most people simply paid what the ticketed price told them, though there were always a few who tried for something more. But she preferred to simply take care of business and the idea of fighting with aggressive bidders had her stomach turning in knots.

"I'm willing to pay you handsomely to retrieve the item," Mrs. McCain continued. "I realize it would be out of your way and you'd have to close down the shop to go to the auction."

"What did you have in mind?" Quinn asked, her curiosity getting the better of her. When Mrs. McCain named her sum, Quinn nearly fell over. She grabbed the edge of the closest shelf to help keep herself on her feet. The amount was enough to help give her a decent cushion for several months. Probably enough to help her get by until the tourist season really got underway.

"The piece is large," Mrs. McCain said. "You'd need a truck of some sort and...I hate to say this...but you'd probably need to take some muscle with you as well."

Quinn blinked. "Muscle?"

"Yes. A man," Mrs. McCain explained. "A slender thing like yourself isn't going to be able to handle the piece. It's bigger than you would think."

Quinn rubbed her forehead. This was all going too fast. She needed a little time to think, but… "When is the auction?" she asked.

"Three days from now."

Quinn choked again. *Guess there's not time to think this over after all.* "I, uh…"

"I know it's last minute, dearie, but I would be so grateful if you would help an old woman out."

Quinn was starting to feel like Mrs. McCain wasn't quite as old as she pretended. She was railroading Quinn in a very clear manner and was coming out successful. Really, when it came down to it, Quinn knew she couldn't turn down this opportunity. She needed the boost…badly. "I'd love to take this on for you, Mrs. McCain. If you'll just tell me the name of the auction house, the name of the piece and your budget, we'll get this all settled."

Quinn spent the next half hour figuring out all the details for her upcoming trip. Well…mostly all the details.

After the conversation was over and Quinn put her phone back in her pocket, she found herself a mixture of excitement and worry. The idea of going to an auction that held actual antique pieces was thrilling and she looked forward to seeing the estate of Mrs. McCain's friend. The set budget was generous and Quinn had no worries that they would be able to win the piece, unless there was someone with a truly unlimited bank account, which didn't happen as often in the little towns of the Oregon Coast as one would think.

But there was still one problem…and it was a doozy. Where in the world was Quinn going to get the "muscle" that Mrs. McCain had spoken about? She understood why the elderly woman had mentioned it. After looking the piece up online, Quinn agreed. It was huge and she would definitely need help. But who?

Although Quinn had met a few men in town, she'd mostly stuck to becoming friendly with the women her age. They were safer.

Quinn tapped the top of her counter. "Maybe Aspen or Maeve would have an idea of someone I could ask. I trust them enough that they wouldn't send me with a creeper." After a few more minutes of thought, Quinn nodded her head. Yes, the Harrison sisters would be the right people to ask. They'd grown up here and knew everyone, so it would be easy for them to help Quinn find what she needed.

Quinn would get on that, just as soon as she closed shop.

* * *

MICHAEL SIGHED as he pulled open the fridge and grabbed the container that held the last of his slice of cake from yesterday. He'd finally, *finally*, finished grading those papers and it had been a worse chore than he'd expected.

Flopping onto his couch, he put his feet on the coffee table and stuffed a large bite of sweet confection into his mouth. Closing his eyes, Michael savored the flavor. Raspberry and white chocolate with a graham cracker bottom had been Aspen's latest invention and it was marvelous. A little on the sweet side, but the tangy raspberry curd made up for it.

He relaxed further, his shoulders settled against the soft cushions and his eyes opened to his empty apartment. Michael was living in the exact apartment that his father had stayed in before his parents were married. It was above the garage of the Gingerbread Inn, and he enjoyed it.

It was quiet, slightly away from town, and his family was close if he decided he wanted to have company. Sometimes, during his summer or winter breaks, he would help out around the inn. His twin younger sisters had left long ago, not interested in the family business and eager to try their hand at bigger cities.

Michael, however, enjoyed the peace and had stuck around. But now he was truly feeling stuck.

He pushed in another bite, but it tasted less like a celebration this time. The fact of the matter was…Michael was lonely. He grumbled under his breath. "So stupid. Grown men don't get lonely." Yet even as he spoke the words to his empty apartment, he knew they were a lie.

Did it make him a sissy to actually want someone to share his life with? Two of his cousins had found their significant others lately... Maybe that was the problem. It had put ideas in his head.

He grabbed the remote off the coffee table and flipped on the television above the fireplace. He skimmed the channels until landing on an action movie that he hoped would take his mind off the pervading sadness he was experiencing, but even blowing up cars and saving the world from destruction weren't quite enough.

Feeling restless, he polished off the cake and stood up, taking his fork to the sink and the container to the garbage. He folded his arms over his chest and tapped his foot. Now what? It was too early to go to bed, but too late to do something with friends. Tomorrow was a work day, after all.

But he needed to move. He needed to try and get rid of this depression. Making up his mind, he turned off the television, grabbed his jacket and walked out into the darkness. The grounds of the inn were large. Maybe he could take a walk without disturbing anyone.

His boots pounded down the steps of his apartment and he took off at a brisk pace to the edge of the property. A dark line of trees was on his left, while the inn in all his glory was far to his right. Leaves, dead grass and other plants crunched under Michael's feet as he walked.

The cold nipped at his nose and the breeze tugged at his longish hair. Soon he was sniffling and working his hands to try and keep himself warm enough to stay outside. He just couldn't quite face his apartment right now. He wasn't one for crowds, but it was still too quiet.

Something had to change. But what? One didn't just make a girlfriend appear out of midair.

His phone buzzed and Michael gratefully pulled it out of his pocket. He smiled in relief. A conversation with his sister would definitely help. "Hey, Alice. What's up?"

"Big brother!" Alice shouted, causing Michael to pull the phone away from his ear. "I need you to settle an argument."

Michael chuckled as he heard multiple voices grumbling in the background.

"Hush!" Alice cried. "My brother's a genius, he'll know the answer."

"Are you sure?" Michael pressed. "You might be better off asking the almighty internet."

"You're better-looking than the internet," Alice teased. "More boring maybe, but better-looking."

"Thanks." Michael had heard all this before. His sisters were much more social and animated than he was, and their favorite joke growing up had been that he was great...but boring.

Tonight, however, the teasing insult hit a little deeper than usual. His quiet calendar, his empty apartment, his restless energy... Was his lack of dates because he was boring? Was there something wrong with him that women just weren't drawn to?

"You there, bro?"

"Yeah...sorry." Michael cleared his throat. "What did you need?"

"Okay...is it 'You've got another *think* coming' or 'You've got another *thing* coming'?"

Michael hung his head. "That's what you're arguing about?"

"Hey, we've got a pizza waiting on this, so please, great, wise wordsmith...enlighten us," Alice said dramatically. "Wait, wait!" she said before he could reply. "Let me put you on speaker." Indistinguishable sounds came over the phone and Michael realized she must have set it somewhere in the middle of the room, because the noises from her guests grew louder. "Okay," Alice called, her voice more tinny than before. "Go ahead."

"It's both."

The room erupted with shouts and Michael waited patiently.

Alice fumbled the phone again and her voice was much closer this time. "Hold on!" she shouted. "Let him talk." The noise dropped. "Explain."

"The phrase is different depending on what part of the country you're from," he explained. Michael kicked at a rock as he continued to explain the transition of the phrase and how it was said differently around the United States.

"Mike...sometimes your knowledge frightens me."

Michael winced. He actually hated the name Mike, and Alice knew it. It was her way of cutting him down to size. *Like she didn't already do that by calling me boring.* "I'll try not to let it go to my head," he said.

Alice laughed and he could tell she'd taken him off speaker. "Looks like everyone's buying their own pizza," she declared. "Bummer."

Michael hesitated. "Are you struggling for money?" he asked softly.

"Oh, no, no," Alice quickly corrected him. "I'm fine. Mom and Dad have been great. I was just hoping that Brad would have to ante up."

Michael relaxed. As a student in her second to last year of college, it would make sense for her to have a tight budget, but he'd thought his parents had been handling it. He was glad to have firm knowledge on it now. "Okay, great."

"Well…thanks!" she chirped. "I knew we could count on you to save the day…or in this case…ruin it."

"At your service, as usual," Michael said, keeping his voice light. When his sister was gone, Michael pocketed the phone and turned back to his apartment. It was too cold and nothing was helping his dark mood. Not even the thought that his sister had been thwarted in her plan to get free pizza.

Boring…too smart… He sighed and pushed his hair out of his face. He really should get it cut. The stairs creaked as he climbed them. "But that's what boring guys do," he said, letting the words hit the night air.

He paused just outside his door, not quite ready to face the dark yet. Boring guys kept their hair short and hid in their apartments eating cake by themselves instead of inviting beautiful women on dinner dates.

Black curls flashed through his mind, just like they had yesterday when Michael had been in at the cake shop. Would Quinn find him too boring? She owned an antique shop. Was that a sign that maybe she enjoyed history and learning? Would she be attracted to a man who preferred books over cocktail hours?

He hesitated, then gripped his doorknob firmly. "Nothing changes, unless something changes," he told himself as he went inside. If he didn't like being called boring and didn't like coming home to an empty apartment, then there was only one person who could do anything about it.

Him.

Tomorrow he would go to the antique shop and meet Quinn officially. If it felt right, he'd even ask her to dinner. She was his last
chance here in Seagull Cove, so if she wasn't interested, then he'd
move on to plan B, and start looking for a job in a bigger city. Time
was ticking and he felt an urgency pounding in the back of his head
that if he didn't do something now...he'd never do anything at all.

CHAPTER 3

Quinn eyed the clock. Lunch time couldn't come soon enough. She was meeting Aspen at the cafe so Quinn could ask about finding someone to help with the bureau she would be acquiring the day after tomorrow.

Rather than explain the situation over the phone, Quinn had wanted to sit down so she could tell Aspen about her worries and concerns about being with a man she wasn't very familiar with. Hopefully, Aspen and Maeve, if she was there, would be able to read between the lines because Quinn had no desire to explain *why* she was so careful around men. She just wanted the women to be willing to help her despite the situation.

After what seemed an eternity, the clock finally struck noon and Quinn closed down the shop for the lunch hour. She didn't always lock the door since she was usually just eating in the back, but today she was leaving so she turned the bolt, checked the windows, then went through the process twice more before rushing out the back.

Aspen's shop was only two doors down and across the street, so it took no time at all for Quinn to arrive. Rather than go to the front, however, she headed to the back door. Aspen had told her it would just be easier than walking through whatever crowd was after their dessert hit for the day.

Quinn knocked, then wrapped her arms around herself. She'd been in such a hurry that she'd left her jacket behind and even though she'd only been outside for a couple of minutes, she was regretting it.

One of her curls blew into her eyes and no matter what Quinn did, it refused to behave.

The door creaked open and a burst of heat hit Quinn in the face, thawing her nose and cheeks. "Oooh, it's warm in there."

Aspen laughed and pushed the door open farther so Quinn could come inside. "Cakes don't bake in freezing temps," she said with a smile. "Come on in before you let it all out."

"As my grandad used to say," Quinn offered, "you're not heating the whole neighborhood."

Aspen nodded and pulled the door closed. "Sounds like something I probably heard a time or two myself." She brushed her hands down her apron. "Your timing was perfect," she said. "I just pulled my last batch of cookies out of the oven, so let's head into the office and we can chat. I think Maeve's still here as well."

"Great. Thank you." Quinn followed Aspen, trying not to feel like a giant compared to the petite, curvy woman. Aspen's looks were something to be envied. Her womanly shape, even when hidden behind an apron, was what every woman dreamed of being. Quinn's taller, leaner figure felt ridiculously childish next to the Italian beauty.

"Hey, Quinn," Maeve greeted as they went into the office. The youngest of the Harrison sisters came around the desk to give Quinn a short hug. "I didn't know you were coming by today."

Quinn shrugged one shoulder. "Aspen was nice enough to agree to meet with me. I have a question for you."

Maeve sat back down in her computer chair and leaned back. "Go for it," she encouraged.

"Have a seat first," Aspen said, her tone scolding her sister.

Quinn laughed softly as the women made faces at each other. She'd always wished for siblings, and seeing their relationship made her slightly jealous. "Thank you." She sat down in one of two chairs and Aspen took the other. Clasping her hands in her lap, Quinn took a deep breath.

"I'm in need of someone to help with a project for work," she said carefully. "And I'm afraid it's kind of short notice."

Aspen nodded encouragingly. "Did you want Estelle to help you decorate or something? Or do you need us to help put together a painting crew?"

Quinn waved her hand in the air. "Oh, no, nothing like that." She forced herself to explain more. "I need a man…"

Aspen grinned and Maeve laughed. "Normally I'd say we all do, but I found mine."

Quinn felt her face go red, though she realized the women were teasing. "Not like that," she said in exasperation.

Maeve only laughed harder. It was nice to see the normally stoic woman had loosened up since she and her fiance had reconciled. From what Quinn had been told, it had been a bumpy ride for a while.

"I need someone to help me bring some furniture back from an estate sale."

Aspen groaned. "That's not nearly as exciting."

Quinn couldn't help but smile. "Which means I need someone who has a truck and who you think can be trusted to go on a little road trip with me."

The laughter stopped and both women studied Quinn.

This was exactly what she'd been afraid of. Quinn knew they were trying to figure out why she was concerned about finding someone safe. But they were female. Couldn't they understand the risks?

"Quinn…" Aspen began. "Did someone—"

"We'd be happy to help you find someone," Maeve interrupted. She gave her sister a significant look and even though Quinn knew exactly what was going on, she was simply grateful that Maeve had seen fit to stop the questions. "When do you need someone by?"

Quinn scrunched her nose. "The day after tomorrow."

"Whoa…you weren't kidding when you said it was a short time-line." Maeve tapped her fingers on the table. "Ethan's working on a board at the moment, so I know he can't go." She raised her eyebrows at her sister. "What about Austin?"

Aspen shook her head and gave Quinn an apologetic look. "Austin is leaving tomorrow for some training down in California. Sorry."

"That's alright," Quinn said quickly, her hopes fizzling. She began to stand. "I'll work something else out."

"No, hold on," Maeve said, holding out a hand. "We've got lots of guy friends. Surely one of them could help." Her face lit up. "What about Gavin? He's strong and has a truck."

Aspen nodded. "Yeah...that could work." She smiled at Quinn. "Gavin's a total teddy bear. Big, but soft."

"I don't think he'd like you calling him soft," Maeve said with a chuckle.

Quinn nodded. "I didn't realize he had a truck. I've met Gavin once or twice. I can ask him."

"It'll depend on his fire schedule," Aspen mused. "I don't know when he's on or when he's available."

"But it's worth asking," Maeve pointed out. She scowled. "Too bad Antonio isn't home. We'd send you with him."

Quinn blinked. "Who's Antonio?"

"Our brother in the military," Aspen replied. "You'd be safe with him."

Quinn nodded. "Can I just get Gavin's number? It sounds like he's a good option."

Aspen got out her phone and began punching buttons.

"Send her Michael's number too," Maeve said. "Friday is a Professional Day at school this week, so he has it off and he has a truck, as well."

"Michael..." Quinn tried to remember who that was. "Which one is he?"

"He's our cousin," Aspen said as she copied and sent contact numbers to Quinn's phone. "Quiet guy, but the sweetest, most helpful man you'll ever meet." Her dark eyes met Quinn's. "I'm sure you've seen him, but most likely he's been sitting in a corner reading rather than chatting."

Quinn nodded, thinking that didn't sound too bad at all. Surely someone like that would be safe to be around. "Okay, then." She slapped her knees. "You two are so amazing. Thank you so much."

"Yeah, for sure," Maeve said. "Let us know how it goes."

"I will." Quinn stood. "Thanks again."

* * *

MICHAEL PUT his stuff in his shoulder bag and headed out of his classroom. His stomach was in knots and he felt like he was going to throw up. Is this what guys who weren't boring felt like? Or was it just because he was the quiet one?

He thought of the laughter coming through the speaker of the phone last night and straightened his shoulders. He was tired of being the picked-on nerd. While he didn't mind that his sisters used him for his knowledge, he wanted to be wanted for more than his brain. Couldn't he simply be Michael? Just a guy who enjoyed books and quiet evenings at home?

He shook his head. No. He'd had enough time in this town to know that that's how everyone would see him until the day he died.

Unless you do something about it.

Today, he was going to execute Plan A. Ask Quinn on a date. If that bombed, then he would move on to Plan B. Get the heck out of Dodge. Not only would it open up his horizons, but how embarrassing would it be to keep spending time with his friends with Quinn there, knowing she had turned him down?

He stuffed his bag in his car and got in the driver's seat, turning the key until the engine turned over. His heart was thumping against his chest and the nausea returned. "Knock it off," he scolded himself. "You're being a baby." If Jayden knew how ridiculous Michael was being, he'd never let him live it down. "If *any* of your friends knew, they'd tease you until the end of time," Michael said, speaking his thoughts out loud.

Main Street was just a couple of minutes away and it only took another two minutes to find a parking spot. The tourists hadn't descended on Seagull Cove quite yet, making parking a non-issue.

He turned off his car and took a moment to breathe. He could do this. He spoke to beautiful women every day. Granted, some of them were his relatives and he wasn't actually attracted romantically to any of the others, but still…it counted…right?

"Suck it up, buttercup," he told himself before getting out of the vehicle. He forced his breathing and heart rate into compliance, threw back his shoulders and strode inside, hoping he looked confident and not cocky.

"I'll be right with you," a voice called from the back.

Michael waited near the door, his eyes traveling around the space. The store was…well…his sisters would say cutesy, but Michael refused to use the word. The antiques had been placed in little collections so it looked like small rooms in a large home, and he had to admit that Quinn had a knack for it.

While history wasn't his specialty, the place felt roomy and inviting. She was apparently a good saleswoman.

"Hi, I'm Quinn…" Her voice trailed off as she rounded the corner. "Oh…" A tentative smile crossed her face. "Can I help you?"

Michael forced a smile of his own, hoping he didn't look as sick as he felt. She was even more beautiful than he remembered. Those dark curls were up in a high bun with a couple trailing down her neck. A neck which was slender and soft-looking, making him want to touch the skin to see if it was as delicate and cool as it appeared. But it was her eyes that held his attention the most. They were gray, or maybe it was a blue that was so light they appeared gray. He wasn't really close enough to tell, but the light eyes against the dark hair was so eye-catching that he now felt sick for a different reason.

Why in the world would a woman as beautiful as that be interested in going out with someone as boring as me?

Quinn blinked. "You're…you're friends with Aspen and Maeve, right? I've seen you around, I think."

Michael shook himself out of his stupor. What a wonderful first impression. Smiling, he stepped forward, hand extended. "Cousin, actually," he stated, knowing he probably sounded like an idiot. "Michael Dunlap. My mother and Mrs. Harrison were cousins."

"Oh…" Quinn's mouth formed a perfect "O," and she shook his hand, only to drop it quickly.

Michael squeezed his fingers into a fist. Her touch was incredible, but she was so out of his league it was laughable. This was a stupid idea. He needed to go straight to Plan B. Plan A was a fairy tale.

Clasping her hands in front of her, Quinn stood tall. "Was there something you needed? Or did Aspen send you?"

Michael frowned. Did Aspen know he was going to come ask Quinn out? How had she heard that? He hadn't told a soul. "Uh…no… Aspen didn't send me. I, uh…" He rubbed the back of his hot neck. "I know we haven't actually met…"

"I believe we just did," Quinn said with a small laugh.

"Right." Michael laughed with her, though the sound nearly choked him. No wonder his sisters made fun of him. This was stupid. "You're, um…you're really beautiful," he blurted, and then his mouth just kept going. "And, uh…I was wondering if you'd like to have dinner with me?"

There. He'd done it. No one could say he wasn't brave. He might still be boring, but he'd managed to ask out the most beautiful woman he'd never seen, though no one would call him a genius at the moment. That had to be the clunkiest date-asking of anyone in the history of asking on dates. She completely tongue-tied him, which wasn't normal for Michael.

He wasn't normally at a complete loss for words, he simply didn't offer them unless asked.

When his eyes came up from the floor to land on her face though, he realized his bumbling was worse than he'd thought. Her pale skin was even more pale and she was the one who looked sick.

"I'm sorry," she rasped, her voice tight and hoarse. "But I don't think that's a good idea." Spinning on her heel, she walked to the back of the shop, leaving Michael in the dust.

"Wow," he murmured, wincing at the pain in his chest. He'd forgotten just how much rejection hurt. This wasn't the first time a woman had turned him down, but it might have been the one that hurt the most, though Michael wasn't really sure why. He barely knew Quinn. All he knew was that he was attracted to her...strongly...and she had seemed like a nice woman.

Pushing back the abnormal amount of pain, Michael straightened, then turned and walked toward the door, pulling it open a little harder than he needed to.

The heavy weight of despair from the other night was back and he found himself frowning the whole way home. The thought of sending out resumes to other schools hurt almost as much as getting rejected did. Michael liked his school, and he loved his family. But Quinn had been his last chance and she, very obviously, wanted nothing to do with him.

"Looks like the hunt starts Friday," he muttered as he drove home. Maybe if he was lucky, Aspen would bring something good by the inn and Michael could sneak a piece from the kitchen. Isn't that what girls did? Eat their feelings?

Well, if any guy had ever needed to follow a female's example, tonight it was Michael. He'd drown himself in sugar and carbs and then on Friday, when school was out, he'd start figuring out where he was going to go next. Quinn wasn't interested, and Michael wasn't interested in any other woman, but surely, in all the millions of people in the world...there was someone who wouldn't care that he stumbled over words and was terrible when it came to asking women out. He just needed a bigger pool to choose from...and he couldn't find that in Seagull Cove.

CHAPTER 4

Once Quinn reached the back room, she shut the door and leaned her back against it, her hand on her racing heart. Why? *WHY?* Why did every conversation have to come back to her looks? Especially from men who looked harmless?

It always seemed to start so innocent, just like it had a couple moments ago. A compliment here and there. A soft smile, a guy who looked nervous, but in reality, he was a raging maniac who took every word, every gesture and twisted it to meet his own purposes. Guys like that were masters of disguise.

No one, not a single person at her school, had believed Quinn when she'd complained about Adam. They all thought he was great. A soft-spoken man who obviously thought she was pretty. Why was that a bad thing?

Slowly, Quinn slid to the floor. *It's a bad thing because he wasn't who he appeared and he stalked me behind everyone's back, until I couldn't even sleep for fear that he would somehow get into my house in the middle of the night without my knowledge.*

She tilted her head back, letting it hit the door, and squeezed her eyes tight. No way would she let tears fall. No way would she mourn how her life turned out. Without Adam's insanity, Quinn would never have had the courage to leave home and start her own business, and even if things were tough right now, she was bound and determined to see this through.

"Even when handsome men with sweet smiles come in and try to ask you out," she whispered into the stillness of her storage room.

Michael had completely caught her off guard. She was pretty sure she had seen him from a distance a few times. Aspen was right. He had always been the guy in the corner, though he seemed friendly. *Seemed.* She snorted. "They always seem friendly." But she'd told herself when she moved across the country that she wouldn't ever fall for a man who was only after her for her looks.

Her unique features had been the source of the problem with Adam, and Quinn wasn't going to make the same mistake twice. It had been costly enough the first time. This time around, she would only consider dating if the man didn't care how she looked, or at least if her looks were low down on his list.

Considering that Michael's first words were "you're beautiful", she knew right away that nothing could ever happen between them. And that didn't even take into account that the man *looked* like Adam. Their features were too close for comfort.

Quinn stared at her hand. Despite her abhorrence at his words, she couldn't quite figure out what had happened when they'd touched. She spread her fingers wide and turned her hand this way and that. Had he been wearing some kind of ring or buzzer? She could have sworn that when they touched, heat traveled up her arm, straight in her chest.

If she thought about it hard enough, Quinn could still feel it. The feeling had a slight pressure, but had been warm and pleasant. In fact, she was crazy enough to want to feel it again. She squeezed her hand into a fist, forcing away the thoughts. *No.* She couldn't go there. She couldn't risk that with another man like Adam.

Michael even resembled Adam. Sandy hair, a little too long, which gave him a charming boyish look with just a hint of a rogue. His demeanor had been a mix of confidence and shyness and tugged at

Quinn's heart strings. She didn't like loud, brassy men, but she'd also learned the hard way that the quiet ones weren't always great either.

She sighed and forced herself to her feet. "I am *not* going to feel bad about turning him down," she told herself. "No matter how attractive he was."

Bracing her shoulders, she walked out of the store room, but the shop was empty. Grateful he'd left, she blew out a long breath and her shoulders relaxed. "It's a good thing Aspen and Maeve gave me two names to call," she muttered, walking to the front of the shop. Her phone was sitting next to the cash register and she picked it up. It probably wasn't the smartest thing to leave it out in the open like that. *At least he proved himself not a thief,* she thought with a snort.

Pulling up Gavin's number, Quinn pressed call. It went to voice-mail. "Hey, Gavin," she said, forcing a bit of cheer in her voice. "This is Quinn Peters. I'm fairly new in town and opened the antique store, Treasures of Seagull Cove." She cleared her throat. "Anyway, I need some help and Aspen thought you might be available. Could you call me back?" She gave him her number, then hung up. "Please let him be available," she whispered. "Please…"

The next couple of hours went by slowly and Quinn was grateful that she had several customers to help pass the time. While she didn't sell anything truly significant, it was nice to know that people were realizing her shop existed at all.

By evening, she was starting to get antsy to hear back from Gavin. Even if he was at work, surely he could have messaged her by now, right? Not wanting to bug him too much, she forced herself to hold off from calling again, instead going through her closing routine.

She flipped the sign, locked the door, checked all the windows, then did the circuit three times until she was absolutely positive that her shop was safe. Once she felt confident enough to leave, she went out the back, carefully locking it behind her and testing the hold before going to her car.

Once at the house, she parked in the garage, took the bat and went inside, doing her usual walk through. After depositing the bat back in the garage, she felt like a rain cloud was hanging over her head. "This is no way to live," she said to her cold, quiet house.

Leaning onto her kitchen counter, she rested her face in her hands. She was too young to be this afraid, but what was she supposed to do? Adam's lesson had been very clear. Even the nice men couldn't be trusted and her looks drew crazy males to her.

She didn't want to be caught unawares ever again, but even as she thought of how frightened she was of Adam, the warm, fuzzy feeling from Michael went back up her arm, counteracting the cold sting of fear.

Quinn shook her hand out. What was that? And why did she want to feel it again? Adam had been sweet-looking and kind on the outside, but his touch left her shriveling in disgust. So why did she want Michael to come brush his fingertips on her arm again? It was stupid. It had to be some kind of fluke.

Her phone buzzed and she dove for it, beyond grateful for the distraction. "Yes, hello?' she panted, having nearly knocked herself off her feet to get the device from the coffee table.

"Quinn?" a deep voice asked. "Is this Quinn Peters?"

She cleared her throat. "Yes."

"Hey. This is Gavin. You left me a message?"

"Oh, yes. Thank you so much for calling me back."

"No problem. I've been out of cell range on a camping trip, but just got back into town. What can I do to help you?" he asked.

Quinn could feel her entire body relaxing as she thought of the safe firefighter helping her save her business. "I mentioned in my message that I own the antique store."

"Yep."

"And I have a large piece of furniture that I need to pick up from an auction house a few hours south of us." Quinn stumbled slightly over her words. "Aspen said you had a truck and might be available?"

"I'm always happy to help," he stated. "What day did you need to go?"

"Day after tomorrow. Friday."

"Aw, man, I'm sorry," he said, causing Quinn's heart to drop. "I start my shift tomorrow morning and it's forty-eight hours. I won't be off until late Friday night. Is Saturday too late?"

Quinn swallowed hard. "I'm afraid so. The auction is around lunch time on Friday, so I'll need to be there."

There was a slight pause. "Well, a buddy of mine also has a truck. He might be able to help you."

Her hope soared.

"His name is Michael Dunlap. He's Aspen and Maeve's cousin. Have you met him?"

"Yes," Quinn croaked. "Yes…I've met him."

* * *

MICHAEL WIPED the sweat and water from his brow as he walked up the steps to his apartment. It was starting to rain, that heavy mist that often sat for days over the Pacific Coastal area. His clothes were stuck to his body and it wasn't all from the actual running.

But the run had gone a long way in helping him feel better, at least mentally. He'd pushed a little longer than normal today and his legs were aching and his lungs burned, which was a good type of pain. Much better than Quinn's immediate rejection had felt.

He pushed a hand through his wet hair, bent over and shook it out and then headed inside. It was ridiculous how much one single word could hurt. It had been so long since Michael had been attracted to someone beyond friendship that he'd been completely caught off guard.

"You're out of practice, old and boring," he grumbled as he worked his way to the bathroom to take a shower. All these years he'd tried not to worry about how his sisters described him and in one fell swoop, a beautiful woman made him realize it was true. Talk about an epiphany.

After the shower, Michael's skin felt less like it would snap and break off, but his stomach was grumbling. He headed to the kitchen and opened the fridge door. His eyes moved over the whole fridge, but he didn't really see anything. Nothing inside sounded appetizing and he found himself not wanting to spend the time to actually cook.

Growling, he shoved his feet in some flip flops, grabbed his keys and headed outside. He winced as soon as he closed the door. He'd forgotten the rain. It was cold and moist and his T-shirt and shorts were far from comfortable. But he wasn't in the mood to go back in and get a jacket.

Ducking his head, he dashed to his car and hopped in the driver's seat. Once inside, he took a moment to actually figure out where he wanted to go. He didn't really want to be around people, but maybe the distraction was exactly what he needed to keep himself from going to that dark place where he considered just how stupid he was being.

Jamming the key in the ignition, he tore out of the driveway and headed to his aunt's house. There was always something cooking at the Harrisons' and if Michael was lucky, Estelle and Maeve would be around to keep his mind busy.

Several cars were in the driveway and he sighed in relief. Everyone appeared to be home. He got out and ran up the front steps, not bothering to knock. "Honey! I'm home!" he teased as he wiped his feet on the door mat.

"Michael?" Estelle came around the corner after a moment, smiling wide. "Hey, stranger. What brings you by?"

Michael made a point of sniffing. "Umm…nothing. Nothing at all."

Estelle laughed. "We're just sitting down. Come on back."

Michael grinned, already feeling better. Nothing cured a case of the blues like a dinner with a loud Italian family. They were the best entertainment around.

"Michael!" Aunt Emory held out her arms and cupped his cheeks. "You get more handsome every day." She frowned and ruffled his hair. "But I think this might be getting a little long."

"Leave him alone, Mom," Estelle said. "I think he looks good."

Micheal rolled his eyes. "I can't decide if I like it or if it's just a nuisance."

"You look younger," Estelle replied, sitting down at her seat.

"Come on over." She smirked. "No one shows up at dinner time without being hungry."

Though he felt the sting of heat hit his cheeks, Michael laughed. Estelle might call him out, but he knew they didn't care if he was there. He walked over and sat across from her. "Thanks."

Uncle Tony shuffled his way over from the couch and Michael felt his humor flee. He hated seeing how weak his uncle was getting. His diagnosis was stealing everything and Michael knew it was only a matter of time before they lost the used-to-be vivacious man.

"Michael," Uncle Tony said with a smile. "How are you?"

Michael nodded. "Fine, thanks. Just plugging away."

"Yeah?" Uncle Tony sat down. "Got a good group of kids this year?"

Michael shrugged. "They're not bad."

"In other words, they're a bunch of hooligans," Uncle Tony said with a snorted laugh.

Michael grinned. Losing this guy was going to be heartbreaking. "They're not the best, most interested group I've ever had, but they're okay."

"Spoken just like your mother," Tony said with a laugh.

Emory smacked her husband's shoulder gently. "Grace is the epitome of her name."

"Exactly my point," Tony defended himself. He waved at his wife. "Do you see what I have to put up with over here? Are you still living in the apartment above the garage?"

Michael nodded, his mouth full of soup.

"Got room for one more?"

Emory threw her head back and groaned.

Estelle chuckled. "Somehow I doubt he wants you interrupting his bachelor ways, Dad."

Tony tapped a gnarled finger on the table. "Are you saying I'm not cool enough to live with someone like him? I can be cool. I'll just pull out the pictures of my younger years and they'll come flocking."

"Who? The imaginary groupies or the ladies at the senior center?"

Tony glared while the rest of the table laughed. He pointed to his wife. "You watch it, young lady. You're the leader of those imaginary groupies."

As much fun as it was to watch his aunt and uncle argue, Michael was desperately seeking an outside opinion. He'd debated during his whole run whether he should speak to someone about his situation and he figured his cousins were his best bet. At least he hoped they were. "Actually..." Michael cleared his throat. "I'm not quite sure how much longer I'll be living above the garage." He quickly put a bite of soup in his mouth, giving himself a moment in case someone pounced on him.

Estelle narrowed her eyes while his aunt and uncle grew quiet. "Okay..." she said warily. "I'll bite. Why?"

Michael looked into his bowl, stirring the contents for a moment. "I've, uh...considered looking for a job in a different town." He winced at the gasp that hit the table.

"Mom, Dad, stop," Estelle said, hushing her parents with a wave of her hand. She leaned forward. "What's going on, Michael?" she asked softly.

He pinched his lips together. "I just...feel like I'm stuck. Like I need to broaden my horizons."

"Like there's no available women," Uncle Tony shot out.

"Would you stop?" his wife chastised.

"That's what he really means," Tony argued. "The pickings are slim. He needs to look in a different part of the ocean."

This was a huge mistake. Michael held in a groan, exchanged an exasperated look with his cousin and settled in. His uncle might be on the right track, but that was *not* what Michael wanted to talk about and he was *never* going to admit it. After all the chatter settled down, maybe he'd be able to explain himself. But he'd have to ride out the whole wave. Something he knew, unfortunately, from personal experience.

CHAPTER 5

Quinn stared at her phone. What now? Gavin couldn't do it, and who did he recommend? The same person Aspen and Maeve did. Their cousin, Michael. The very man she not only rejected, but walked away from earlier this afternoon. The man who sent tingles up her arm, who was glaringly handsome, and who had blurted out that she was pretty in a way that said nothing else mattered.

She groaned and put her face in her hands. Life was such a mess. She needed to get that bureau. The finder's fee would be an enormous help in getting her business the kick start it needed to survive until tourist season.

"Moving companies," she muttered, scrambling for her phone. "What about a moving company?" She quickly pulled up a search engine on her phone and began searching for nearby companies. Fifteen minutes later, she fell back in disgust. It was useless. None of them were even close to her area. From glancing at a few websites, the amount of money it would take for them to deliver to Seagull Cove would eat up half of her profit. She couldn't afford that.

She stared at the phone screen again. Could she do it? Would Michael even be *willing* to hear her out? Maybe if she apologized for being so abrupt with him, he would be willing to let her hire him. She didn't want him to have any disillusions about why she was calling him.

"It's either deal with him, or eat Ramen for the next couple of months," she muttered. Her stomach churned at the thought. She was a well educated woman who had been hired into a very nice position out of college. Unfortunately, that meant her tolerance for cheap eats had dropped dramatically ever since getting her first paycheck. "No…" she whispered, setting the phone to the side. "I can do it. I can survive."

Mrs. McCain's white head popped into her mind and guilt dripped down Quinn's spine. What would happen to the bureau? Would Mrs. McCain be able to get anyone else on such short notice? The elderly woman certainly couldn't do it herself. Was there anyone else nearby who could do it for her?

Quinn closed her phone and let her chin fall to her chest. No. The answer was no. This was Quinn's area of expertise, no one else's. The odds of them being able to handle the auction and subsequent paperwork and delivery were slim.

She reached over, her eyes still closed and grabbed the phone. Her joints felt stiff and her breathing was shallow. "Everyone is vouching for him," she reminded herself. "He's not Adam. Just because he thinks I'm pretty doesn't mean he's going to stalk or threaten me. Aspen wouldn't send me with a man that she thought would hurt me." Quinn took a deep breath. "He comes from a good family. It'll all be okay."

Forcing her breathing to slow, Quinn punched in the number that Aspen had given her. The phone rang five times before going to voice-mail. Part of her was relieved and part of Quinn just wanted this over with.

"Hi, Michael," she croaked. "This is Quinn. We, uh, met today at my shop. The antique store." Quinn shook her head. That might not have been the best thing to bring up. "Um…Aspen gave me your name and number because I need someone with a pick up truck to help me. Can you…call me back? I'd appreciate it. Thanks."

She hung up and set the phone on the coffee table, then headed into the kitchen to brew a cup of tea. She'd only made it about halfway there when her phone rang. Rushing back, Quinn grabbed the device, feeling equal parts excited and full of dread at speaking to the person on the other side of the line. "Hello?"

"Quinn?" the deep voice said. "This is Michael. You left me a message?"

"Yeah…" Quinn cleared her throat and pushed an errant curl out of her face. "I was told you have a truck and that you might have Friday off. Is that correct?" It was probably best not to bring up this afternoon at all. Maybe it could just disappear into the stratosphere like it had never happened?

If only luck were that kind.

"Yeah, I do. What do you need?"

Quinn began to pace the room, the whole story spilling out without any filtering. "So…I'm kind of in a desperate situation," she said at the end. "I really need some help, but I don't really know many people and Gavin was already busy and I know you and I didn't really hit it off this afternoon…"

Crud. Crud, crud, crud! I wasn't supposed to talk about that.

Quinn slapped her forehead. She was the world's biggest idiot. "Sorry. I…" Her shoulders fell. "I'm sorry. I was rude this afternoon and—"

"No, no," he hurried to reassure her. "It's fine. You were very clear in your feelings and that's…that's great."

Quinn shook her head. Why was he sugarcoating it? The afternoon had been a disaster and now she was trying to throw them together for an entire day. What was wrong with her? "Still…I should have been nicer about it." She cleared her throat again. "But anyway, I'll pay you for your time. And gas. And mileage." Maybe if she threw in enough extras she could entice him to overlook her rudeness.

A deep chuckle came across the line and it did funny things to Quinn's stomach. She put a hand there, trying to calm butterflies. What was this? Why were her hormones going crazy for a guy that was too much like Adam to be safe?

"Quinn…it's alright. I'm happy to help. And you don't need to pay me. That's what friends are for, right?"

"I'd feel better if I paid you," she said firmly. No way was she going to let him come back at some point demanding recompense. Having something like this open between them was definitely asking for trouble.

"I really don't want to take your money. Put it towards getting your business off the ground. Besides," he continued, "you're doing me a favor. I had no idea what I was going to do on Friday and this gives me something to keep me busy. So really…you're helping me out."

Quinn bit her lip. This guy was too nice. Just one more glaring red flag. Men never did anything this big for no recognition. "I don't want to argue," she said, working hard to keep her tone soft but firm. "But I really would feel better if I paid you. I'm fully aware this is an imposition and I don't feel right taking advantage of you, especially on such short notice."

A long sigh came from the other side of the line. "Okay," he said, capitulating. "Whatever you think is best."

"Thank you. I appreciate it." Feeling marginally better, Quinn finally sat down on the couch, her heart rate calming down for the first time since they'd been speaking. "So, we'll need to leave first thing Friday morning."

"What's considered first thing?" he asked.

Quinn scrunched up her face. This was going to be tricky. Not everyone was a morning person. "Um…we need to leave at like four in the morning." There was silence on the other end of the line and she worried for a moment that she lost him.

"Have you thought about just going up the night before?" Michael asked. "That might save us both some grief."

Quinn rubbed her forehead. She had thought about it, but she didn't want to pay for a hotel room. It was just another unnecessary expense…at least it was for her.

"Tell you what," Michael ventured. "How about instead of you paying me for the trip, you pay for two hotel rooms? That way the money goes to a good cause, I don't have to feel bad about taking it from a friend and we both get a good night's sleep so we're not completely cranky during our hours together in the truck."

"Oh, we're not driving together," Quinn blurted out before she could think better of it.

"Oh. We're taking two cars?"

"Yeah, I figured you could follow me." There was no way she was riding in a cab with a man she barely knew for like six hours. Did everyone assume she had a death wish?

"You want to pay for the gas for two of us to drive when we could easily fit in my truck?"

"Yes." There was no question. Quinn absolutely would not put herself in that kind of vulnerable position. She'd learned how to protect herself in the last year and a half, and not getting into a car with strangers was high on the list.

It sounded like he grumbled something under his breath. "Okay. If that's what you want. But I still propose that you put the money toward a night in a hotel. Or maybe I'll drive up the night before and meet you there in the morning."

Quinn pursed her lips in thought. It really would be a good idea to go up the night before. While she didn't mind early mornings, getting up at three so they could head out at four was a little extreme. Surely there was a cheap hotel that wouldn't hurt her budget too much. "Okay," she said. "We'll head out tomorrow night. I close shop at six. Can you be ready then?"

"Yep. School gets out earlier than that."

Quinn froze. "You're a teacher?"

"Yeah. I teach middle school English."

Why did life hate her so much? The comparisons between Adam and Michael, other than the weird hormonal thing when they touched, were getting out of control.

"Is that a problem?"

"No," she croaked out. "Just meet me at the shop at six fifteen."

* * *

THE NEXT DAY AT WORK, Michael couldn't seem to stop looking at the clock. He was more eager to get free for the long weekend than his kids were and that was saying something.

Finally, the bell rang and the classroom emptied in a flurry of papers, sneakers and shouts of glee. It would be one of those rare weekends where the students didn't have any homework and Michael was glad to not have any papers to correct. He still hadn't quite recovered from the last essays.

Mentally calculating how many hours it was going to be until he and Quinn left, Michael frowned at the answer. He still had a long time to wait. Shaking his head, he forced himself to sit down at his desk and get the little bit of work he had done.

"It's not like this is a date," he reminded himself. In fact, Quinn had gone out of her way to make sure Michael was under no illusion that this was anything other than desperation to save her business.

She'd even mentioned that she had asked Gavin before asking him. So not only was Quinn desperate for help, but Michael's assistance had been at the very bottom of the barrel.

That same depressive cloud he'd been under the last couple of days threatened to swallow him whole, but Michael pushed it back. "She's just one woman," he reminded himself. "One woman who, for no apparent reason, hates my guts." He cocked his head. "Or maybe it's because I'm as lame as my sisters say. Quinn certainly didn't sound impressed that I was a teacher."

He probably shouldn't have taken on the job, but Quinn really had sounded in need of help and Michael didn't have any other suggestions as to whom she could ask for help. If he'd had someone to pass her off to, it might have been smart to do that. But he didn't...and he couldn't ignore the fact that despite her disdain, he actually was looking forward to spending a little more time with her.

He knew it was dumb, after the way she'd turned him down, but what man didn't want to spend time watching a beautiful woman?

"One last hurrah before leaving town," he muttered. He'd come to the very firm decision after speaking with his aunt and uncle that leaving was the thing to do. He simply had nothing keeping him here, other than nostalgia. It was time to try something new. Maybe he'd even try teaching a different grade. Older or younger, it didn't matter. He just needed a change.

After finishing his work, he headed home to wait out the last couple of hours before leaving with Quinn. The time couldn't move fast enough, and yet he was sort of dreading the trip. Beautiful as she was, every time he looked at her, Michael knew full well he'd see her rejection.

Hopefully she could ignore her dislike for enough time to get through the next two days without too much trouble.

After grabbing a few supplies, packing some snacks and filling up the truck, Michael headed to the little antique shop. The front looked dark, but he parked and waited. If Quinn didn't appear in the next couple of moments, he'd go knock on the door. But she seemed to be pretty set in how she wanted this to go and it was going to involve as little contact with him as possible. Michael would do his admiring from afar.

It took less than two minutes for a lean silhouette to walk around the side of the building, heading straight for him.

Michael rolled down his window. "Good evening, Ms. Peters."

A smile tugged at her lips, but she held it at bay. "Hello, Michael. Are you ready to get going?"

Michael patted the dash of the truck. "She'll get me there and back. You all set?"

Quinn nodded. "Thank you again for being willing to do this." Her light eyes searched his, and her cheeks turned a light pink. "I feel like I need to apologize again for the other day."

Michael waved a hand through the air. "Seriously. It's okay. I realize I was pretty bold, coming in and blurting all that out. Can we just be friends and pretend it never happened?"

Those cheeks turned a little darker and Michael was fascinated with the matching warmth it created in him. "I think that would be fine."

He nodded, pretending he wasn't still admiring her beauty. "Great. Then what do you say we get on the road?"

Quinn nodded in return. "I'm the red car, right over there."

Michael followed the direction of her slender finger. It landed on a very tame sedan. Not quite what he would have expected for someone as exotic-looking as her. "The red will make you easy to follow," he said with a smile.

"Right." With one last almost-smile, Quinn left, heading to her car and pulling out onto the road.

Michael followed, turning south and gauging her speed as they worked their way down Main Street. He let out a sigh of relief when they got to the outskirts of town and could go over twenty-five miles an hour. After a few minutes, the treeline became a little more sparse and a long line of dead road lay ahead of them.

Michael frowned. It was evening in the spring and he had plenty of experience to know that storms popped up at all times on the coast, but the black horizon had him slightly worried. This wasn't just a spring drizzle they were driving into. It was a full coastal barrage.

He pushed his lips to the side. "Let's hope we make it to our destination before it hits." Considering his luck lately, Michael's confidence was less than stellar.

CHAPTER 6

Quinn's heart was so deep into her throat, she thought she would choke on it. Her speed had reduced dramatically, her windshield wipers were going so fast, she was sure they were going to fly off, and she still couldn't see but two feet in front of the car.

This type of storm was something she had not yet experienced while living on the West Coast, though she'd heard about it. There'd been several storms throughout the last six months, some she would even go so far as to call miserable, but this was something else.

The night had come on faster than normal and now it was pitch black, she was on a lonely stretch of highway surrounded by trees that were bowing to the strength of the wind and her only comfort was the man she was desperately trying to ignore even existed.

Those two headlights behind her were helping give Quinn a little boost, knowing she wasn't alone. Not that she wanted to rely on Michael for anything beyond retrieving the bureau and getting it to Mrs. McCain, but knowing that he was around if something happened was a balm to her mind.

She gripped the steering wheel and clenched her teeth when she felt her car hydroplane for just a split second. Once she had grip again, she lowered her speed one more time. At this rate it would take twice as long as normal to reach the town of Gold Beach. What was she thinking? Traveling at night rather than in the bright light of morning?

"It's not like you knew how deserted this stretch of highway was," she muttered. "But Michael did." A small flash of anger rose up in her, but she squashed it down. This wasn't his fault, as much as she would love to have someone to blame it on. How could he have known such a storm was about to descend on the entire Oregon Coast? She certainly hadn't checked the weather.

Giving herself a mental and physical shake, Quinn leaned forward, forcing herself to focus. They couldn't be that far from civilization. In the next town, they could grab a hotel room and wait out the storm, then finish the drive in the morning. It would require an early morning, which they'd been trying to avoid, but there was no helping that now.

She jerked when something dark moved ahead of her. Quinn gasped when she realized a small herd of deer had sprung into the road. Even as her foot slammed on the brakes, she knew it was too late. With her limited visibility, she hadn't been able to see them in time.

She was going to crash.

Time seemed to slow as she felt her tires slide on the water, leaving her moving faster than she should have with her brakes engaged. A dark hide met with the front of her car and the animal flipped up and over, its rump landing on Quinn's windshield on the passenger side.

Her head jolted forward, smashing into the airbag as it deployed, and stealing her breath. She felt her head hit the back of the seat and then the world went black.

"Quinn?" a deep voice came through the haze. "Quinn? Can you hear me?"

The voice was in the middle of a heavy buzzing tone that Quinn couldn't place. She wasn't quite sure who was talking to her either. "What?" she rasped.

The man mumbled something under his breath. "Can you open your eyes?"

Warm fingers cupped her cheek and a sensation of warm electricity went through her, crawling down her neck and into her chest. Quinn sighed and leaned into the touch.

"Quinn, I need you to open your eyes," the voice persisted.

But they're so heavy. She tried to follow the command, but was only able to manage a groan. She wanted to just slip back into oblivion. The more her mind awoke, the more she realized how much she was hurting. Her neck hurt, her face hurt…in fact, her entire body ached. Why did she hurt so much? She couldn't remember having done anything to cause it.

The only part of her that was pain free was where the man's hand was against the side of her face.

"Please, Quinn. I need to see if you have a concussion," the voice said. "And we need to get you out of this car before you get too wet and become hypothermic."

"W-what?" She tried shaking her head, but the pain was intense and she stopped. She worked on her eyes instead. Surely that wouldn't hurt too much. Her lids began to flutter.

"That's it," the man cooed. "Come on. You can do it. Come back to me."

Quinn tried harder, but the movement in her eyelids didn't seem to be leading to anything. When she finally felt as if she had them open, she still was only seeing dark.

"Can you see me?"

Quinn slowly turned her head to find a drenched man staring at her. His strong jawline was impressive and his longish hair was plastered to the side of his head, yet still managed to look manly and attractive. She wondered if he had stubble on his chin and her fingers began to twitch before…

"AHHHH!" Quinn screamed, jerking away. "Go away, Adam!"

Adam backed up, his hands in the air. "Quinn…it's me. Michael. Michael Dunlap."

Quinn ignored the pain in her neck and head as she scrambled to the far side of the car, but when her hands landed on something sharp she whimpered and folded into herself.

"Quinn," Adam said more softly, as if approaching a frightened animal. "It's Michael. I'm not this Adam guy. Remember? We were going to Gold Beach to buy that furniture for your customer?"

Slowly, Quinn's brain came back to life and the pieces slid into place. "Oh my gosh…" she breathed, twisting to look at Michael. He was still standing on the downpour, hands up as if he were waiting to be arrested. "Michael…I'm so sorry. I didn't…" Quinn swallowed her words and gulped, closing her stinging eyes. How could she have thought he was Adam? What would Michael now think of her?

It doesn't matter, she reminded herself. *He's here to do a job. You already turned him down flat for anything else.*

She cleared her throat. "I'm sorry," she said, her voice tight and strained. "I mistook you for someone else." Looking around, Quinn's eyes landed on the cause of the accident. The deer lay on the hood of her car, her windshield was crushed and the glass shattered. She looked down at her hands. That must have been what hurt when she started to crawl over the console.

"May I look?" Michael asked, patiently waiting for her to show him her wounds.

Still feeling slightly fuzzy and unsure, Quinn didn't have it in her to fight. She nodded and held out her hands. The light glow of headlights cast heavy shadows inside her car. And she could understand why waking up had been such a struggle.

The wind moaned, rocking the car, and she realized they were in a vulnerable position. "We probably should move somewhere else. Ouch!"

"Sorry," Michael murmured as he pulled another piece of glass out of her palm. "I don't want to leave these in, but there's not enough light to see either." He glanced back at his truck, the rain sluicing down his face.

Guilt swam in Quinn's gut, adding to the nausea that was already there from killing a deer and getting in an accident.

"Let's get you to my truck," he finally said. "You can rest while I drive us to the nearest town and we'll get you to an emergency room." His hand came to her forehead and he frowned. "I'm almost positive you have a concussion and you might need some stitches."

"What about the car?"

"You slid off the road," Michael explained quietly. "It's not going to be in anyone's way."

* * *

MICHAEL WATCHED as Quinn considered the situation, then nodded, only to wince at the movement. Yeah…there was no way she hadn't gotten a concussion. They were lucky she hadn't received a broken nose as well. Her head must have been turned slightly to have avoided that when she hit the airbag.

But the blood dripping from the split in her forehead and the cuts all over her hands from the broken glass were enough to frighten ten years off his life. Rejection or no, Michael would never wish ill will on anyone.

Bracing himself near the door, he helped Quinn climb onto unsteady feet. He was already drenched through to the skin, but he hated that Quinn was about to be the same. This storm was one for the record books. Or maybe it was just the fact that he was out in the middle of it. Michael had been through some doozies in his time living on the coast, but this seemed to be one of the worst.

Why hadn't he received any kind of storm warning? The weather service was pretty good about letting them know if there was the possibility of something resembling a typhoon.

"Easy does it," Michael murmured, carrying as much of her weight as she would allow. Even though her legs were far from steady, she still leaned away from him as they walked, as if being anywhere near him was painful for her.

It didn't seem that way when she was still partially unconscious.

Michael could have sworn that Quinn had leaned into his touch when he'd cupped her cheek. He'd been trying to move her head slightly to help her regain consciousness and it sure seemed like she had burrowed into his hand. Why was his arm around her waist so distasteful now?

Maybe it had to do with the Adam guy?

Yeah…that was weird. Just who was Adam? And why was Quinn so terrified of him? Was he the reason Quinn was so blunt about refusing to date Michael?

Michael shook his head, dislodging water from his eyes. Right now, they were in trouble. Quinn needed medical attention and Adam, her continual rejection and Michael's attraction for the woman in his arms really didn't matter.

"Okay, hang on," Michael said in her ear. The wind and storm were so loud that he wasn't sure if she could hear him, but she seemed to understand. Taking one arm off her, Michael reached out and yanked open the passenger door of his truck.

The seat, which had been dry up until this point, was immediately slammed with the rain. Michael tried wiping his face, but it didn't last long enough to be helpful. So he gritted his teeth and went back to work. He had no idea where they were, but he prayed that the next town was close enough that they would be able to get dry quickly.

Good thing his truck was newer and there would be no question about a heater. But as water-logged as they were…it would just be better if they could get changed…and quickly.

"Up we go," he said next to her ear again.

A shiver rocked her body and Michael bit back a curse. He had to get her settled. When her hand slipped off the handle with her first attempt, he decided he'd had enough. Sweeping his arm under her legs, he ignored her squeal and lifted her into the truck. She wasn't the lightest woman he'd ever raised up. Quinn was slender, but tall, and right now Michael was more grateful than ever that despite his bookish ways, he had friends who pushed him to work out.

It was all well and good for a woman to want to be independent, but everyone needed help once in a while, and now was one of those times.

Quinn must have realized it as well because she gave him a tremulous smile before mouthing, *Thank you.*

Michael nodded, then closed the door. Slogging his way through the mud back to Quinn's car, he retrieved her suitcase, purse, keys and phone. It took him several minutes because they were knocked all over the vehicle from the crash, but he was simply grateful to have found them.

Climbing back out, he locked the door and slammed it hard. With as bent as the front end was, he wasn't sure how secure the car was, but any thief would be hard-pressed to actually remove it from the area.

With a regretful glance at the dead animal, Michael slogged his way back to the truck. He opened the back door and put her things inside, hanging onto the keys and phone. After climbing into his own seat, he handed them over. "Thought you might want these."

Quinn's hands were like ice and her whole body was shaking as she reached over. "Thank you."

"Engine should still be warm," he assured her as he turned the key. "We'll get the heater turned on in just a second." His truck roared to life and Michael immediately went about turning all the vents on his passenger, blasting the warm air as high as it would go. He smiled at her sigh of relief even as his own skin began to prickle with a chill. Great...now he needed to get them both warm.

The cab will be hot soon enough.

Leaving the air blowing her direction, he buckled up and put the truck in drive. Glancing around, more for other deer rather than vehicles, Michael pressed the gas pedal. The engine revved, but he didn't move. Frowning, Michael pressed harder. The gauge on his dash flared up, but other than some rocking, the truck didn't move. "You've got to be kidding me."

Panic, which he'd been able to hold at bay since the accident, began to climb up his chest and into his throat. He'd been able to stay calm because he knew he could drive them to safety. At least once he knew Quinn was alright, that had been the case. But now...he seemed to be stuck, and that was ruining his ability to stay cool and collected.

"Hang on a sec." Before Quinn could say anything, Michael jumped from the truck, turned on the flashlight of his phone and began walking around the vehicle. When he reached a tire that was a foot down in mud, he swore.

Kicking out a little, he nearly fell over since the entire side of the road was a boggy quagmire. The rain was doing more than ruining visibility, it was taking the landscaping with it.

Hanging his head, Michael walked back to the truck and got inside. "I have good news and bad news."

Quinn's light eyes looked over at him, so wide and innocent. She was shaking too hard to answer him and Michael swore in his mind all over again.

He pushed a hand through his soggy hair, trying to get the strands to stay out of his eyes. Who cared about looking young and cool? Right now he just wanted it out of his face. "The bad news is the back tire is stuck."

Her eyes widened. "Stuck? And we can't do anything about it?"

Michael shook his head. "I'd guestimate it's in a foot of mud. I cleaned out the bed to make room for your furniture, so there's absolutely nothing in here that can help us get out."

Quinn closed her eyes and leaned her head back against the seat. "You said there was good news?" she whispered.

"The good news is that I still have a mostly full tank of gas. We can sit in here as long as we need to with the heater running."

Quinn huffed and smiled slightly. "That's one way to look at the bright side." Turning her head, her eyes glassy with pain and despair. "How long do you think it'll take for us to get rescued?"

Michael shook his head. "No idea. With this storm, it could take a little longer than usual. But hopefully, at least by morning."

Her pale face went even whiter and Michael felt like an idiot, but it wasn't like he would lie to her. She was an adult. She needed to know what was going on.

"I'm sorry," he said sincerely. "If I felt like there was anything I could do to make this situation better, I would. I do have some medicine in the glove compartment, so maybe we can at least ease your headache a little. But I'm not a doctor, so I can't do anything about the cuts or your concussion." He watched her make a face when she moved her head. "Or the whiplash."

"It's not your fault," Quinn assured him, her eyes closed. "I should have seen the deer."

"Not sure how you could have," Michael said. Even now, they were talking fairly loudly just to be heard over the pounding of the rain on the roof. "I haven't seen a storm like this, well…ever."

"Ever?" Quinn cracked one eye. "I thought your family had been here a long time."

"Born and raised in Seagull Cove," he stated, hoping the change of subject would help her feel better about spending so much time together. "Someday I'll have to tell you the story about my mom coming to help her grandmother and never leaving, but the point is, I've been through some nasty storms and this one takes the cake."

Quinn hummed. "Cake. Must run in the family." She shivered again.

Michael chuckled, wondering what he could do to help her. He held out a palm. "Give me your hand," he said in a way to let her know she could refuse.

Quinn narrowed her eyes.

"I realize you don't like me, Quinn," he said softly. "But if we don't get you warmed up, we're going to be getting a lot closer than I think you'll be comfortable with."

Those eyes grew very wide again and she finally offered him one of her hands.

Michael began to hold it between his own, trying to bring blood and warmth back to her limbs. With the cuts she'd sustained, he couldn't rub it too hard, but he could use his own heat to help.

Her touch, however, heated him far more than it ever would her. As attracted to her as he was, he couldn't help but enjoy the soft, though cold, skin. If given half a chance, he knew he'd hold on for a long time…and that was when he realized just how much trouble they were in for the foreseeable future.

CHAPTER 7

Quinn swallowed, trying to keep her panic down in the bottom of her gut where it belonged. Going crazy wouldn't help. She knew it wouldn't. But the panic she was fighting didn't seem to believe her. It felt like it was clawing through her chest and it was all she could do to keep it contained.

The storm of the century was here. She'd wrecked her car. A deer was dead. Her head felt fuzzy. Blood was dripping down the side of her face. Her hands were sore and cut, but the one highlight was the warm tingle that Michael's massaging was creating.

But the fact that the man who reminded her of her stalker was the one doing the massaging? Yeah...that just added more fuel to the panic fire.

She finally pulled back her hand, though her hormones screamed not to. "Thank you," she said hoarsely. "My fingers are definitely more awake now." *What?* "I mean, warmer." *Oh my word...I don't just have a concussion, I have mouth diarrhea!*

"No problem," Michael said, his voice completely at ease.

She peeked out one of her eyes to see him settle deeper into his seat.

"So…" he ventured. "This isn't quite how I planned on spending the night."

Quinn couldn't help but grin. "Oh? How exactly did you picture your evening?"

He glanced over at her. "In front of the television with some takeout from the nearest fast food restaurant."

She chuckled.

"It was going to be glorious."

Quinn's laughter grew. "It sounds like quite the date." *Mouth diarrhea indeed.* She could have smacked herself, if the steering wheel hadn't already done a bang up job. Why did she have to bring up a date? That was absolutely the most awkward and wrong thing she could ever say to Michael.

"Speaking of…"

Oh no…

He rubbed the back of his neck. "I, uh…well…I'm curious."

Quinn swallowed down her bile.

"And I promise this isn't me trying to convince you of anything, but could I ask why you dislike me so much?" He gave her a curious look. "I'm fully aware I was your last choice to take this little trip with. And you made yourself very clear the other day when I asked you out, but what I can't figure out is what I've ever done to upset you. We'd never actually spoken before I walked into your store, but you had some very strong, very focused feelings and I'm just curious what I did that I don't remember."

Quinn turned her head, wincing at the movement, and looked out the rain drenched window. She needed to answer him. Despite her struggles, Michael had been nothing but kind. Yes, he'd brought up her looks, which she hated, but otherwise, he really hadn't done anything wrong, other than looking like the man who stole Quinn's confidence and security. "You didn't do anything," she said softly, turning back to him to make sure he knew she was telling the truth. "You…simply…remind me of someone."

Michael's brows pulled together. "That Adam guy? What did he do? And what have I done that's like him?"

Quinn faced front, laid her head back and closed her eyes. There was no way she was telling Michael that story. They weren't friends. They were barely acquaintances, and though she wanted him to know he hadn't done anything untoward, she definitely wasn't sharing the purgatory she'd been through for the last couple of years. Or how much it had messed up her life ever since.

There was silence followed by shuffling. Michael apparently got her message. As the silence drew out, Quinn knew the night was going to be long...very long. Truthfully, she was sleepy. She could probably drift off right now, but she couldn't remember if that was an okay thing to do with a concussion or not.

Were they supposed to sleep? Or were they *not* supposed to sleep? Hadn't the research on it changed lately? So did doctors say it was safe to sleep? Or...

Quinn opened her eyes. "Michael, do you know if it's safe to sleep when you have a concussion?" She twisted her head just enough to see him. "I can't seem to remember if research said you should sleep or shouldn't? And my head is kinda fuzzy, so..."

Michael pinched his lips together. "I'm afraid my expertise is middle school literature." He gave her a sheepish grin. "I can quote you *Moby Dick* all night, but medical advice?" He shrugged.

An unconscious smile spread across Quinn's face. "You teach literature?" It was so nice to have something different from Adam to put on this guy. Adam had been a fifth grade teacher. Large and strongly built, just like Michael. Kind of shy and quiet spoken, just like Michael. But hearing that he was a bookworm made Quinn think that possibly, Michael's behavior was sincere, where Adam's had been a facade.

I mean...it's not like I can date him, but maybe he's not going to be quite as bad as I thought.

Michael nodded. "Yeah." He rubbed the back of his neck, then tried to wipe the water on his jeans, but they were also soaked.

Quinn didn't miss the shiver that wracked his large chest. "You're cold."

He glanced her way before staring out the windshield. "The cab'll warm up in a minute."

It was only then that Quinn realized that every vent in the entire truck was aimed in her direction. She had a moment of alarm, not quite sure of his motives. Had he done it because he was worried about her? Or was it just like Adam? A way to back her into a corner for taking care of her?

"Quinn?" Michael asked tentatively. "You look like you're going to be sick. Is the concussion making you nauseous?"

That had to be it. She squeezed her eyes shut tight, swallowed hard. "Yeah…" She rasped. "Something like that." Her brain and head hurt far too much for her to be able to keep this all straight.

Why did Michael have to look and remind her of Adam? Aspen had said her cousin was a good guy, but Quinn just couldn't shake the thought that everything he did was just like the man she'd run away from. On one hand, it wasn't fair to Michael. On the other hand, she was too scared to let down her guard.

"Do you want me to turn down the heat?" he asked. "Or crack the window for a second?"

She heard shuffling and the truck rocked a bit.

"I don't think we want the window open for long because we don't want to lose heat. It would be too easy to get hypothermia from being wet and the cold night air, but if a burst of cool air would help calm your stomach, I think we can manage it for a moment."

Something brushed against her and Quinn squealed, her eyes shooting open as she pressed herself away from his arm and body, which were only a few inches from her.

"Whoa, whoa, whoa…" Michael backed up quickly and put his hands up again, the same way he had outside her car. "I'm sorry," he said quickly. "I was just trying to press the button for you to get some air."

"Can't you do it from your side?" she panted.

He cleared his throat. "I know this is going to sound stupid, but I bought the truck used and two of the window buttons don't work on my side." He scrunched his nose. "And I haven't bothered to get them fixed since I don't often have passengers."

* * *

Even as he said the words, Michael knew they sounded like a line. Why hadn't he just had the truck fixed? At first it hadn't seemed like a big deal. He got a little better deal on the truck because of it and he almost never had anyone in the passenger seat, so who cared?

Now he cared. He cared a lot. A woman, whom he was beginning to think had been abused in some way, was sitting in his truck, terrified because he'd reached across to the window. All because he hadn't bothered to pay for a tiny little repair.

His curiosity was eating him alive, but Michael wouldn't ask again. It was clear from earlier that it was not a topic she was willing to share. Maybe he should just draw her attention elsewhere? That was safe, right?

He grabbed his phone. "I'm not sure why I didn't think of it," he grumbled. "But we should totally look up info about concussions, not to mention call for help."

Quinn relaxed slightly back into her seat.

"Or not..."

She stiffened.

Michael set the phone down. "There's, uh...no signal."

"So no help either."

Michael shook his head. He was starting to think he was secretly a serial killer. Every time he opened his mouth, his words and their situation could be twisted into something dark and horrible. No wonder Quinn was so scared. "But don't worry. When the rain lets up, I'm sure we'll be able to get that tire out of the mud and get you to the auction before it's too big of a deal."

She nodded. Her mouth drooped, along with her eyes. It was clear she was tired, but Michael wasn't sure if she should sleep. He was just as clueless as she was.

"So...tell me about your store," he said, hoping it was a safe conversation. "Have you always been into antiques?"

When her lips softened and she smiled, he sent a prayer of thanks up. "Sort of, I guess," she said. "I was raised by my grandfather. I wouldn't say he was into antiques as much as he just never threw anything away."

Michael chuckled. "Hoarder?"

"You could say that," Quinn said, her smile growing. "Grandpa was raised in the Depression and he simply never threw anything away."

"And you inherited the trait? Is the shop just a cover for your own hoard?"

Quinn laughed, then winced, but her smile remained. "Nothing so nefarious, I'm afraid. I…" She cleared her throat. "Had to leave my last job and was looking for something new." Her eyes stayed on the windshield. "I wanted a fresh start, so I gave into my childhood curiosities and decided to open an antique store."

"And how's it been going for you?" Michael pressed. "You mentioned that this job was going to be very helpful."

"Yeah…I hadn't planned to let myself be hired out as an acquisition person, but it kind of fell in my lap and since…" She looked sideways at him. "Since business is slow at the moment, it seemed ideal."

Michael nodded. "I hear that. It seems like the only shops in town that stay busy year round are Aspen's cafe and the candy shop." He grinned at her. "I think it's because they still pull the taffy in house, rather than ship it in. Between that and the fudge, the locals come as well as the tourists."

Quinn smiled tiredly at him. "That sounds about right."

"But don't worry," he assured her. "I have no doubt that when tourist season picks up in a couple of months, they'll flock to your store like crazy." He chuckled. "I always thought it was weird we didn't have an antique shop. It seems that every town, no matter the size, on the Oregon Coast has at least three and we didn't have any."

"When I was working on opening, I had a few people tell me that a woman had one several years ago, but she'd gotten sick and moved into an assisted living place," Quinn offered.

Michael pursed his lips, nodding slowly. "Yeah…I think I remember that. It was when I was just a kid though, so I didn't really pay too much attention to it." He snorted. "It seems that that's the only way people ever get out of our town. Either they die, or they're taken out against their will."

"And that's a bad thing?"

He shrugged. "I guess it depends on what you're looking for in life." The pause was awkward and Michael knew his bitterness could be heard in his tone. He hadn't meant to spill so much, but it was out there now. It's not like he was ashamed of the fact that he was growing antsy and thinking of leaving. It just…well…it just was some-thing most other people never considered, so it was kind of a taboo topic.

"I know I hit my head and all, but I'm trying to figure out if you're saying that you want to leave Seagull Cove."

Michael looked over at her pale face and wide eyes. Man, she was beautiful. Even with her curls hanging heavy with water and the color gone from her face. Regret that she wasn't interested in him fell into his belly like a full sized dictionary. She had been his last chance, but the sign had been clear. He shook his head when she raised her eyebrows. "Doesn't matter," he said. "I wouldn't really expect you to understand."

If he wanted color brought back to her cheeks, he'd just found a good way to do it. Quinn looked on the verge of livid and her gray eyes flashed. "Why wouldn't I understand?" she demanded. "Do small towns like this teach you that women can't handle the same thing as the big strong men?"

Michael waited until her tirade was over. "Wow. That was a lot."

She huffed and turned her face away. "Sorry. Sore subject."

He chuckled, the sound growing when she glared at him. "For the record, I come from a family of women who run their households as well as independent businesses. Take Aspen for example, with her cakes. My grandmother ran a family inn that my parents still work at together. Maeve does books full time and Estelle is working on breaking into the wedding industry." He huffed. "I have two younger sisters. Twins. One is going to finish college in the next couple of years with a masters degree and the other just started her first corpo-rate job."

The color had only grown deeper with his words. "Sorry," Quinn muttered.

"It's fine. You don't really know me, but believe it or not, even us small town folk grow with the times."

Quinn nodded. "I know, I just…like I said, it's a sore subject."

"Well, I pity whoever told you to stay home rather than work. I imagine they had their man card handed to them on a platter."

Quinn laughed, then made a pained face. "I shouldn't laugh," she said, rubbing her forehead and breaking open the cut.

"Here." Michael hesitated. He could learn when the situation called for it. "There are napkins in the glove compartment. We should press them against your forehead. Would you like to get them? Or would you like help?"

Quinn gave him a curious look. "I can do it," she said, her tone soft. "Thank you." She retrieved the napkins and used one to clean her face a little. "Out of curiosity, then, why do you think I won't understand?"

Michael took in a long breath. The answer was pushing boundaries just a touch, but what did it matter at this point? They'd both said things they probably shouldn't have. "You mentioned you were forced to leave your last job. At your age, it was probably your first, or at least close to your first one." He scratched his jawline. "I'm afraid I've reached the point where I…where I feel like I'm stuck. I've done all I can here and now maybe it's time to move on."

"So you *do* want to leave Seagull Cove."

He couldn't tell if she thought that was good or bad. "Yeah, I suppose I do."

Quinn blinked several times. "Huh."

Huh? That's it? Huh? He mentally rolled his eyes. What did it matter? She had no say in it and there was nothing keeping him here. He would find someone just as beautiful as she where he went and that would be that.

Michael relaxed in his seat, praying the hours would go by quickly. They'd only been stuck for a couple of hours and the conversation was deeper than he normally shared. Just what might come up by the time the sun rose?

CHAPTER 8

Quinn slowly came into wakefulness, realizing that at some point during the night she had slept. But as her ears registered rain still blasting the truck, and the cab was still fairly dark, she figured it couldn't have been very long.

She blinked a few times, adjusting to the small amount of light.

"Good morning," a gruff voice said.

Quinn turned, pausing when her head spun. Apparently, her concussion was far from healed. "Morning?" she croaked.

Michael gave her a small smile. "Yep. It's five a.m."

Quinn's eyes flared. "You've got to be kidding me."

He shook his head, then leaned over the steering wheel and looked outside. "I'm not seeing an end to this storm and I still can't get anything on my phone."

Quinn felt like crying. How many things could go wrong in one little trip? *A lot, apparently.* She sighed, then tensed when her body began to talk to her. "Uh..."

Michael turned her way and raised his eyebrows.

Quinn made a face. "I need to go to the bathroom," she whispered. *Why did I whisper? It's not like he doesn't know that humans have to go. Even if men are like camels and can hold it forever, he still knows it's a bodily function.* But the heat in her cheeks wouldn't abate. No matter how natural it was, she was completely embarrassed to have brought it up.

Michael pinched his lips. "I guess that means we're headed out in the rain." He pushed a hand through his hair. "Good thing we can use the heater to dry off again."

"We?" Quinn gasped. "What do you mean, we?"

How did the man not look completely nonplussed? Did nothing rattle him? Even last night during the accident, he'd stayed cool as a cucumber. He hadn't argued when she'd rejected him. He'd still agreed to help her without giving her a hard time. And now he was talking about taking her to the bathroom like it was yesterday's news.

He is nothing *like Adam.*

Those words actually caused her shoulders to involuntarily relax. Each time she saw something in Michael that helped differentiate between the two men, she found herself softening. The problem was, she wasn't sure if that was good or bad.

"Do you think you can walk?" Michael asked softly, bringing Quinn's mind back to the conversation at hand.

She frowned, but had to force her brow to relax when the movement hurt. "Uh…I think so?"

Michael nodded. "Okay, well, I'll just come open your door and make sure you're steady on your feet. If you can handle it, I'll let you go by yourself."

"And if I can't?" she challenged.

"Then I'll help you get where you want to go."

"You're not coming with me while I use a bush," Quinn said adamantly. She'd hold it for the next two days before that happened.

Michael's lips twitched. "I'll let you have some time to yourself and turn my back, okay? But the last thing we need is you falling and hitting your head again."

Quinn narrowed her eyes at him. Could she trust him to keep his word? Would he really turn his back? *Yes…*a little voice in the back of her head was whispering and Quinn wasn't sure where it was coming from. Ever since dealing with Adam, she found herself quite sarcastic and cynical in her thoughts, even if she didn't speak them all out loud. But this voice felt…familiar. Like it belonged to the Quinn she had once been. The one who trusted and felt safe without having to recheck every lock a dozen times before going to bed. A craving unlike anything she had ever felt before slammed into her gut.

She wanted that Quinn back.

"Scout's honor," Michael said, raising two fingers in the air.

Quinn couldn't stop the smile tugging at her lips. "Were you even a Scout?"

"I was," Michael said with a nod. "Made it all the way to Eagle."

Quinn laughed. "Wow. I didn't think those existed anymore."

He chuckled with her. "They do in small towns. Some of the things we hold on to are good."

Quinn cringed inside. She had reacted badly to him last night when Michael had been trying to help her. Maybe it was time to give him the benefit of the doubt. Just because he was similar to Adam in looks and career, didn't mean they were the same men. "If you're willing to help and give me some privacy, I'd appreciate your help."

Michael responded by getting out of the truck.

Quinn shook her head, watching him get soaked immediately. This storm was something else. She was equal parts amazed and disgusted. Why did the storm have to come now? Couldn't it have waited forty-eight hours? Her door opened and Michael scooped her up before she could say anything.

"Hang onto my neck," he hollered over the wind and rain. "The whole place is a mud pit. I'll carry you."

"That doesn't seem fair!" Quinn shouted.

Michael gave her a grim smile. "Least I can do is save your shoes from being ruined," he called back.

Quinn followed orders and wrapped her arms around his neck. She leaned into his hold deeper and her weight shifted, causing her to lean comfortably into his broad chest. That same pleasant burning that had been bothering her every time they touched was now spreading through her whole body.

It was as if she could feel him skin to skin, but that was impossible.

Between clothes, rain and flying debris, there was no way she should have had such a reaction. In fact, there couldn't have been a less romantic situation than this storm. But her hormones seemed to have a mind of their own and Quinn's heart fluttered, following their lead.

Ridiculous, she scolded herself.

Ducking her head into his neck, she let Michael take charge. She had been ticked off about having to go on this trip with him, but right now, she was so grateful he was there. She felt him slip a couple of times, but he caught himself quickly and kept her safe and secure, exactly how Quinn needed it to be.

"Okay." Michael's voice was softer. "This little cubby is a bit less crazy."

Quinn lifted her head and opened her eyes. Sure enough, he'd found a tight knit group of trees that were effectively blocking enough of the storm for it to feel a little more calm.

"I'm going to put your legs down," Michael said. "See if you can stand, alright?"

Quinn nodded and tensed her muscles while he followed through. Slowly, her weight was transferred to her own limbs and Quinn tightly gripped his shoulders. Her knees shook, but she felt like she was able to keep them firm enough. "I think I can do it," she said, feigning a confidence she didn't feel.

Michael looked skeptical, but he didn't argue. Another point in his favor. His arm was still around her waist and for just a split second, his eyes darted down to her lips before coming back up. "That's fine," he said, his tone a little lower than before. "Why don't you just go around the back of this tree. I'll wait here."

But his arm didn't move and Quinn didn't either. She found herself strangely reluctant to move away from his hold. Whether or not her legs would hold her didn't matter. She didn't want to lose his warmth and the intense look in his eyes as he stared at her.

Relieving herself felt far less urgent at the moment than it had back at the truck.

* * *

SHE WASN'T MOVING. Quinn's eyes were wide and looking at Michael as if she was trying to figure out the key to the universe.

His heart thumped against his chest and his fingers flexed against her back. He didn't want to let go and have her fall, but maybe she was waiting for him to make the first move.

It was taking every bit of willpower he had to keep his eyes on hers instead of looking down at those lips. They haunted him. When was the last time a woman had driven him so crazy?

Never.

Michael wasn't sure he could ever remember a time when he'd been so taken with someone. Holding her was like heaven, even with the water pouring down his neck and soaking every part of him. And when she'd ducked her head, resting against his shoulder as if she trusted him with every part of her? He'd nearly begun strutting like a peacock.

He couldn't help but wonder what it would be like to press his lips to hers. To pull her tighter, closer…

He shook his head and forced himself to step back. "Sorry," he said gruffly, rubbing his heated neck. "I'll turn my back."

Quinn looked slightly shell-shocked, and swayed slightly, causing Michael to lunge forward to catch her. This time, however, he only cupped her elbow. Holding her fully against him was dangerous to his willpower.

"You okay?"

She nodded jerkily. "Yeah. Sorry." She pointed to the trees. "I'll just…go back there."

Michael nodded and let go of her again, stepping back. As soon as Quinn had disappeared, he turned his back to her, standing guard and trying to listen for any vehicles that might be coming their way.

He'd purposefully taken her in the opposite direction of her car. He didn't want her seeing the carnage last night's accident had caused. The mangled deer wasn't pretty and her car was even worse. It was a complete miracle she had walked away with nothing but a concussion and a small split on her forehead.

Speaking of…he should probably take a look at that when they got back to the truck. The rain might cause it to open up again.

"All done." Quinn held onto the tree while she came back his way. "Wet jeans should never have to be pulled up," she grumbled, tugging at the waist of her pants.

Michael chuckled. He understood the sentiment. He probably should take the opportunity to go to the bathroom himself while they were out here. That way he didn't have to get wet twice. But as he opened his mouth, something in the distance caught his eye.

"What?" Quinn asked. She dragged a chunk of curls from her forehead.

"Just a second." Michael started to walk away, then paused. He didn't like leaving her alone. The storm was still horrible, even if their little grove was calmer. But who knew what might come crawling through the area? "Are you willing to take a small detour?"

"What? Why?"

Michael pointed deeper into the trees. "I think there might be a cabin over there."

Quinn spun, but tilted to the side.

Michael didn't even hesitate, just picked her up, cradling her right back where she belonged. *She doesn't* belong *there,* his inner voice scolded. *She just feels good there.* He snorted. *Semantics,* he shot back.

"What's so funny?" Quinn asked.

"Just being an idiot," he told her. "Come on. Let's check it out." Michael ducked his head and headed back out into the bulk of the storm. He couldn't see a road, but there had to be a way to get to the cabin.

His sneakers slipped through the mud a couple of times, and he worried that he was going to splat them both in the bog that the forest had turned into, but somehow, they managed to get into the clearing.

"There's the road," Quinn said loudly, pointing to the other side of the cabin.

"Must come in from a different one than we were on," Michael responded. There were no cars around the area and the windows were dark. Even though the sun should have been rising by now, the daylight wasn't appearing. The moisture-heavy clouds still covered the horizon, letting Michael know there wasn't an end in sight.

He hurried up the steps of the porch, noting that the wood looked sturdy, though far from luxurious. "Probably a hunting cabin," he muttered. Turning his head, he put his hand in his hair and shook it all, trying to rid himself of as much moisture as possible. He scrubbed his hands down his face, his fingers noting the shadow of a beard, and he grimaced. He hated facial hair. It made him look ten years older than he was and right now that was *not* something he wanted.

Quinn took that opportunity to knock on the door. "Hello? Is anyone there?"

They waited a couple of heartbeats, but there was no sound. At least not that they could hear over the whine of the wind.

Quinn wrapped her arms around herself, her clothes blowing against her. They were both soaked clear through again, and Michael felt like his clothes were trying to kill him.

He stepped up, banging with his fist. "Hey! Open up!" Still, there was no response. "They're not here," he said unnecessarily to Quinn.

She nodded. "Now what? Go back to the truck?"

Michael shook his head. He tried the knob, but it was locked, just like he'd expected. "No. This shelter will be much better than the truck." He grinned. "There might even be a toilet."

Quinn rolled her eyes. "Great. Now that I've already gone."

Michael chuckled. "Let me check the windows." He tucked into himself for protection and ran around the entire cabin, checking to see if anything had been left unlocked. On the backside, just above waist level, luck was finally on his side. One window was not only unlocked, but open about two inches.

When he went to push it up higher, Michael realized why the window was still in that position, even with no one home.

Cursing under his breath, he looked around to find something he could use for leverage on the stuck window. The opening wasn't large enough for either of them to shimmy inside, but maybe he could break the seal. He would pay the owner later.

Finding a large, sturdy stick, Michael put it in the frame and tried pulling on it. The window creaked, but didn't budge. He let his legs go and hung his weight a little, but only gained another two inches. Shaking his head, Michael got to his feet and prepped himself to jump. If he broke the window, so be it. Leaping off the ground, he landed his upper body on the branch, effectively snapping the branch and sending the window shooting upward at an odd angle.

Tossing the remnants of the stick to the side, Michael pulled himself onto the ledge and tumbled inside. Water immediately pooled at his feet and the wind and rain from outside came rushing through the opening.

He knew he would need to find a way to close up the opening, but right now he had other priorities. Not caring that he was dragging mud and water through the entire front room, he ran to the front door, unlocked the deadbolt and threw it open. "Welcome, miss. May I offer you shelter from the storm?"

Quinn gave a shaky laugh and stepped inside. "Thank you, good sir," she responded, her teeth chattering. "You wouldn't happen to have a fire handy, would you?"

Michael looked around and spotted the fireplace. His small bit of luck was holding. There was dry wood piled inside. "Step one," he said after closing the door. "Man starts fire." He walked away from her and grinned over his shoulder. "Step two. Man gets dry and warm."

"That better include woman."

"Of course," Michael said, waving a hand through the air. "Equal rights and all that."

Quinn's smile was shaky, but seemed genuine. "I'm glad to see there are still some gentlemen in the world."

He gave her a smile, but inside he couldn't help but wonder about the man she spoke of earlier…Adam. It didn't sound like he'd been a gentleman at all. Michael shook his head. *Later.* He promised himself. Right now they were back to being in danger of hypothermia, and as much as he'd enjoy warming Quinn up with body heat, he had a feeling the tentative friendship they'd been nurturing would go up in smoke.

CHAPTER 9

The sound inside the cabin was much easier to take than being out in the storm. Quinn was almost positive that when they finally got home, they would discover they'd been in the middle of a typhoon.

She shivered as she watched Michael try to light a fire. "Hopefully those Eagle Scout skills come in handy now," she teased, trying to tighten her jaw to keep it from shattering.

Michael nodded. "You and me both."

Quinn smiled and looked around the space. It wasn't large by any means, but it was clean. Well…it had been clean. Now there was water on the floor, muddy footprints and a window in the corner was wonky, allowing wind and rain to come inside.

Deciding that moving was better, Quinn forced her stiff and sore muscles to shift as she walked over to push down the window, but it was at an odd angle and she couldn't seem to get it to close.

"I'll get it in a minute," Michael called her way. "It was stuck open and I had to use a branch to jam it up enough to climb inside."

Quinn nodded, hugging herself to try and preserve warmth. Her body was growing stiffer by the minute and she wasn't sure how much was from the cold and how much was from the accident.

The soft crackling of dry wood caught her attention and she gasped, limping over to see the first flickers of flame as they licked some tinder underneath a large stack of wood. "You're a miracle worker," she breathed, holding out her hands.

Michael laughed and leaned back on his heels. "I wouldn't say that. Whoever owns this place was prepared." He held up a small box. "There were matches at the ready."

"God bless hunters," she whispered.

Michael laughed a little more before groaning and climbing to his feet. "It'll take a moment for the wood to catch, but hang tight, the heat's coming." He shuffled his way to the window.

Quinn couldn't help but watch as he tried to close the dang thing. His back muscles were clearly visible through his long sleeved shirt and she watched them bunch and move as he did all he could to force the glass into obedience.

Warmth stirred in her belly and she realized her body was reacting the same way it did when he touched her. Just what was going on here?

You're attracted to him, dummy.

Quinn blinked and turned back to the small fire just as Michael huffed and turned back to the room. She'd almost been caught ogling, but that wasn't the part that had her cheeks flaming. Since when was she attracted to Michael Dunlap? While she had admitted from the beginning that he was a handsome man, he looked so much like Adam that she'd nearly been repulsed by him when they'd originally met.

But somehow Michael was starting to break down her barriers and the longer Quinn stared, the less Michael looked like Adam.

"Aha!" Michael shouted triumphantly. He came back into the gathering room from a hallway, with a crowbar in his hands.

Quinn raised her eyebrows. "You plan to smash the window to smithereens?"

He smirked at her, causing her heart to skip a beat. "I think every man has had that fantasy at least once."

Quinn laughed. "I'm guessing you're a fan of action movies."

Michael was smiling as he shrugged. "I enjoy them as much as the next guy."

She allowed her eyes to feast on his back and arms again while he used the crowbar to work the stubborn window back down. True to what he'd said earlier, it refused to close all the way, leaving about a two inch gap where the wind easily found its way inside.

Michael stepped sideways and grabbed an old quilt off a stool. "I hate to ruin this for the owner, but we need to keep the heat in." He rolled it up and stuffed the crafted fabric along the bottom of the window, doing a decent job of creating a plug. Michael stepped back, hands on his hips. "It's not perfect, but it's enough."

When he turned to face her, Quinn couldn't look away. The shadows of the room danced along the sharp angles of his face, and just like when he'd been holding her in the forest, she was mesmerized.

What would it be like to run her fingers along the stubble that was growing on his chin and cheeks? Or to have his hands at her waist again? What if his lips touched her cheek…heck, what if he full-on kissed her?

Quinn didn't need the fire anymore. She was warm inside and out at this point and she cleared her throat, turning to the flames that were nicely filling the space. "Thank you," she said, her tone slightly raspy.

Michael didn't answer right away, and she looked over to see him slipping off his shoes and socks. He gave her a commiserating look. "Sorry. I'm soaked through and I think I'll warm up better without having wet feet." When Quinn didn't react, he raised his eyebrows. "Would you like to do the same? I think it'll help."

"Oh!" she exclaimed, feeling foolish that she hadn't caught onto his suggestion. "Yeah. Sorry. I was drifting." She shifted onto her backside, biting back a wince, and began taking off her shoes. He was right. The heat against her toes was heavenly and she immediately felt a difference.

Michael frowned and came over, kneeling beside her.

Quinn couldn't move while his hand went to her forehead.

"Does it still hurt?" he asked softly, his thumb caressing the curve of her brow.

No. Not at all. Quinn gulped. What was wrong with her? It had to be the concussion. That's it. She wasn't thinking clearly because she'd hit her head. "It's sore," she said softly.

Michael's gaze never left hers. "Do you want me to go back to the truck for more medicine?"

Quinn shook her head, but stopped when it felt like a bowling ball was rolling around. "No. I'll be fine."

His hand dropped to her cheek and his thumb went to her cheekbone. "You don't look fine," he said, his concern evident. "You're really pale."

Quinn tried to give him a smile, but she didn't really feel like smiling. The moment was thick and heavy, like molasses, but it wasn't humorous. "I'm always pale," she managed.

Michael's spreading of his lips was more like placating than a smile, but it was enough to break the spell between them. "You fit right in on the Oregon Coast," he quipped. His hand dropped and he stood up.

Quinn sucked in a deep breath, grateful for the oxygen. She hadn't noticed just how little she'd been breathing since he'd crouched down in front of her. She heard a slurping sound and looked up again, only to nearly fall over in shock. "What are you doing?"

Michael carefully held his shirt in his fist. "I'm trying to get as dry as possible," he said.

It was no wonder that warm firelight was used in almost every romantic movie scene. The dancing flames were cheery enough by themselves, but add a strong, shirtless man and Quinn wasn't sure she'd ever be the same. "Oh," she said weakly. She'd be lucky if she survived this...and all with a man she rejected less than forty-eight hours before.

* * *

MICHAEL COULD PRACTICALLY FEEL Quinn's eyes boring into his back as he walked across the room to the front door. He wasn't sure whether he should tease her or just put the stupid shirt back on. He lived on a beach. Men walked around without their shirts on all the time. One side of his mouth quirked up. *Boy, won't she be in for a surprise come tourist season?*

Once outside, he wrung the shirt out as best he could. With the rain driving sideways, he actually got a little more wet being outside, but the amount of water that came out of his shirt was enough to fill a couple of glasses and he was grateful to have it gone.

He stepped back in and eyed the room. Quinn had gone back to watching the fire, though the stiffness of her back said she was completely aware of him. Finally spying what he was looking for, Michael grabbed a wooden dining chair and brought it over to the flames. He set it up on the side and draped his shirt over it. "There. That should be dry in no time."

The heat from the fire was pleasant on his skin and he hoped it would fill the cabin quickly. Plugging that window should help the heat distribute a little better, but the most important thing was for them to get dry. Even with the fire, staying wet was asking for illness or something worse.

"I'm going to explore. Do you want to come?" he asked her. Quinn's cheeks were bright pink and she wouldn't meet his eyes. A little imp on Michael's shoulder wanted him to flex or bounce his pecs, but he held back. He was, however, more grateful than ever that his friend Gavin talked him into putting away a book once in a while and lifting a set of weights. A little niggling feeling in the back of Michael's head said that Quinn wasn't keeping her gaze averted because she didn't like what she saw.

Guess that only makes things fair, he thought.

"Um…" Quinn scrunched up her face. "I don't really want to sit here by myself, but I also don't want to leave the fire."

Michael chuckled. "Sounds like quite the conundrum."

She gave him a playful glare and Michael's heart leapt at the flirting. Sighing, Quinn rose to her feet, looking uncomfortably stiff. "The cabin's not very big," she said, as if reminding herself. "We'll be back by the fire in just a few minutes."

"Right." Michael held out his hand. When she stared at it, he smiled reassuringly. "Just don't want you to feel alone." *Liar, liar, pants on fire,* his inner conscience chanted. Yep. Michael was completely lying. Well…mostly. He *did* want her to feel comfortable, but he also wanted to have an excuse to touch her again. He wasn't enough of a playboy to take complete advantage of their isolation, but who would blame him for pushing the lines just a tiny bit?

And if Quinn grew to welcome the attention? Maybe his plans to send in those resumes could be put on hold for just a touch longer.

Quinn's hand was trembling, though Michael wasn't sure if it had to do with him or the cold. It could go either way.

Giving her hand a little squeeze, he smiled and waved toward the hallway. "Let's see what the bedroom looks like."

Quinn didn't move and Michael pulled back. She was completely ashen and Michael realized just how his words sounded.

He shook his head and smacked his forehead, before turning to her and stepping up close enough that she knew he was serious. "Okay, Quinn…I'm only going to say this once, alright? I don't think it needs to be talked about or rehashed a million times, but I do want to make myself clear."

She just stared.

"We both know I'm attracted to you. You're a beautiful woman." He grinned. "Even when soaking wet."

Her demeanor didn't change.

"But I was also raised with what many people would consider old fashioned standards. I would *never*, under any circumstances, do anything to violate you in any way shape or form. Any touch…" He held up their hands as an example. "Will be welcomed by you, or it won't happen." He raised his eyebrows. "Do you understand?"

She blinked, the first movement she'd made in a while, and slowly nodded. "Yes…but how do I know you mean it?"

He gave her a grim smile. "I have nothing but my reputation and past behavior to offer you," he said. "I'm a man of my word, but you haven't known me long enough to have many examples of that."

She tilted her head, her look becoming considering.

An epiphany hit Michael. "I'm not Adam," he said in a low, but firm tone. He was beginning to think every skittish behavior from her had to do with this guy. It made Michael want to go wring the dude's neck, and Michael was far from the violent type.

She softened even further. "I think I'm beginning to see that."

Michael offered her a friendly smile. "Great. Then let's go see if there's a place for you to rest...*alone*..." he emphasized. "Because I'm still worried about your concussion." He looked pointedly to the window. "And it doesn't look like this storm is going anywhere, anytime soon."

Quinn's shoulders deflated. "I'm not getting to that auction, am I?"

"I'm sorry," Michael responded sincerely. He hated to see her miss an opportunity that was supposed to help her business. She might not be interested in him, but Michael didn't want to see her hurt.

She took in a long breath through her nose and visibly straightened her shoulders. "Thank you for all your help. If I'd hit that deer and been on my own, I'd be in a much worse situation."

"If you'd waited until morning, you probably wouldn't have ever left," Michael grumbled. He shook his head. "The fact that we're stranded is all my fault."

Quinn frowned. "I don't blame you. Knowing myself, I would have thought it worth the risk and headed out anyway. Then where would I be?"

The guilt still hung heavy, though Michael appreciated her words. "Still...I'm sorry. I should have checked the weather report."

"You and I both," she said. "Now...how about that tour?"

Michael began to walk, grateful that Quinn walked with him. His curiosity over the story with Adam grew and so did Michael's frustration. Adam had obviously been a jerk and had wounded Quinn in some way. But how exactly?

Quinn was a stunning woman, who was obviously independent

and intelligent and capable. Just what could that bozo have done to her?

There were two doors at the back of the hallway. Michael threw open one and was hit with a blast of cool air. A double bed sat in the middle with neatly folded blankets, a night stand with a lamp, a small dresser and not much else.

"Hang on." Michael walked over to what he assumed was a closet. The door was thin and small, but his hunch was correct and to his relief, there were a couple of clothing items left behind.

He grabbed a large sweatshirt and tossed it to Quinn. "Now let's see if we can find you some pants."

"What about you?" she asked, fingering the dry clothing.

"We'll make it work," he muttered. She was the one with the injury, it was far more important to take care of her than himself. After jerking open all the dresser drawers, he was relieved to see a couple pairs of pajama pants. "Look. One for each of us." He held up the plaid items.

Quinn grinned. "Matchy, matchy."

Michael smiled back. Her comment had bolstered the fire of attraction inside him, though he wasn't sure why. No guy cared about matching someone else, but if it brought a smile to Quinn's face? Michael would do it all day long.

CHAPTER 10

Quinn kept having to swallow her giggles, all while trying to pry her gaze away from Michael's lovely physique. They were both dressed in matching plaid pajama bottoms, though she was also drowning in a massive sweatshirt, with Michael still shirtless.

Even with the rain beating on the windows and the wind wailing against the sides of the cabin, the moment felt almost...cheery.

Fire danced in the grate, doing a nice job of heating the small sitting room and bringing light to the small house. The electricity wasn't on, probably due to the storm, though Michael said in a bit he would walk around to see if perhaps the owner had turned it off while they weren't staying there.

But with the two of them sitting in front of the fire, the shivering mostly gone and wearing their new warm clothes...it was just about the most intimate moment Quinn had ever had with a man. At least one that she wasn't terrified of.

She hugged her knees harder, ignoring the pain in her head and her hands, while squeezing her eyes shut, pressing them into her kneecaps. The longer she was with Michael and away from her old home, the more she was beginning to understand just how much Adam had stolen from her…and Quinn hated it.

"Are you okay?"

Quinn snapped her head up, her messy bun of wet curls bouncing dangerously against her scalp. She probably should let them down to dry and to ease the horrible whiplash in her neck and shoulders, but the feel of her hair on her skin was driving her nuts right now and she decided she would rather deal with the pain. "Yeah," she croaked out. "I'm fine."

Michael wasn't convinced. "You know," he said softly, "I'm a pretty good listener." His smile was tentative. "And there's no one out here to hear us if you want to say something you don't want others to know."

Quinn stared. Was a man really offering to listen to her problems? It seemed unreal. Her grandfather had been the one exception in Quinn's life. Otherwise, the men she knew would rather gouge their eyes out than listen to a woman prattle on about her fears, worries and issues. She had begun to think it was something programmed into their DNA and her grandpa had been some kind of mutant.

Then she recalled Aspen's description of her cousin. How he was the quiet one, the people watcher. Gavin had mentioned the same thing about Michael sitting on the sidelines, but being a really good guy.

Quinn's own recent experience had given her similar results. His touch was warm and pleasant, and never forced. When he'd offered his hand to help her stay steady, there had been no deceit or ulterior motive in his eyes. Instead they'd been clear blue, open and honest.

It was a refreshing change from the dark blue ones she'd come to learn held nothing but trouble.

And Michael's promise to honor her boundaries? Quinn's knees had nearly buckled and it had nothing to do with being weak from the accident. He had been so *serious*. Like there was nothing in the world that could make him break that line of respect and for the first time in a really long time, Quinn had felt safe.

"Quinn?" Michael said. "Did you hear me?"

She blinked, coming out of her wandering thoughts. "Oh, yeah…

sorry." Giving him a weak smile, she shrugged. "My mind has been wandering."

His look was concerned. "Do you think it's the concussion? Should I go back to the truck and get you some medicine?" He looked over his shoulder. "Maybe you need something to eat. It's been a while and I should probably check out the kitchen."

Quinn put her hand on his arm before he could stand up. "Thank you," she said with as much sincerity as she could create. "For taking care of me."

His smile was warm and his eyes soft. "Anytime." He stood and walked away from her and Quinn felt oddly colder, though the fire was only a few feet away.

She watched him rummage through the cupboards, pulling a few things out and putting them on the counter. It only took a few minutes before he came back and crouched down.

"It looks like we've got beef stew...or beef stew," he said with a chagrined smile.

Quinn rested the side of her head against her knees, smiling back. "I think the beef stew sounds like a good option."

Michael chuckled and the sound did more to warm Quinn than the flames. "Beef stew it is. Give me ten minutes."

Quinn waited quietly, sneaking glances over her shoulder every once in a while. She couldn't seem to help it. Michael was proving to be everything that everyone said he was and in proving himself, she was having a harder and harder time figuring out why she'd compared him to Adam in the first place.

Just because two men both have blond hair and blue eyes doesn't mean they're both crazy.

Guilt sat uneasily in her gut. She'd judged this man before he'd ever spoken more than ten words to her and it made her feel like a jerk. A tiny voice in the back of Quinn's head wasn't quite ready to just give into everything stirring inside of her, but Quinn knew if Michael continued down the road he was on, she wouldn't be strong enough to keep holding him off forever...and truthfully, she wasn't sure she wanted to.

But the question is...is Michael still interested? He said he was attracted to me, but that doesn't mean he still wants to take me out. Especially after the way I treated him.

"Do you want to eat at the table?" Michael called out. "Or should we stick close to the fire?"

Quinn debated. Her backside was going numb from sitting on the hardwood floor, but she wasn't sure she was ready to be away from the heat quite yet. "Can we pull chairs up to the fire?"

Michael chuckled. "I think we can manage that."

"Thank you." Quinn stumbled to her feet, reaching out to catch her balance when her head spun with vertigo and pain. Man...she must have hit her head really hard.

"Easy now." Michael's smooth tones were right next to her.

Quinn opened her eyes to see him waiting beside her with his hands out, ready to catch her. "Just a little dizzy," she whispered, wincing at the pain in her head. Maybe she should take Michael up on his offer to go get that headache medicine. *No...he's already gone above and beyond. Let him stay dry.*

Swallowing down the nausea in her stomach from moving around, she forced her protesting muscles into action and grabbed a dining chair.

"Let me get that," Michael said. "You've been through enough." He took the chair and easily carried it to the fire, setting it up so she was close without being too close, then held out his hand. "Come sit down and I'll grab your bowl."

Quinn sighed inwardly. She was in so much trouble with this guy. She took his hand, relishing his strong grip and the pulsing going up her arm, and let him help her sit. "Thank you," she said and laughed. "I feel like that's all I say anymore."

Michael winked at her. "There are worse phrases to get stuck on." He spun and walked to the kitchen, coming back with two bowls. He handed one to her. "You okay to eat? You're not nauseous? Are your hands too shaky?"

Quinn laughed again. "I'm okay, as long as I'm not walking around too much. *Thank you*," she said, emphasizing the words, bringing out the chuckle she was beginning to like a little too much.

Michael nodded, then walked over to grab his own chair and come up close to her side. He paused before eating. "Do you mind if we say grace?"

Quinn's heart took off. He really was too good to be true. "That would be great."

* * *

MICHAEL IGNORED the shocked look on Quinn's face and bent his chin, saying a simple prayer over the food. He couldn't tell if she was shocked because she didn't usually pray herself, or if she was simply shocked that he did.

It wasn't like Michael went around proclaiming the fact that he went to church. But he wasn't trying to hide it either.

Quinn laughed before she spoke. "And for the hundredth time, thank you."

Michael snorted a laugh as well. "And for the hundredth time, you're welcome." They were quiet for a moment as they dug into their meals. His stomach had felt like it was going to eat itself. He hadn't wanted to say anything to Quinn because he didn't want to make her hunger worse and he had no idea if there was any food, but he was grateful that whoever owned this place kept an emergency supply of food on hand.

Canned beef stew had just become Michael's favorite meal.

His bowl was empty much faster than Quinn's and he went back for more. There were enough cans in the pantry that he wasn't worried about running out. This storm wouldn't last forever, so although they might be stuck for a day, maybe even two, it shouldn't be much beyond that.

He came back and sat down. "Do you feel like you need to lie down?" he asked, secretly wishing she would say no. He liked her company, though she'd been very quiet lately. Was it him? Or the concussion? He still wasn't sure, though there were times she looked at him in a way that made him positive she was attracted to him. And she was definitely welcoming his casual touch more. Michael wasn't complaining about that one bit.

Quinn smiled at him and shook her head very gently. "No. Not yet." She set her empty bowl in her lap.

Scarfing down the rest of the stew, he held out his hand for the bowl.

Quinn started laughing. "Should I say it again?"

"You don't have to," he flirted, "but I enjoy hearing your voice." He smiled to himself when her cheeks turned bright red. Her light skin made it so easy to see her blush and he found himself oddly attracted to it.

After taking the bowls to the sink, he came and sank down, sighing as the heat of the fire hit him. The cabin was definitely warming up, but it was amazing the temperature difference between the kitchen and the sitting room.

Only the whipping of the wind and the lashing of the rain could be heard for a few heartbeats and Michael tried to figure out if he should break the silence when Quinn beat him to it.

"I'm sorry I compared you to Adam," she said softly.

He turned to her and shrugged. "I'm sure you had your reasons."

Quinn scrunched up her face. "I did, but you're showing me they weren't very good reasons."

Michael held his breath. His curiosity was killing him and he was digging for an excuse to pummel this guy into the ground for whatever he did to Quinn.

She sighed and sunk in her seat enough that she could rest her head against the top of the back of the chair. "We worked together," she said lazily.

Michael watched her relax. "Did you own an antique store in your last town?"

"No…" Her light eyes darted his way. "I was a teacher."

Michael straightened. "You were?" What were the odds that she was as much of a nerd as he was?

She smiled at his eager reaction. "I taught kindergarten."

MIchael nodded thoughtfully. "That makes sense." He smiled. "I can see you doing that."

Quinn's smile widened, then fell. "Adam taught fifth grade." Her eyes went back to the fire. "He was one of those guys who seemed really shy at first." She snorted derisively. "When he spoke, he spoke quietly and presented himself as a history-loving, sweet man."

The fire in Michael's belly began to burn hotter than the one in the grate. No wonder she had been so opposed to him without even knowing him. Quiet and knowledge-loving were Michael's middle names.

She glanced at him again. "He also had blond hair and blue eyes." Her eyes grew sad. "I'm sorry I treated you badly because of him. It wasn't fair."

Michael huffed. "Sounds to me like it was a learned behavior."

She closed her eyes and sighed. "I suppose it was. We only went out a couple of times, but he…"

Michael's jaw clenched. If Quinn said that Adam forced himself on her, Michael wouldn't be held responsible for his actions. Storm or no storm, he'd find the sicko and take care of him.

"He wouldn't leave me alone." Her eyes opened again. "I told him I didn't want to go out again. On our dates, I could see that he wasn't quite as soft spoken and easy-going as he appeared at school, but I just kept feeling like something was off."

Michael nodded. Mental red flags were a good thing, but often easy to ignore. He was glad that Quinn stuck to her guns.

"He kept coming into my classroom after work, or waiting by my car, even though I told him to stop. He was always commenting on my…looks. Said I was *so beautiful* he couldn't help himself." Her eyes were misty. "I tried complaining to the principal, but he told me that I should be flattered. My looks were something to be proud of." She laughed, the sound entirely without humor, then wiped at her eyes.

Michael's fists clenched.

"Principal Stephens also mentioned that Adam wasn't breaking any laws, so technically there was nothing he could do anyway." She sighed heavily. "Then Adam showed up at my home."

The low growl that slipped out had been unintentional, but it caught Quinn's attention.

"I don't have to continue."

Michael nodded. "Please do. I'd like to understand, and give you an opportunity to talk it out." He gave her a sheepish grin. "I have two younger sisters. I've been their sounding board for years."

Quinn's face softened. "That's very sweet, thank you." She blew out a breath. "It's hard to want to share it. Nobody has bothered to believe me."

"I do," he said with conviction. "No doubt."

Quinn laughed softly. "Thank you, for the one hundred and tenth time."

Michael wanted to smile back, but he could only nod.

"He didn't come in the first time, I just saw him outside my window one evening."

It was taking every ounce of effort to keep from grabbing Quinn and wrapping his arms around her, hiding and protecting her from the world. How could this beautiful woman have endured so much? No wonder she was skittish.

"I called the police, but he was gone by the time they got there and no one could find evidence of him." Quinn tucked a curl behind her ear, but it sprang out again. "That happened a couple more times, but without evidence and without any actual threats, no one, not the school board, the principal or the police could do anything. Adam was questioned multiple times and always walked away without so much as a warning."

Michael shook his head, waiting for the last shoe to drop. He could feel it coming.

"Then one night, I got home from a date with my girlfriends and he…" She took in a shuddering breath. "He was in the house." She started to shake her head, but stopped and rubbed at her cut. "I don't know how he got in, but he was there and…"

"Did he touch you?" Michael asked, recognizing the threat in his own tone.

Quinn let her head turn his direction. "He didn't have the chance.

A few words were exchanged, but I threw my keys at him, which star-tled him just enough for me to run to the neighbors." She turned back to the fire. "I called the police and then called my principal and quit. I knew the drill and I was done. So I packed up and moved, not leaving anyone any information about where I was going or what I was doing." A tear trailed down her cheek.

Michael took a chance and reached out, touching her hand softly. To his surprise, she gripped him back, her thin fingers stronger than he would have expected. "I'm sorry," he whispered. When she looked his way, he leaned in, making sure there was no mistaking his next words. "I believe you and if that guy ever shows his face in this area of the country...I'll protect you."

CHAPTER 11

Quinn couldn't breathe. Her lungs had completely frozen over at the intensity in Michael's gaze and words. She believed him...and he believed her.

The same trust and respect that he was offering to her right now, the trust she had looked for for over two years while Adam's behavior had escalated, was burning brightly inside of her and she wanted nothing more than to offer it wholly and completely back to Michael.

He's not Adam, her soft, old self stated unnecessarily. *This is Michael. And he's exactly what has been missing in your life.*

Those last words made her blink and the spell over her lungs broke, allowing her to pull in a deep, life saving breath.

Though she could breathe again, her heart was still racing at a hundred miles an hour as she and Michael continued to stare at each other. "Thank you," she finally whispered. "But I hope it doesn't come down to that," she quipped weakly, desperate to break up some of the tension between them.

As wonderful as she was realizing he was, as much as her feminine hormones were screaming for her to give in and see where this could go, Quinn kept herself under control...mostly. She couldn't just jump in his lap and declare her undying love and have them live happily ever after.

She barely knew him. They needed time to get to know each other, if he was willing of course. Maybe this little storm and accident were a blessing in disguise. What else would have forced her to slow down enough to consider Michael as someone she wanted to get to know?

Nothing.

Michael made a face. "Me too. I'll be honest, I've never been much of a fighter, but the thought of someone abusing you like that…" He shook his head, his cheeks red. It was clear he was more than just bothered on her behalf. "Men like that belong in jail."

"Agreed," Quinn said, giving his hand a squeeze. She wasn't ready to let go of it. It felt too good. "But there's nothing I can do about it," she said with a shrug. "The police's hands were tied and otherwise it was a 'he said, she said' scenario."

"But why believe him over you?"

Quinn slumped. "I'm not sure. I thought I was friends with the people I worked with, but…Adam had worked there a lot longer than I had. He was several years older than me and I think no one could imagine the quiet man they worked with doing the insane stalking I was talking about."

"More than likely, no one wanted to deal with it," Michael growled. He leaned forward, still holding her hand, but resting his elbows on his knees as he stared into the fire. "It's amazing what we let people get away with simply because we're too afraid to take a stand." He glanced her way. "Very few people are willing to stand alone. Good for you for not giving in and keeping quiet."

She gave him a sad smile. "It didn't do any good."

Michael smiled back, but it was brighter than hers. "It brought you here."

Quinn laughed softly, then rubbed her temple. Man, was she sore. It seemed that with every passing moment, she got worse. Getting out of the truck to go to the bathroom this morning had been torture, but it appeared her body wasn't done going downhill.

"You need that medicine," Michael said bluntly. He dropped her hand and stood up.

"No...wait..." Quinn wasn't sure where her panic was coming from, but she didn't want him to leave, even if it meant some help with the pain she was experiencing. "I'll be fine." She pointed to the windows. "You've already done so much. You don't need to go out in that weather just for some headache medicine."

He stared at her for a moment, his face softening. "I can tell you're hurting," he said softly.

Quinn nodded slowly. "And yet, it's all superficial. I have a headache and I have bumps and bruises. Nothing that can't heal just fine with some rest."

Michael snorted. "Rest. In a damp cabin in the woods with no electricity? I don't know if you noticed, but that bedroom back there was twenty degrees cooler than out here." He looked agitated as he waved an arm toward the short hallway. "You won't be able to rest well at all if we don't get you back soon. And what if..." He stopped, clenching his jaw.

"What?" Quinn asked, honestly curious. Why was Michael so upset?

His chin fell to his chest and his shoulders slumped like a little boy being denied a treat. "I just worry that your concussion will cause some problems that could have been helped if I got you help on time."

Quinn's eyebrows rose up. "You think I might have brain damage?"

He scowled and shifted away. "I didn't say brain damage. But what if there's something wrong we can't see? And I was too stupid to park my truck in a better place, so now we're trapped out here and you would have been just fine if I'd made different choices?"

"Ah..." Quinn nodded. "So you're still blaming yourself for all this."

He didn't respond, just pushed a hand through his hair.

Quinn stood, ignoring the pain in her back and thighs. Why in the world did her quads hurt? The human body was a strange thing. She stepped a little closer to him, ignoring his wary stare, and rested her bruised hands against his chest.

MISTAKE! her brain screamed when she remembered he wasn't

wearing a shirt. HIs heated skin felt nearly scalding against her palms, though she wasn't sure if it was from the fire or something else.

Forcing herself to stay put, she looked up and met his gaze. "This. Is. Not. Your. Fault." She paused, waiting for those words to sink in. "I don't blame you for one iota of it," she further pressed. "Your suggestion to go the night before was a smart choice and unless you have some magical powers I'm unaware of, you have no control over the weather or a random group of deer. You also aren't a seer who could tell in that black abyss we escaped from that the side of the road was a mud pit." She patted his chest, then pulled her hands back before she began petting him. "So if you're some all-knowing god, please tell me. Otherwise, please let it go."

He snorted and an amused smirk played on his lips. "All-knowing god?"

Quinn shrugged, the movement pinching in her neck, and she raised a hand to rub the spot. "Who knows? I'm gonna bet with your job that you're a big reader. There's a multitude of knowledge in books. Perhaps you've gained more than the rest of us."

He put his hand on her arm, softly and slowly rubbing his palm up and down. Quinn wished it was against her skin rather than a too-big sweatshirt. "Well, I hate to disappoint us both, but I'm far from all-knowing. Unless you're looking for themes of Shakespeare or the life details of Jane Austen, or which books contain middle school kids' favorite swear words, I'm probably not your guy."

Quinn smiled.

Michael's easy smile came back. "Would you let me rub your neck? It looks like it's hurting you."

Quinn nodded, feeling slightly like a Bobblehead doll. "I'd like that. Thank you."

Michael looked around. "Hang on." He gently pushed her to the side. "Not sure why I didn't do this before," he grumbled, then held up a hand when Quinn glared at him. With a mighty heave, he began to maneuver the couch in the small space until it sat directly in front of the fire. It would be much more comfortable than the wooden chairs they'd been using. "Have a seat," he said, waving his hand toward the old, plaid cushions. "I'll stand back here and see if we can work out some of your tightness."

"So you've read a book on being a masseuse, is that what you're telling me?" Quinn teased as she sat down. She nearly jumped out of her seat when Michael's voice came right in her ear as he leaned over the back of the couch.

"No…but I do have a soft spot for a…woman in distress."

There was no way to miss the fact that he hadn't called her beautiful, which stirred odd feelings of conflict inside Quinn. She was beyond grateful he had listened to her story and was acting accordingly, but…she also found herself *wanting* Michael to think she was beautiful. Her attraction to him was growing by the moment, and her traitorous heart wanted it to be the same for him.

* * *

MICHAEL STRAIGHTENED, feeling like he'd pushed the boundaries enough for the moment. He'd seen enough from her in the last couple of hours to think that she was truly softening toward him, giving him courage to push the flirting and touching a little. He didn't mind if she knew he was attracted to her, but the biggest thing was, he wanted her to understand he understood boundaries and wouldn't break them.

Especially after her dealings with that pervert.

Michael took a deep breath, bracing himself for the riot of sensations that always followed when he touched Quinn. Her hands on his chest had almost brought him to his knees. Despite his concerns for her health and safety, there was a small part of him that was grateful they were stuck in the cabin. That the barriers between them were being broken down and that he was beginning to see more of her than just the stunning face she displayed in public.

"Tell me if I squeeze too hard," he said, as his fingers gently danced over her skin. She had to be hurting something awful. The two pills she'd taken last night would be long gone and with as bad as the front end of her car was, Michael was positive that her whiplash was nearly unbearable.

Her ability to keep going, to talk to him, to stay awake, it all spoke to her strength of character and he found himself even more drawn to that than her intriguing gray eyes.

"So…" she said, relaxing under his touch. "I've shared all my deep, dark secrets. Doesn't that make it your turn?"

Michael chuckled. "If I had them, I still don't know if I'd share them."

"Hey!" she cried in mock outrage.

His smile was starting to feel like a permanent fixture on his face. Aspen would be proud. "In all seriousness, I'm more of a what you see is what you get type of guy. I love books, that led me to my current job. My dad and mom run the Gingerbread Inn, taken over from my mom's grandmother many years ago. I'm the oldest of three kids, with twin sisters I already mentioned. I have way too many cousins and we seem to dot every corner of Seagull Cove."

Quinn laughed softly.

"And…that's about it."

"You obviously do more than read books," she said. "I know a lot of bookworms and none of them can carry a full grown woman all the way through the woods without breaking a sweat."

His cheeks were starting to ache with how much he was smiling. Good thing no one was around with a camera. "My cousin, Jayden, likes to be active and my best friend is a firefighter. Jayden has enough energy for twenty people and Gavin refuses to let me be a couch potato in peace."

"From what I've seen of Jayden, I'm guessing he's not the type to be active alone?"

"Something like that."

Quinn nodded and laid her head to the side, allowing him a little deeper access to the tight muscles. "And your sisters? Are they as into books as you are?"

Michael snorted. "Not a chance. Our mother was a librarian, so I came by my interest honestly, but my sisters are more like my dad. They like adventure in real life rather than between the pages. In fact, I think the most common insult I've received during my growing up years was how horrible it was to have such a boring brother." He probably shouldn't have shared that. Quinn already had shut Michael down once. He was just now starting to get through to her, and now he was telling her about how lame his own family finds him. *Niiiice. Exactly what every woman wants to hear.*

Quinn turned to look over her shoulder, then shifted her body when that apparently hurt. "They think you're boring?"

Michael shrugged. "I suppose I am. It's fine."

Those light gray eyes were warm as she said softly, "I don't think you're boring."

Michael laughed, a little uncomfortable, though the words landed dead center in his chest. Warm and welcome. He scratched the back of his head. "Thanks."

"No, I mean it," she persisted. "Just because you don't like the same things as them doesn't make you boring. I taught kindergarten. I know the good a paper adventure can do." She smiled. "Don't let them get you down."

He nodded, unsure what else to say. He had been so set on helping her and making sure she was taken care of, yet every time he turned around, Quinn was comforting him instead! Easing his guilt and building his confidence. It made him all the more eager to try his hand at going out again, but he reined in the urge.

Too soon.

"Do you want to lie down?" he asked. "You probably should sleep some."

Quinn's eyebrows pulled together. "Actually, I think I'm going to walk around a little, try to loosen my muscles, and then maybe I'll nap." She gave him a sheepish look. "Can I nap on the couch? I know that means you don't get to sit on the cushioned seats, but I really don't want to go back in that back room all by myself."

Michael couldn't blame her. The wind, if anything, had only grown stronger in the last hour and he was surprised some of the windows hadn't been broken in yet. If one of the trees in the yard broke, they were going to be in a world of hurt. "I don't mind at all. I just want you to be comfortable."

Quinn stood, stretching her back and groaning. "Well, you're doing a great job."

"Says the woman who's moaning in pain," he teased.

Quinn laughed. "I suppose I spoke too soon." She began to shuffle, following the outer walls of the room. "What's your favorite book?"

He sat down in one of the chairs. The space was just big enough that there were a few places that kept him out of her way. "Favorite? Like absolute favorite?" He snorted. "That's like asking a mom who her favorite kid is."

"Okay...what genres do you read?"

"Anything."

"Anything?" Quinn raised an eyebrow. "Even romance?"

He shrugged. "Sometimes. If it's got other elements in it as well."

She nodded. "Okay. Favorite sci-fi?"

Michael tilted his head back in thought. "Good question..." he muttered. "I've got a couple series I love. When I was a kid I was like everyone else and completely under the *Star Wars* spell, and I still enjoy those. But I'll be honest. I don't know that I have favorites, as much as I just have those I like enough to keep thinking about." He shrugged. "In the moment, whatever book I'm reading is my favorite."

"Fair enough." She rotated her shoulders and stretched her arms over her head.

Michael was more than grateful the sweatshirt was too large for him to see the lines of her body. He didn't need anything else attracting him to this woman. He was already gone, hook, line and sinker. "How about you? Siblings? Family? Favorite activities?"

Quinn shook her head. "Only child. Raised by my grandad, and he's gone."

"I'm sorry."

Quinn shrugged. "It's fine. It was several years ago and he was sick, so it was better that he got relief."

Michael nodded.

"I mean, I miss him. He was great, but I'm glad he's not in pain anymore."

"I get it and that's a really great way to look at it."

Quinn's cheeks turned red. "Thanks." She pushed a curl back, but as usual, it sprung forward again.

"Your hair…" Michael ventured. "And your gray eyes. They're…"

"Weird? Quirky?" she supplied with a smile.

"Unusual." Michael finished for her. "Are they from your parents?"

Quinn shook her head and finished her third lap by coming back to the couch and sitting on the edge. "Nope. Believe it or not, if my grandpa is to be believed, they came from my grandmother." Quinn raised her eyebrows. "I never met her, but Grandpa says the curse skipped my dad and landed on me."

Michael leaned in. Slowly, so she could stop him if she wanted, he reached out and pulled on the curl, stretching it, then letting it spring back. "That's not a curse," he said softly. His fingertips skimmed under her eyes, noting the dark circles, but paying more attention to the light gray orbs. "It's eye-catching and should be viewed as a blessing." Their stares held and the tension crackled louder than the fire.

"For time one-hundred and twenty-one," she whispered, "thank you."

CHAPTER 12

Quinn's eyes fluttered as she slowly came out of her nap. She and Michael had been talking and she hadn't even realized she had fallen asleep. Something soft was under her head and a warm blanket was draped over her shoulders.

After adjusting to the semi-darkness, she looked around. Firelight was still flickering to her right and she turned her head to see Michael up close, leaning on his knees. His blond hair looked dark in the shadows and the scruff on his chin was becoming easier to see.

The wind still sounded as if it was trying to tear down the whole forest and a few heavy thuds let her know that the tree branches were whacking the house as they moved. "How long did I sleep?" she croaked, then cleared her throat.

She began to push herself, but the pain in her head and neck made her hiss and lay back down.

"Easy," Michael said in a deep, soothing tone. He rushed to her side, squatting at the side of the couch.

When she had regained her eyesight, she turned to him.

Michael smiled, tilting his head adorably to the side. "Hey," he whispered.

"Hey," Quinn couldn't help but whisper back. How did she ever think he looked like Adam? Michael's demeanor was so different, so sweet, so wonderful. Quinn couldn't believe she had pushed him away without ever getting to know him.

He started to reach out, but cleared his own throat and pulled back. "I think it's late evening," he told her. "You slept a few hours."

Quinn felt her eyes widen. "Seriously? And the storm is still here?"

Michael nodded and rubbed the back of his neck, glancing at the window. He stood, his knees creaking slightly. "Yeah. It's a doozy for sure. We have rainstorms that'll last days, but I can't remember one quite this bad before."

Quinn started to rise again, this time much more carefully, and Michael bent over to help.

"Easy does it," he soothed, offering support on her shoulders until she was seated upright.

"Thank you," Quinn murmured. She rubbed at her eyes and grimaced at the light smear of mascara she found on the heel of her palms. "I must look a fright," she muttered, not really directing the comment at Michael.

"You look wonderful," he answered.

Quinn looked up. "Why do I get the feeling you'd say that to anyone?"

Michael shrugged, dropping his eyes from hers. "Truthfully? I probably would. Life's too short to be rude. But in this case…" He brought his eyes back to hers and held them. He didn't need to finish his sentence. Once again, he was declaring that he thought she was attractive and this time, Quinn's heart soared.

She patted the seat next to her. "Want to try something not hard?" she asked.

Michael chuckled and sat down, though he left a respectful distance between them. "Ahh… much nicer," he agreed, leaning back against the cushions.

"It certainly feels better than those wooden ones," Quinn said. "Though I shudder to think of how much dirt and other germs are stuck in this fabric."

Michael's eyes were closed, but he grinned. "I recommend *not* thinking about it."

"Good plan." Quinn leaned back as well. She was tempted to rest her head on his shoulder, but didn't want to be too forward. It looked like they had another night together. She would let things unfold as they may.

"Guess what I found while you were sleeping?" Michael asked.

"Evidence of Bigfoot?"

Michael's confused face slowly turned toward her. "You're a believer?"

Quinn laughed, even though it hurt her chest. "No," she said, waving a hand in the air. "I mean…I totally get why people are. The woods on this side of the country are pretty amazing and who knows what's hiding in them, but nope…not a believer." She quirked an eyebrow, grateful the stinging sensation in her chest was dying down. "But you asked and I came up with the most outrageous answer I could think of."

He chuckled. "It was that. I was sitting here thinking I had totally misjudged you."

"Oh? Being a believer would change your opinion of me?"

Michael shrugged. "Maybe." He looked her up and down like he was sizing her up. "Or maybe I just would have thought you hit your head harder than I thought."

"Hey!" Quinn pushed against his arm, regretting the pain the movement brought, but not regretting the fun flirting going on between them. "I'll have you know my grandfather always said I had a hard head. It can certainly withstand a car crash."

"You have a hard head? Or he said you were hard-headed?"

Quinn sniffed and stuck her nose in the air. "I heard what I heard." Michael's low laughter was like a balm to her wounds. Quinn could have listened to it all night long. His sisters thought he was boring? No way. Michael was fun, intelligent, kind, handsome and the best part of all…sincere.

"You still haven't figured out what I found," he hedged.

"Oh…yeah." Quinn took a moment to think. "Something other

than beef stew."

Michael made a face. "As much as I'd like to say 'yes,' I'm afraid that's a negative. But!" He held a finger up in the air. "I found a bunch of bottled water under the bed and I found a pack of cards in one of the drawers."

"Hydration and distraction, two of my favorite things," Quinn teased.

"I thought as much." He stood and walked away for only a moment before coming back with both of his treasures. "Here. Drink up."

Quinn followed orders. The beef stew had helped her stomach earlier, but it definitely had done very little to slake her thirst. The water in the cabin had been turned off when they arrived and as far as Quinn knew, Michael hadn't figured out how to turn it on yet. Though, she had been disappointed to note that when she opened her eyes, he was wearing his shirt again.

It must have dried enough while she was sleeping and he'd put it back on. If Quinn had been brave enough, she'd have complained. It had been a wonderful view to help distract her from the weather raging outside.

"I also have good news," Michael said as he began shuffling the cards.

"What's that?"

"I think the storm is beginning to wane."

Quinn's head immediately jerked toward the window, causing a sharp twinge in her neck. "Ow."

Michael tsked his tongue and shook his head. "It's still going to be there even if you'd take an extra two seconds to move," he scolded.

Quinn rubbed her neck. "I suppose so, but you caught me off guard. I can still hear the wind."

Michael nodded. "Yeah. But I'm pretty sure the rain is less than it was. It sounds more like a swarm of bees now, rather than an angry mob of hornets."

She cocked her head and sure enough, Michael was right. The rain was still plenty steady, but it wasn't so dire-sounding. "Huh. Maybe we will get out of here before we're both old and gray."

"Maybe so." He finished passing out the cards. "Ever played poker?" he asked.

"I know the basics, I think," Quinn said. "But what about betting? We don't have anything."

Michael's lips twitched. "Then I suppose we'll have to get creative."

* * *

She was sizing him up. Michael could see it in her eyes. Just how serious was he and what did he want? The words were practically written across her bruised forehead.

"Okay…" she hedged. "Remind me how we start?"

Michael picked up his hand. "Look at your cards. Do you know what makes a good hand?"

"I think so," she said, eyeing what she'd been dealt.

"Okay. So first, we make our bets, then you can trade in cards to the dealer."

She nodded. "It's coming back to me. Seems like the kid next door taught me to play once when we were being babysat together."

Michael chuckled. "Was he trying to impress you?"

Quinn shrugged and moved her cards around. "I don't know. We were betting chocolate chips, so it's not like it was going to get too crazy." She folded her cards in her lap. "Okay. I'm ready."

Michael nodded. "You go first."

She grinned. "If I win, you have to shout that you're an old maid, out into the storm."

Michael's eyebrows shot up. "Where in the world did you come up with that?"

She laughed, her shoulders shaking slightly, only to wince afterwards. He really should have taken the time to go get those pills while she was sleeping. But Michael had been reluctant to leave her. She'd looked so peaceful and the way the firelight danced on her porcelain cheeks had been mesmerizing. So instead of getting her help, he'd sat around like a voyeur and watched her rest.

"I had a roommate at college who used to do that when we played

Old Maid. The loser always had to shout it out the front door. I think the other apartments thought we were nuts."

He rubbed the back of his neck. "Right, well…if that's what you want to bet. You realize there's no one around to witness my humiliation?"

"Oooh, so you have a bad hand, huh? I should have bet something like a foot massage."

"I didn't say that," Michael shot back.

"But you implied you were going to lose."

"Maybe I was going to let you win."

"Don't go easy on me," she demanded. "If you're going to win, then win. I'll hold my own."

He grinned at her. "I didn't realize you were competitive."

Quinn rolled her eyes and rubbed her forehead afterward. "I'm not usually. But when it comes to games? I don't like to be at the bottom of the pack."

"There are only two of us."

"Yep," she agreed.

"That means the odds of being on the bottom of the pack are fifty-fifty."

"Yep."

He smiled. "Okay, then. How many cards do you want?"

"Wait, wait, wait. You haven't said your bet."

Michael pursed his lips. He knew what he wanted, but he figured he should work his way up to it. Play a few rounds and then toss it in when she was least expecting it. After all…he'd been a saint during their time there, and there was a long night looming ahead. Surely what he wanted was attainable if he played his cards right.

"I'll reiterate yours. Loser has to shout to the woodland animals."

Quinn narrowed her eyes. "Deal." She looked at her hand again. "Three cards."

"That doesn't sound like a number from someone super confident in their ability to win."

"Shhh…" she scolded. "I'm working here."

Michael couldn't have stopped smiling if his life depended on it.

This was so much better than taking a woman to the movies or a fancy restaurant. Well…it was better if you took away Quinn's injuries and the crazy storm outside.

But there was something so enticing about the intimacy of the fire and their proximity and the sweet hum of attraction between them. They were flirting, laughing and having fun getting to know each other and there was no pretense or need to put on a show. One of the things he hated most about dating was trying to actually get to know the other person, the one behind the mask and behind the best behavior they displayed in public.

"Are you done yet?" he asked.

She glared over her cards. "Patience is a virtue."

"It's also something only old people have."

She laughed. "Is that your way of telling me you're young?"

Michael scratched his jawline. "Actually, I think I need to remind myself once in a while. According to my sisters, I've been an old fuddy duddy since I was ten."

Quinn shook her head. "Your sisters and I need to have words."

He grinned at that and swapped out two cards. "Time to lay 'em down."

She frowned, then shrugged. "If you say so." She spread her cards out, the smile she was trying to contain spreading across her face. "What do they say? Read 'em and weep?" She pointed and counted out each of her four kings.

Michael didn't even bother to lay down his hand. It was too fun watching her be excited to win. "Well done, Padawan. You are now ready to become the Master."

"Uh, uh, uh," she said, pointing to the door. "Not until you've fulfilled your end of the bargain."

Michael stood and shuffled to the door, hoping he looked depressed. Acting wasn't his strong suit, but he was enjoying her amusement. He peeked through the door and looked back over his shoulder. "It's dark. And wet. And windy."

Quinn pointed imperiously toward the outside.

He rolled his eyes, straightened his shoulders and yanked the door open. "I'M THE OLD MAID!" he bellowed before slamming the door shut again.

Quinn was laughing and holding her ribs. "That's awesome. I wish my phone was working."

He shook a finger at her. "Recording it wasn't part of the deal."

"Next time, then," she said.

Michael frowned as he watched her stretch. "Do your ribs hurt? Does it hurt to breathe?" Once again, his concern that there were injuries he wasn't seeing came rushing to the surface.

She waved him off. "Just bruised. I can breathe fine, but if I laugh hard, it aches. It'll be okay."

He shook his head. This woman got more amazing by the minute. Five more hands went by with them splitting the victories before Michael decided to make his move. The mood was light, the camaraderie warm, and he'd waited long enough.

He bit the inside of his cheek to keep back his smile. His poker face wasn't as good as Jayden's, but hopefully it would be enough. "Bet?" he asked her.

Quinn tapped her bottom lip, spiking Michael's blood pressure. He was going to die of internal combustion before he went through with his plan. "Loser has to tell about a time they got in trouble that was public and embarrassing."

Michael nodded. "Wow. Going for the deep stuff now."

"Absolutely."

"I accept that bet, but this time, I'm making my own."

"Oh?" Quinn raised her eyebrows and tilted her head slightly. "Now we're getting somewhere. What do you bet?"

Forcing himself to take his time, Michael slowly leaned in. The tension grew with each inch and he could see her breath catch. It was all he could do to keep his eyes on hers rather than her pink, plump lips. He moved until their noses were only a few inches apart. "I want to bet…a kiss."

CHAPTER 13

as she sweating? Quinn was positive there was a trickle of sweat working its way down her back even though the room was barely tolerable temperature-wise. If she moved even a foot or two away from the fire, she would break out in goose-bumps, but right now, she felt flushed all over.

"A...what?" She gasped.

Michael's smug smirk was a mix of adorable and annoying. "If I win, I want a kiss."

"Why?" The word came out before she could stop it, and once it hung between them, Quinn wanted to smack her already aching fore-head. *Are you kidding me? Who asks a guy why he wants to kiss? All guys like to kiss. Most don't even ask permission.*

Michael's right eyebrow slowly rose. "I guess I haven't been as clear about it as I thought," he muttered. Tilting his head to the side, he said, "Quinn, I think you're amazing. You're strong and intelligent and while I know you don't like the word *beautiful*, you need to know that I definitely find myself attracted to you on the inside just as much as I do on the outside." He smiled again and leaned in slightly. "So I don't think it's that crazy that a guy like me would want to steal a kiss from a girl like you."

"Steal," she teased breathlessly. "You just asked permission."

"I've never been a very good thief," he said casually, leaning back again. "Once tried to take a Popsicle without Mom's permission when I was little and I nearly puked."

Quinn laughed, her fear slowly subsiding and being replaced with anticipation. She couldn't deny that she had thought about what it would be like to kiss him, but she hadn't planned for him to make such a big deal out of it either. Usually a kiss just…happened. Talking about it like this kind of made her nervous. "I guess I can see why your sisters made fun of you." She smiled to ease the tease. "But I still think they're wrong."

He shrugged. "Prove it."

Quinn glanced at her hand, guessing her odds. She had a good start, but it wasn't great. "I won't lose on purpose," she warned him. The thought of making him work for it a little was actually kind of intriguing. What woman didn't enjoy a little chase before a kiss?

"I wouldn't expect you to," he responded. "How many cards?"

Quinn pursed her lips, trying to gauge her odds of what might be coming through the deck. There were only two of them, so there were lots of cards to draw and she needed something specific if she was going to put this guy in his place. "Two, please," she said, handing hers over.

Not bad… She put the queen next to the other, which gave her two pairs. They weren't fantastic, but she had a solid hand. Would it be enough?

"I'll take two as well," Michael stated, passing his own cards in and out. He frowned, moving his hand around, and Quinn wondered if he was regretting his move.

Her heart began to pound the longer the moment stretched. "Well? Are you ready?" she asked, her tone offering a little too much of her impatience.

Michael grinned at her. "Nervous?"

She put on the most innocent face she could. "Not at all, I'm just eager to hear your deep, dark secret before it's time for dinner. The Popsicle story didn't count."

Michael snorted and shifted his cards one more time. "Call," he said.

Quinn set down her cards. "Two pair."

Michael nodded slowly. "Not bad."

"Michael," she growled, knowing he was holding out on her on purpose. "I'm starting to think you're a sore loser."

He shrugged. "You're right. I am." He set down his cards, showing his own two pairs.

"Oh…how does that work?" she asked. "If we have the same?"

"Well, normally it would come down to who has the highest value of pairs, but…" With a sharp, deliberate movement, he set down his last card, creating a full house, which even Quinn knew soundly beat her cards.

Heat immediately shot up her neck and into her cheeks.

"I do believe the victory is mine," Michael said as he gathered the cards.

Quinn cleared her throat. "Yep," she squeaked, clearing her throat again. "You're right." Her fingers grew restless and she began to tap them on her knee, but she stopped quickly when she reached a sore spot.

She looked down at her body. At the oversized sweatshirt, the too-big pajama bottoms. If she looked underneath, she'd see the black and blue of her skin and the physical evidence of the accident that had forced them together. Her body ached, her head was screaming, she knew she had to look like something from a B rated zombie flick, and yet he wanted to kiss her?

"What's going on in that curly head of yours?" Michael asked. How in the world did he seem so casual about the whole thing?

Had she misread him? Did he do this all the time? Now that she was finally starting to trust him, would his real intentions come out? Had he planned that accident because she'd rejected him?

Squeezing her eyes shut, despite the pain, Quinn forced her breathing to slow down. *Stop it,* she told herself. *You're being ridiculous. Michael doesn't give off any of the red flags that Adam did. You CANNOT judge one from the other.*

"Hey…" Warm fingertips traced along her jaw. The feeling was amazing despite her sensitive skin.

Quinn opened her eyes.

"I would never take that which isn't freely given," he said in a soft but steely tone. "If it freaks you out that much, just say so." He gave her a sad smile. "It was only a game. It wasn't meant to cause a panic attack."

Quinn wasn't quite sure what to say. How did she explain the war going on inside of her? That one part of her worried it really was all a game. Even the kiss. That he would turn out to be just like Adam…a wolf in sheep's clothing.

Yet the other part of her, the part that had been silent for far too long, the *old* Quinn, thought the idea of kissing him was the best thing she'd ever heard. She loved the feel of his touch. She was beginning to crave the tingles of electricity that went up her arm every time he brushed her fingers, and the idea of seeing what would happen with a kiss, well…it had her tied in knots…good knots.

"I'm just nervous," she whispered, hoping he wouldn't ask for too many details. "It's been a long time—" she began, but cut off. He didn't need to know how long it had been. She had kissed Adam, but Quinn had decided those couple of kisses didn't count.

They hadn't been pleasant and they hadn't been mutually wanted. Which meant she didn't have to acknowledge they existed and it also meant her kissing was more than likely out of practice.

"Here." Michael set aside the cards and stood up, holding out his hand to her.

Quinn's fingers were shaking as she put her hand in his, but the heat of his skin helped soothe her frayed nerves. She allowed him to help her gently to her feet.

"Are you sure you're okay with this?" he whispered, his beautiful blue eyes roaming over her face.

"If you really want to kiss this hideousness," she croaked, "I won't stop you."

He brushed his nose against hers. "I don't see anything even close to hideous, but the real question is, do you want it, Quinn? Forget the bet. Do you want to kiss me too?"

Her chest heaved and her heart tried to beat straight out of her chest. Her knees, which were already shaky, began to knock together and she knew it would only add to her injuries if she didn't get herself under control. Her hands quickly went to his chest and she gripped his T-shirt tightly to hold herself up.

Michael's arms went around her waist, supporting her while being ever so gentle. It was his soft touch that finally answered the question for her. Michael had won the kiss fair and square, yet not only was he offering her a choice, but he was holding her like she was the most precious object on Earth. He wasn't just taking, he was offering and doing so in a way that wouldn't bring any harm to her or her injuries. She knew exactly what to say.

"Yes."

* * *

MICHAEL HAD NEVER BEEN QUITE SO nervous when holding a woman. What was it about Quinn that was different? He couldn't place his finger on it. He'd kissed several lovely, wonderful women before, but none of them had his heart racing like a horse at the Kentucky Derby or made his hands shake like a young teenage boy on his first date.

He flexed his fingers against her back, being as careful as he possibly could while still offering her support. She seemed a little shaky and the grip she had on his shirt was tight enough to tear the fabric.

When she had finally answered his question, Michael had been sure he would be the one needing to be held up. Her soft, breathless *yes* was everything a guy could hope for.

Michael shifted himself closer and ran his nose along her damaged cheek. The heat from her skin burned clear through him, landing smack in the middle of his chest. His fingers itched to move and touch her hair, letting her curls fall through his fingers, but he kept them still.

He needed to remember she wasn't well. Now wasn't the type to get aggressive. She needed care, affection and tenderness and he was determined to show her that he was nothing like Adam. He would treat her the exact way she deserved to be treated, and then, when the real world broke into their bubble, he would wait to see if it was enough. He'd offer her himself and let her decide.

Her breathing grew shallow the longer he prolonged the kiss and Michael found his own following suit. He ran his nose along her ear, then nuzzled in just behind her jawline. How did she smell so good? She smelled of forest and rain, maybe from their drenching in the storm, but whatever it was, Michael was positive he'd never smelled anything so enticing.

"Michael," she breathed. "Please…"

He squeezed his eyes, holding onto his last shred of self control. But how could he deny her whispered request? Instead of continuing to build the moment, he brought his mouth up to hers, just barely keeping distance between them, as he forced the tension up another notch or two in anticipation of the kiss.

Something inside of him insisted that the moment would be amazing, and he didn't want to rush it, but her plea had him picking up the pace. "You're so beautiful," he whispered against her lips, forgetting that she hated the word.

Her answer was to speed up her breathing and he felt her straining in his direction.

Feeling like he had tortured them both enough, Michael brushed his lips ever so slightly against her, the touch zinging to his gut. He paused just long enough to breathe and enjoy the moment one more time before pressing his lips fully to hers.

His gut instinct had been wrong. Dead wrong. This wasn't amazing, it was earth-shattering and Michael didn't know if he'd ever be able to come up for air.

Her lips were soft and pliant and she followed his lead as if she were made to kiss him.

Slowly, so as not to hurt her, he pulled her closer into his body. Her hands left his shirt and wrapped around his neck, tangling in the back of his hair, the sharp tug mixing with the pleasure of the kiss and giving him a jolt he wouldn't soon forget.

Not wanting to overtax her, he forced their lips apart and kissed his way down to her jaw, where he peppered any skin that wasn't discolored with tender and sincere worshiping touches.

He ducked his head slightly to get under her jawline and she tilted her head to offer more access. Michael almost growled in approval as he explored every inch of skin he could. He never would have imagined something could be this good. Now he just had to figure out how to keep this woman in his life for longer than the raging storm outside.

Would she be open to that? Would she be willing to give this a shot? Or was this all just the result of a warm, romantic fire and their forced companionship?

She cupped his cheeks and brought their mouths back together and Michael's thoughts flew out the window. He didn't care. Not one bit. All he cared about was the here and now and the riot of sensations the stunningly delicate woman in his arms was creating inside of him.

Tomorrow could take care of itself.

Eventually, her hold on him started to relax and Michael took the signal to ease up. He slowed the intensity of their kissing and slowly brought his head up, breaking their touch. He stared into her wide, gray eyes. She looked disheveled and shocked, like she wasn't quite sure what had happened between them.

That makes two of us.

He let his fingers dance along her cheek. "I think that was the best bet I ever made," he said, his voice low and hoarse.

Quinn's lips twitched and she eventually gave into the smile. "I'm not sure I've ever enjoyed losing quite so much."

Michael chuckled and tucked her under his chin, holding her against his chest. "Thank you."

She jerked a little, pulling back to look at him again. "Thank you?"

Michael nodded. "You didn't have to give so much, but I'm grateful you did."

After a moment, she sighed and laid back against his chest. "I suppose I should say the same, but we both know I'm like a broken record at this point, so I'll just say 'ditto'."

Michael smiled and kissed the top of her head, then simply held her. They stood for several minutes, leaning into each other and letting the desire between them slowly come down to something more manageable.

When she began to shake, he realized he'd waited too long to get her off her feet. "Sorry," he said gruffly. "Let's get you back down on the couch." He guided her, careful of her cuts and bruises. "Are you hungry? Do you want me to fix dinner?"

Quinn looked up from under her eyelashes and the look was intoxicating. "I'm afraid I'm not in the mood for beef stew," she said softly.

Daaaang... Michael choked and straightened, putting a little distance between them as he caught his breath. This woman was going to be the death of him. The glorious, totally worth it, death.

"Uh…" He rubbed the back of his head. "While I'm all too happy to oblige, I think I need to take a little time to get myself back under control before doing that again." He shook his head. "You have no idea what you do to me."

Her face fell and she leaned back, frightening Michael.

"He used to say that, didn't he?" Michael snarled.

Quinn shrugged.

Stepping away from her, he shoved his hands in his hair. "Is there anything I can say to you that won't sound tainted?" He spun, facing her. "How do I help you understand how wonderful you are if half the words in the English language sound like a pervert?"

Quinn gave him a sad smile. "You're doing just fine," she said. "I think the problem is with me, not you." She took in a shuddering breath. "You called me beautiful earlier, and for the first time in a long time…I didn't feel like throwing up."

Michael hurried back to her side, sitting on the edge of the couch and grasping her hands. "Quinn…I know I'm not suave or all as outspoken as other guys, but what just happened between us? It was totally sincere from my end." He dropped his head, afraid to look at her in that moment. "If you'd be willing to give me another chance, I… I'd still love to take you out to dinner."

Quinn pulled her hand away from his and Michael's heart fell until he felt her pull him up by his chin.

"How about we start right now with that beef stew?" she asked.

He smiled, his fear floating away with the wind outside. "I'll be right back."

CHAPTER 14

Quinn couldn't seem to stop staring at Michael, and at least she didn't seem to be the only one. They were both hunkered over their bowls, but their eyes kept bouncing back to each other, as if some magnetic pull kept them from staying away too long.

Each time they caught each other, Quinn found herself blushing and she caught Michael's ears turning red. Then they would laugh, only slightly uncomfortably, and turn back to their dinner.

Quinn was so caught up in the game they were playing, she didn't even register the bland flavor of the dinner like she had earlier. She was guessing it was pretty late at night at this point, but she was anything but tired.

Kissing Michael had made Quinn feel as if she'd downed a dozen energy drinks and she was practically buzzing with excitement. Currently, she was simply hoping that unlike a stimulant, she wouldn't end up with a horrible energy crash at the end of their time together.

"All done?" Michael asked, holding out his hand.

Quinn smiled and handed him her bowl. "For the two-hundreth time, thank you."

He smiled in return as he stood. "I'm impressed you're keeping track."

Quinn laughed softly, but sobered quickly as well. She had a sudden, odd urge to be the one taking the dishes to the sink. She wasn't one to let people take care of her the same way Michael had been helping during the last couple of days.

She knew it was because she was injured and she was grateful for it, but she also wanted a way to show her own appreciation, and nothing was coming to mind. Normally, she would do something like bake someone cookies or bread or offer them something unique from her store, but she didn't have access to any of those things right now. Maybe she could simply plan to do something later?

"What's your favorite dessert?" she called over her shoulder.

"Dessert?" Michael asked, causing her to jump. He had come back faster than she'd expected and was walking toward the fireplace. He crouched down in front of the fire, frowning as he put a few more logs on it, shifting the ashes to make sure the heat never wavered. "I'm not sure." Spinning on his toes, he faced her. "I eat a lot of cake and enjoy it."

Quinn laughed. "Let me guess. A hazard of being related to Aspen?"

Michael shrugged and stood up, stretching his arms over his head.

Quinn couldn't have torn her eyes from his arms and chest if her life had depended on it. She knew exactly what it felt like to be held by those strong arms. If she hadn't known his profession, she never would have guessed that he was a teacher. Her old school hadn't boasted men that looked like Michael Dunlap. Adam had been in shape, but much softer than Michael.

"Aspen's mom is a professionally trained baker and her dad was a famous chocolate sculptor." He grinned. "I ate a lot of good food growing up."

"I'll bet you did." Quinn tucked a curl back up in her messy bun. It popped back down in her eyes. "Ugh," she groaned, yanking out the ponytail. Her curls had air dried and were a mass of tangles and kinks. What she wouldn't give for her anti-frizz serum right about now.

She paused for a moment as the pain of her movement passed, then began trying to pull the curls apart enough to manage a new bun.

"Let me."

Quinn froze. Michael's eyes were on her hair and his fingers gently took the chunk from her.

The moment was sticky and thick as he slowly pulled her curls apart, working until each one hung independently. Once that chunk was done, he took another and began the same process, his eyes glued to her hair.

She'd never seen someone so fascinated with it before. Sure, she had people mention how tight her curls were. But Michael didn't simply look passingly interested. He looked completely spellbound, like a young boy seeing Santa Claus for the first time, and that look did more to ease any lingering fears Quinn had held onto than their half hour of crazy kissing.

This man liked her. A lot. And he was willing to do anything, including carry her through storms, cook her dinner, massage her sore joints, and untangle her chaotic curls, all in the name of easing her discomfort, even though she'd rejected him on sight.

That familiar wave of guilt swept through her, ushered out quickly by a tsunami of deliciously sharp attraction.

There were very few men in the world like Michael. And Quinn had won the relationship lottery to have a chance to give this a try.

Quinn closed her eyes and relaxed into his touch. The wind was still howling, but the pounding of the rain was slower and the crackling of the fire seemed louder. The smell of wood and their dinner permeated the area and Quinn sent a quick prayer heavenward that she didn't stink as badly as she feared.

"All done," Michael said. His voice was low and husky, a testament to how much the act had affected him as well.

Quinn opened her eyes straight into his bright blue ones. "Number two-hundred and one. Thank you."

He smiled and leaned forward, leaving a kiss on her forehead. Laying back against the couch, he tenderly pulled her into his side and she sighed in contentment as she rested her head against his shoulder and neck. This was far more comfortable than sleeping in the car had been, or even her nap on the couch.

Her eyes began to droop as he rubbed his hand up and down her arm. She wished she were wearing short sleeves so she could feel the touch against her direct skin, but she didn't have anything else to change into.

Probably a good thing anyway, she thought wryly. *My attraction to him is starting to get out of control, especially with us tucked away all by ourselves.*

"You never answered the question," she murmured as she toyed with the edge of sleep.

"I think my sweet tooth will eat just about anything," Michael responded, his mouth pressed against the top of her head. "But baked goods are probably my weakness."

Quinn smiled. "Like cookies and cake?" She felt him nod.

"Exactly like cookies and cake." He shifted slightly. "But shhh… sleep," he encouraged. "I've got you. You're safe. Sleep."

"Hmm…" Quinn hummed contently. She pulled up her legs onto the couch, twisting until she was completely draped over his chest. "This is really nice." She bounced slightly as he chuckled and could have sworn she heard him mutter, "A little too nice," right before she gave into the pain-free darkness.

* * *

MICHAEL FELT the exact moment that Quinn fell asleep. Her weight settled into him completely and her breathing changed. His arm tightened momentarily around her as he reveled in the moment of Quinn lying in his arms.

After her adamant rejection only a couple of days ago, he would never have imagined this happening.

When he'd first noticed her across the room at Maeve and Ethan's engagement party, he'd been so struck by her beauty that he'd found himself pushing aside his plans to leave Seagull Cove. Shortly after, he'd been slapped in the face by her turning him down, and now she was cuddled into his chest as if she trusted him more than anyone else in the world and Michael was struggling to remember why he had bothered to update his resume.

He reached up with his free hand and rubbed the back of his neck. It almost felt as if he had whiplash as badly as Quinn did. But still…he couldn't find himself arguing with the outcome.

His gaze drifted to the window. The rain looked like it had nearly stopped, and the sound of the wind had lessened, he was sure of it. The darkness looked foreboding, but Michael began to wonder just how much longer he had with her.

Who would have thought Oregon's worst storm in years would be the very thing he needed to get Quinn's attention.

She shifted against him and groaned quietly, and Michael frowned. He needed to go back to the truck and get her that medicine. It wasn't much, but it was better than nothing. They hadn't had any medical supplies and Michael had restrained from telling her that the cut on her forehead would more than likely leave a scar since they'd lacked the ability to close it up properly.

He squished his lips to the side. He was tired. Dog tired, but Quinn needed to come first. Carefully, as carefully as he'd ever done anything in his entire life, Michael shifted her until he was able to slip out and put her head on a pillow.

The loss of her hold cut him to the core and he realized his attraction was becoming much deeper than anything he'd ever experienced before. If he didn't know any better, he would say he was on the verge of falling in love with this woman.

He let his fingers trail along her bruised cheekbone and remove a curl that had slipped over her forehead. He didn't want to go, but he wanted her to feel better more.

Taking a deep breath, he headed to the door. "Crud." Before leaving, he went back to the icy cold bedroom and changed into his original clothes. "At least that means I'll have something dry to come back to," he muttered as he jerked on his stiff jeans. Who knew that denim wasn't a fan of mud and rain?

After getting himself as settled as he could, he went to the door again, his hand on the knob, and hesitated. Glancing over his shoulder, he took in her face once more, his eyes memorizing every curve and angle that the firelight highlighted. He had an odd feeling in his gut and didn't want to leave.

Michael shook his head. "Stop being an idiot," he grumbled. Saying a quick prayer for her safety and forcing himself to quit being a sap, he slipped outside. The first thing that caught him off guard was how cold it was.

The wind wasn't nearly as strong as before, but the temperature had dropped by probably close to twenty degrees. *Dang those Pacific storms.* Hunching his shoulders, Michael took off, walking as fast he could. He'd brought his phone with him, but he squinted into the darkness, trying not to waste the battery.

Only a few steps into the forest, his foot slipped and he had to catch himself on a tree. Cursing under his breath, he powered up his phone and turned on the flashlight, only to curse again. The ground was covered in a thin sheet of ice. Standing back up, Michael tapped it with his sneakered foot. The spot cracked and let him know just how thin it was, but it didn't really matter. Ice was ice and this wasn't a good sign.

He glanced back at the cabin, suddenly worried about the fire. No...he needed to keep going. The pain medication would be more important than ever if this new development meant they were stuck for longer than just tomorrow. An idea popped and he quickly turned toward the road, hurrying as fast as he could.

Slipping and sliding, he made his way to the side of the pavement. Climbing up the shallow incline was harder than it should have been and the first thing he checked was the stuck tire. Frowning, Michael squatted, careful not to lose his balance on the slippery slope.

"What the heck happened?" he grumbled. His tire was visibly flat. With the frozen ground, Michael had hoped he would be able to drive out of the hole, but he couldn't drive like this. They wouldn't make it anywhere on a metal rim.

Grumbling under his breath at their rotten luck, Micheal unlocked the cab and climbed inside. Rummaging around, he pocketed the medicine first, then searched for anything else that would be helpful to them. A sweatshirt he must have thrown in the back at some point was lying dirty on the floor, but he didn't care and tucked it under his arm. He grabbed a small bag of tools, and the small cooler he'd packed with his dinner the day before. His meat sandwich was probably no good, but the apples and bottled water would be welcome.

Not finding anything else, Michael climbed back out, locked the door and walked around to the road. Turning his phone back on, he waited, but to his consternation, he still had no signal.

He shivered as the wind curled around him, causing sharp pinpricks against any skin that was exposed to the elements. Gritting his teeth, he bit back another round of cursing. This wasn't good.

Holding his breath, he turned on the flashlight and passed it over the road. Visibility was far from great, but he couldn't find any sign that any other cars had passed along this highway. The faint frost and icy patches looked completely untouched other than the marks from his shoes.

Unsure how to proceed other than to get back to Quinn as quickly as possible, Michael shut down his phone, stuffed it in his back pocket, and hurried back to the cabin.

The faint glow of the fire through the window in the dark woods was like the world's best welcome. Despite everything that he'd just learned about their situation, Michael felt a smile spread across his face and his pace picked up.

He wiped his feet off as best he could, then slipped inside and froze. Quinn wasn't on the couch.

"Michael?" came her voice. Even without seeing her, he could hear the panic in her tone.

"It's me!" he hollered.

Quinn came limping down the hallway, visibly relaxing when she saw him. "Oh my goodness, I'm so glad you're back."

"Sorry about that," he said quickly as he shut the door and bolted it. "I decided while you were sleeping was the perfect time to run back to the truck." He reached in his pocket, then pulled out the bottle of pills and shook it. "Did someone call for some pain relief?"

Quinn gave him a small, tired smile. "While I appreciate the effort, I wish you'd told me you were going."

Michael walked over and kissed her cheek. "I'm sorry," he whispered. "Next time, I won't sneak off like a thief in the night."

She looked up at him and Michael wanted to puff up his chest at the trusting look she sent his way. "Thank you…" She smiled and laughed lightly. "For the two-hundred and twenty-sixth time."

Michael chuckled along with her. Walking away, he began setting his retrieved treasures on the small table.

"What's all this?" she asked.

"Stuff I found in my truck."

"Why bring it back?" she asked. "Aren't we heading out once it's light?"

Michael hesitated. He hated being the bearer of bad news, but he also wasn't about to lie to her. Turning toward her, he sighed. "I don't know," he said honestly. "When I went outside, I discovered that the temperature was dropping and…"

"And?" she pressed, her eyes wide.

"And there was ice all over the ground." He reached out and lightly gripped her upper arms. "The road was covered in ice and I couldn't see that any other cars had driven down it. Plus, I still have no signal."

She swayed and he pulled her into his chest. "What does it all mean?" she whispered.

Michael rubbed her back, being careful of how sore she was. "It means we might be here a little longer than planned," he said softly. "But don't worry. I'll get us out of here…eventually."

CHAPTER 15

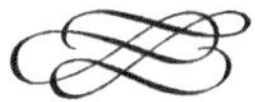

Quinn was confused. Ice? Why was there ice outside? What did it mean? Michael made it sound so ominous. Was it really that big of a deal? "I…don't quite understand," she stammered, rubbing her forehead. "Has the temperature really dropped that much? And if the storm is passing, why does it matter if there's ice?"

Michael nodded and took in a deep breath. "If we're getting ice, it means an arctic storm is moving in." He glanced at the window. "Which tells me that we're not going to be saved quite as quickly as I had hoped." His bright blue eyes came back to hers. "My phone still couldn't pick up a signal, but with an ice-covered road and the wind still heavy, we might be seeing some snow soon."

"Snow!" Quinn cried. "It's mid-spring."

Michael shrugged. "As crazy as it sounds, it *does* happen once in a while. We get air flows down from Alaska and Canada sometimes that carry arctic winds and they blast through with winter weather, but they don't last very long."

"I think I need to sit down," Quinn said weakly. How did she not know this about the Pacific Northwest? It had seemed like such a calm, lovely place when she'd done her research. The perfect setting for an antique shop, right on the water. Yes, she knew they got a lot of rain, but she could handle rain. Icy, arctic snow storms? She definitely hadn't signed up for that.

Michael's arm was immediately around her waist and she took comfort in his warm, strong touch. "Don't worry," he assured her. "The storm shouldn't last too long and then we'll get ourselves out of here. If I have to walk a few miles down the road until I find a signal, I will."

"Don't leave me," she said, grasping his shirt. "I don't want to be left alone." She hadn't had the chance to tell him, but there had been a few noises while he was gone that had terrified her. Logically, she knew that it was just the wind causing the trees to hit the house, but they had sounded like a person and it had caused her to hide in the back room.

Just another thing that Adam stole from me, she thought bitterly. *My ability to think rationally under pressure.*

Michael groaned and pulled her in close, burying his face in her neck. "I'm not leaving you," he whispered against her skin before leaving a soft kiss just under her ear. "But you aren't going to be up for a hike, even in a day or two, and especially not in this weather."

Quinn had a sudden thought. "Wait...if the ground is freezing, then you should be able to get the truck out, right? The mud is gone?" He pulled up so he could look at her, sorrow in his eyes. Quinn knew she wouldn't like what he had to say.

"I must have run over something when I pulled off the road," he said, regret dripping from the tone. "My rear tire is completely flat."

Fear squeezed Quinn's chest. "Michael...are you sure you ran over something?"

"What else could it be?" he asked. "I don't think a deer or bear would do something to it."

She pulled back from his hold, needing to be released from the calming effect he had on her. "Do you think there's a chance that I... we...were followed here?"

Michael frowned. "I don't understand."

Quinn spun back to him. "What if Adam followed me here?"

Michael shook his head. "Ah, Quinn. Do you really think that guy came all the way across the country? You said you didn't tell anyone where you went. Plus, why would he wait this long? You've been in town for six months. Not to mention, how could he be surviving out in that storm we just went through?"

Quinn thought about his words. They made sense, but her fear refused to go away completely. "You're right," she said, nodding rapidly, though it pained her head. "I know you're right. I...I guess I'm just freaked out that Murphy's Law seems to be against us."

He chuckled and put his hands at her waist. "It does seem that way, doesn't it?" Pulling her closer, he kissed her forehead, lingering just enough to get her blood pumping. "Although, there's a selfish part of me that's grateful I was given the chance to really get to know you."

Quinn gave him a sad smile. "It's probably the only way it would have happened, right? I kind of shut you down immediately."

He shrugged, rubbing her arms. "It's fine. I understand why you did it."

She shook her head and rested her hands against his chest. When did she become so comfortable touching him? That kiss they shared seemed to have broken layers upon layers of barriers and it was all happening so fast that Quinn's brain couldn't seem to keep up.

And I'm not sure that I want to.

Nothing about her situation with Michael was creating red flags or sending her into a panic, so she was doing her best to roll with the punches. Each time he touched her, her heart nearly went into cardiac arrest, but it was the most wonderful sensation she'd ever felt. No kiss, no touch, no other man had ever created such a riot of emotions in her and she was enjoying every minute of it. Which surprised her.

"While I'm grateful you're so forgiving," she said, "I shouldn't have jumped to conclusions. Just because you have a couple of physical traits similar to Adam didn't mean you were like him."

"Maybe it was the fact that I tend to be quiet," Michael offered. "Or that I'm a teacher just like him."

"You're not helping your case here," she teased.

He chuckled. "My point was just that I understand. I'm sorry that guy ever was in your life at all, but I'm grateful you're here. Same with the storm. I'm sorry you crashed and that you got hurt, I'm really sorry about your car and your business, but I'm grateful for the chance to get to know you."

Quinn laid her head on his chest. "Me too," she said softly. "Me too." She stayed in his arms longer than was polite, but she just didn't want to move. They probably needed to get to sleep or their morning would be rough. And despite Michael's conviction that a winter storm was coming, there was always a chance that in the light of day, things might look better and they could take that walk down the road.

And she *would* be with him when he walked down the road to get a signal. Quinn wasn't going to be left behind. She would crawl on her hands and knees if she had to, but more time spent alone in the cold cabin was definitely not happening.

"Come on," Michael urged. "You need rest and I definitely need to sleep. We'll tackle the morning, in the morning."

"Is that just another way of saying don't borrow trouble?"

"Probably, but it's a saying for a reason, right?"

She nodded and curled into his side on the couch. Man, he was comfortable. Going back to real life after this was going to be heartbreaking. "I'm guessing you have a whole list of sayings that like, Mr. Literature Teacher."

He gave an exaggerated type of sigh. "I hate to brag, but I am pretty handy if you're ever playing Scrabble."

Quinn grinned, her eyes beginning to droop again. Now that Michael was back, the fears she'd been struggling with were calmly disappearing and she felt safe enough to relax.

"Or if you want to insult someone using words they don't understand."

She huffed a laugh and smacked his chest. "Stop making me laugh. I'm trying to follow orders and go to sleep."

His arms came around her and she felt him press his lips to her temple. "Sleep, lovely Quinn. You're safe with me."

The last bit of her heart that had been holding back from the man holding her melted like ice cream on the Fourth of July. He really was a wordsmith. He knew exactly what she needed to hear, and it was enough to have her dropping off, knowing everything would be just fine.

* * *

MICHAEL CLOSED his eyes and let his head rest against the back of the couch. He hated that she'd been afraid while he was gone. The more time he spent with her and the more he learned about Adam, the more Michael realized just how much that man had terrified Quinn.

She hadn't just turned Michael down. She'd been frightened of him. It had manifested when she'd tried to get away from him after the crash and her brain hadn't caught onto what was going on. She'd been frightened enough to climb over broken glass to get away from him. Simply having a similar color of hair and eyes to Adam had been enough that she'd turned him down and run away without ever getting to know him.

She'd been scared enough that when you slipped out for an hour, she hid in the back room.

His chest ached with the desire to growl out his frustrations, but he didn't want to disturb Quinn. His protectiveness of her was all-encompassing and reminded him of how strongly he felt about his sisters, though he had no desire to hold or kiss his sisters the same way he did Quinn, of course.

But she'd become important to him and the more he came to know her, the deeper he was falling.

No coming up for air now, he thought with a mental chuckle. She had him, hook, line and sinker and unless she decided to cut him loose, Michael had a prophetic feeling that he was in for good.

The sounds of the wind and the crackling fire began to die away as he slipped into sleep, but in what seemed only moments later, he jerked awake.

"What is it?" Quinn murmured, shifting her position on his shoulder.

"Nothing," Michael grunted, raising himself up a little higher. "Just slept wrong. Go back to sleep."

She yawned and nodded, drifting off immediately.

Michael, however, was wide awake. He could have sworn that he heard a voice. And it wasn't the sweet tones of Quinn's sleepy murmuring. It could possibly be rescuers, but there was something about it that rubbed Michael wrong.

His eyes went to the window, but it was too dark outside for him to see anything except the waving of tree limbs. It looked like the wind was picking back up and Michael knew his instincts about an arctic storm were coming true.

The sound of a branch snapping had his gut clenching. It could have been the wind, but having it follow in the edge of the voice-like sound put him on edge.

Carefully, he began to move, trying to shift Quinn to a pillow, but she woke up. "I'm just going to check the windows," he whispered, caressing her warm cheek. "I don't want us to lose any more heat out of here than necessary. Be back in just a moment."

Her eyes were wide and far too alert. "You're not going outside?"

Shoot. He wanted to investigate but wouldn't be able to do so fully from the inside. "No. I'm not going outside."

She hesitated, then nodded. "Okay."

Michael smiled reassuringly at her, then walked to the window with the blanket plug. They probably needed that blanket if the temperature was going to drop any more, but they needed the wind blocked even more.

He ran his hand around the edges, feeling the icy bite of the wind as it made it through in a small stream, but his focus was on the outside. His eyes were wide as they tried to peer into every shadow and crevice visible through the window.

Not seeing anything of interest, he made his way to the other windows in turn, but nothing looked out of place, other than the heavy sway of branches in the wind and the growing layer of ice.

He wondered if they would get sleet or snow, because their location on the coastline could mean either. Snow would allow them to go home sooner, but ice seemed more likely after the moisture they'd already had.

It was a good thing it was the weekend, but come Monday, if he was still trapped, he hoped that school was out for a day or two. Otherwise, his boss would be ticked that he'd missed teaching and left no warning.

Quinn's scream sent Michael's heart into his throat and he spun, rushing back to the couch.

"He was there," she rasped, pointing to the window and curling into herself. "He was there!"

Michael spun, but the window was dark. He could only see the firelight reflecting in the paned glass. "Who was there?" he asked, though he had his assumptions. "What did you see?"

Quinn whimpered and practically climbed into his lap. "Adam," she whispered, as if saying the name out loud would summon his spirit. "I saw Adam."

Michael rubbed her back, feeling her trembling from head to toe. "You *saw* him?" he pressed. "Can you tell me about it?"

Her voice broke on a sob. "I don't know," she admitted. "I was halfway asleep when movement in the window caught my attention and when I looked up, there he was. Just standing there. Staring at me. Just like he used to do at school."

Michael swallowed bile. Were her earlier worries correct? Could he really have followed her here? But why now? And how would he find her in the woods like this? It just seemed too illogical and fantastic. What were the odds, really?

Quinn picked up her head. "You don't believe me," she said flatly.

Michael shook his head. No way was he going there. He pushed his concerns aside. He'd promised he believed her and he wasn't going to break it, though he knew his face probably looked skeptical. "Why don't you wait here and I'll go check outside?"

Quinn's shaking grew to epic proportions. "No! Don't leave me! He'll come back!"

"Quinn," Michael said calmly. "Quinn, sweetheart, if there's a man outside, I need to go track him down."

She burrowed into him. "Please don't go."

His hold on her tightened. Michael hated how afraid she was, but he really needed to go look outside. Walking around to the windows had given him a chance to assure they were each locked, and he knew he'd locked the front door when he came back from the truck, but still…

"Please," she begged again.

Michael sighed. "I won't leave you," he said, kissing the top of her head. He grunted as he shifted on the couch until he was comfortable and Quinn was held tightly in his arms. He rubbed her back and arms, talking soothing nonsense until he felt her drift off again.

It hadn't been nearly as hard as he'd thought it would be to get her to sleep and it made him question the situation all over again. She said she'd been on the verge of sleep. Could it have been a dream? A nightmare? The fact that he rocked her into sleep so quickly let him know she was still partly asleep during her panic attack.

Or maybe she just feels safe with you.

Michael snorted quietly. She didn't know him well enough to feel that safe. If she really thought she saw Adam, Michael shouldn't have been able to calm her so quickly. He was definitely falling for her, but he knew it would take longer for her own feelings to catch up.

Sighing, he braced himself for a long, sleepless night. His mind was torn as to what was happening. Quinn seemed so sure of herself and Michael didn't want to be lumped in with everyone else who didn't believe her story, but the odds of what she was talking…

He shook his head. It just didn't seem possible.

*Still…*It really didn't matter. He was awake and he would stay awake. If by some nightmarish miracle, Adam really was out there… then Michael would be ready for him. This time, the pervert wouldn't be able to wiggle his way out of anything.

CHAPTER 16

Quinn woke up so warm, it was slightly stifling, but whatever she was curled against was amazingly comfortable and she didn't really want to move. Shifting just enough to try and stretch her muscles, she froze when she heard a grunt.

Her eyes popped open immediately and she gasped, scuttling backward and nearly falling on the floor. Her muscles protested every bit of the move, but she needed to give herself enough room to think properly and she couldn't do that as long as she was SITTING IN MICHAEL'S LAP!

Quinn sat pressed up against the arm of the couch, breathing heavily and watching the amused look on Michael's face.

"How...um..." She cleared her throat and pushed a riot of curls out of her face. She felt heat climb up her neck and wasn't sure how to even ask her question. It sounded ridiculous! But she'd been so tired when she went to bed that she had very little recollection of what happened last night.

"How did you end up in my lap?" he asked, his lips twitching.

At least he was trying to curb his desire to laugh, but the twinkle in his eye and his lips kept giving him away.

"Uh, yeah...that."

Michael gave in and chuckled. He reached over and patted her foot. "You got scared, remember? You thought you saw…something… and begged me to protect you."

"I did *not*," she stated automatically and emphatically. Adam might have taken away some of her courage, but she wasn't the type to curl up and ask a man for his protection. She'd moved halfway across the country *on her own*, for heaven's sake. She wasn't some ninny who couldn't handle herself.

"Suit yourself," he said, standing and stretching his arms toward the ceiling.

Quinn forced herself to look away. Geez, he was handsome in the morning. Her eyes shot back to his face. *Other than the dark circles, of course.* Why did he have such dark circles? Didn't he…?

"Oh…" she breathed. "You didn't sleep. Did you?"

Michael hesitated for a second before shaking his head. "No. But I'm fine. I can handle a night without."

Quinn buried her face in her hands. "Except it's not just a night without, is it? It's been a couple of nights without good sleep for you." She groaned. "I'm so sorry. I don't remember being such a mess."

The couch tilted slightly as he sat back down. "Quinn, it's fine. When we get back home I'll sleep for a week if I need to. A couple of nights aren't going to kill me."

She looked up, feeling like a horrible burden. "You should have just put me down. I don't even remember what scared me so badly. I'm so, so, so, so sorry."

He smiled, though it looked slightly forced, and ran a finger along her jawline, sending a shiver down Quinn's spine. "It's fine. Now, come on. I'm starved. Do you want beef stew? Or beef stew?"

"Hmm…tough choice," she hedged. "Maybe beef stew?"

Michael stood and nodded. "That's what I was thinking too." He began to walk away and Quinn had to grip the couch as an irrational gush of fear slammed into her.

Why was she scared to let Michael go to the kitchen? It's not like she couldn't see him, or anything. He was only a few feet away. And why in the world would she have been so terrified last night that she would climb into his lap in order to sleep? It was so unlike her, not to mention she couldn't remember a thing. It had to have been important enough to have her acting dramatically, but why couldn't she remember it, then?

Her wandering mind came back as Michael made noise in the kitchen and Quinn stood up from the couch. She needed to visit the restroom and take care of her needs before breakfast. She began to shuffle away from the fire, shivering as she did.

She paused at the table, frowning. "How did the headache medicine get here?"

Michael looked over his shoulder. "I went and got it last night while you were sleeping."

Something tickled the edge of her brain. "Was this before or after I climbed into your lap?"

He paused, his shoulders stiff like he was bracing for a blow. "Before."

Quinn fingered the bottle. There was something she needed to remember. Something important… She suddenly realized just how light the cabin was and her eyes jerked to the window. She gasped. The windows were fully covered in frost. "Oh my gosh…"

An arctic storm...

Her eyes widened and she turned back to Michael. "The storm," she croaked. "You were right…after you came back, you said it was too cold…and then I saw, I saw…" She swallowed and bent over, resting her hands on her knees. He'd been here. Adam had been here! He was out there, somewhere in the storm, stalking her again. He'd followed her all the way across the country.

"Easy, Quinn," Michael said just before his hand landed on her back. "It's all going to be okay."

"No, it's not!" she cried, her fear hitting her like a baseball bat to the gut. She spun, slapping his hand away, and the room spun with her. Pausing, she gripped the dining chair until her knuckles felt like they would break, as she tried to steady her breathing. "He's here," she whispered thickly. She managed to open her eyes and stare Michael down. "Somewhere out there…" She pointed toward the outer wall of the cabin. "Is a madman. He's here. He followed me," she ground out. "Don't tell me it's going to be alright. You didn't even believe me last night!"

Michael put up his hands. "I do believe you," he reassured her.

Quinn shook her head. "No, you don't. I can see it in your face."

Michael hesitated slightly. "Quinn...sweetheart...let's just calm down here. Every window, and the only door in the cabin, are locked tight. If Adam is out there, the only person he's hurting is himself. It's below freezing, the snow has already accumulated a couple of inches and there's no shelter anywhere but in here."

"That just means he's going to try and get inside," she argued.

Michael shook his head. "It means he'd have to be mentally insane to follow you over here."

Quinn snorted. "Any man who would stalk a woman is mentally insane."

Michael's shoulders drooped. "Fair enough. But still...this is much more extreme than following you around work. How would he have found out you were here?"

"I..." Quinn hesitated. She had no idea how Adam would have found her. When she'd left town, she'd cut every friend and acquaintance she had loose. None had been close enough that she'd been willing to risk herself or them for the relationship. She hadn't been back on social media or called anyone. There really was very little way for Adam to have found her. In fact... She hung her head. "He can't be here, can he?" she whispered.

"Probably not," Michael replied.

She looked up. "So I'm the crazy one?"

He shook his head. "No. Absolutely not. You're traumatized from a past experience and you were half asleep. I think it was simply a nightmare."

She nodded as her logical side finally got the scared side of her brain to calm down. "I'm sorry." She scrubbed at her face. "I don't know what came over me."

Michael took a hesitant step toward her, then moved more swiftly when she reached for him. He wrapped her up tight against his broad, strong chest. "Being stuck here with me is more than likely the real nightmare," he teased, his lips moving against her forehead. "It's understandable that between your concussion, the trauma and cabin fever, your brain would be going a little stir crazy."

"Why are you so nice?" she muttered into his chest. His chest shook with a light chuckle and Quinn found herself smiling at the feel and sound of it.

"Because life's too short to be rude," he said. Turning her toward the hall he gave her a gentle nudge. "Go take care of what you need to and then we'll get you fed."

Still smiling, Quinn went to do just that. She was completely embarrassed about her hallucination, and yet here she was, smiling like a teenager in the throes of their first crush.

Michael was so amazing and it looked like she was going to get a little more time with him than they'd thought. She should have been frustrated that everything was going wrong, but secretly...Quinn couldn't help but be very, very pleased.

* * *

MICHAEL WAS EXHAUSTED, but his muscles were so tight that he was ready to spring any second. He'd been a little relieved at first when Quinn woke up and didn't remember last night. It had just reiterated the fact that she had probably dreamed the whole thing, which was exactly what he'd suspected, but then she'd remembered and chaos had ensued.

It had physically hurt him when she'd pushed him away, but the fear from her was nearly palpable. He'd known she wasn't thinking straight. His determination to have it out with Adam seemed to grow every time Michael witnessed how much Quinn had been affected by his stalking.

He glanced at the window. He knew that she had been dreaming last night, but something just kept tickling at the back of his mind. The sound of the branch, his flat tire, Quinn's dream... Could Adam be there?

Michael shook his head. There was no way someone from the east side of the country had followed Quinn and was out here in the woods with them. Michael had found this cabin by complete accident. It would be impossible for Adam to have found them here, especially not with the weather they were currently experiencing.

Michael went back to opening cans and sent a quick prayer of thanks heavenward that they actually had food, even if it was the same thing over and over again. At least they wouldn't both starve while staying in this dang cabin.

He dumped the stew into the pot and began to stir it, looking up when Quinn came walking back in. She had changed out of the pajama pants, back into her jeans from the first night they'd arrived, though she still had the sweatshirt on.

"Feeling better?" he asked.

She gave him a shy smile. "A shower would go a long way."

"You can give it a try, but I don't know if there's a water heater."

She shrugged. "I should probably risk the icy cold because I'm sure by this point I stink, but the idea of a cold shower somehow doesn't do it for me."

Michael laughed and held out his arm. She swiftly came over and hugged into his side, wrapping her arms around his waist.

Michael kissed her temple. "I'd be happy to help get you warm again," he whispered.

A shiver went through her and Michael's smile grew.

"Well, then, maybe I'll risk it," she teased. "And try brushing my teeth."

"I brought back our bags, so that shouldn't be too hard to do."

Her eyes widened. "Seriously?"

Michael pointed to the table. "I grabbed them last night."

Quinn left his side and limped over.

"Why don't you take a couple of pills with breakfast?" Michael said. He hated seeing her move like an old woman, especially since he knew how capable she was when she wasn't injured.

"Oh my goodness, yes..." Quinn gushed.

Michael looked over to see her clutching her clothes to her chest. "Women and their clothes," he grumbled. "I just don't get it."

She pointed a finger at him. "These aren't just clothes," she retorted. "These are clean clothes. Clothes that aren't crunchy with mud and water."

"Ah..." Michael nodded slowly. "I'm beginning to understand. So women buy so many clothes because they like clean ones? Even though they also own washing machines?"

Quinn put her hands on her hips and gave him a look. "Watch it, buster. Or I won't pretty myself up for you."

He made a considering face. "Can you get prettier than you are now? I'm not sure it's possible."

Quinn's shoulders softened. "I didn't think men like you existed," she said.

Michael frowned. "Uh..."

"How do you always know the right thing to say?" she asked.

He chuckled uncomfortably and scratched at his chin. "Is this where I'm supposed to admit that I'm simply quoting some romance book that I read?"

"Do you read romances?"

"Not unless they were assigned for school."

Quinn grinned. "Then probably not. I'd hate for you to lose your street cred."

Michael snorted. "My sisters would tell you that I don't even know what street cred is."

Quinn rolled her eyes and walked back his way. "You pay way too much attention to what your sisters say."

Michael couldn't stop watching her. The sway of her hips as she walked his way. There was nothing in her movements at the moment that said she was hurting and Michael was caught in her tractor beam.

Quinn stopped right in front of him and tapped her fingers against his chest.

Michael felt his heart beat the same rhythm as her fingers. He felt like he couldn't breathe.

"Did you hear me?"

Michael blinked. "What?"

Quinn's lips curled into a tiny smirk.

"I said…I think you pay too much time to what your sisters say."

It still took a moment for Michael to break out of his attraction-induced haze to figure out what Quinn was saying, but eventually the words sunk into his brain. "You…don't think they're right?"

Quinn shook her head. "Nope." She leaned up on tiptoe and kissed his jawline. "You don't have to be like them to be awesome. Besides…can they claim your gift with words?"

He smiled back and shook his head. "No. In fact, they called just the other day and asked me to solve a bet for them."

"So they make fun of you, but still use you for their gain?"

Michael blinked. "Yeah…I suppose they do."

Quinn tsked her tongue and shook her head. "Don't worry…I won't take you for granted that way." She started to walk away, hedging toward the bathroom again. "I only want you for your muscles." With a short laugh and a wink, she disappeared inside the small wooden door.

Michael stared at the door until the smell of something burning caused his nose to twitch. Holding back a sneeze, he cursed under his breath and spun to the stove, jerking the pot off the flame.

He stirred it and sniffed, hoping it wasn't too scalded to be edible. Odds were they had enough food to throw this away, but with the way their luck had been going lately, Michael wasn't taking any chances.

A squeal from the bathroom had him jumping and nearly dropping the pot back onto the stove. But when the sound was followed by angry shouting, Michael paused to listen only a moment before laughing under his breath and dealing with the food again.

He hummed to himself while pouring the soup into two bowls. He wasn't looking forward to his own cold shower after Quinn was finished, but listening to her complain about the freezing temperature did have him anticipating holding her until they both warmed up.

Perhaps another one of those cliches he knew too much about really was true…this one might have to do with a silver lining.

CHAPTER 17

Quinn was freezing and her headache was about to kill her, but she'd never felt quite so invigorated…well, except when she and Michael had kissed for the first time. But right now her skin and hair were clean and she was in fresh, if inappropriate, clothes. The slacks and blouse she had packed for the auction were hardly what she needed to be wearing in a dirty cabin in the woods, but no one was taking that clean feeling from her today.

She wadded her hair back up, not wanting to deal with it, and padded to the kitchen area. Michael stood up from the table and his eyes went up and down her, like he was in complete awe and Quinn's heart melted even further.

Yes, she was in nicer clothes, but though she'd teased about making herself pretty, she had no real hair products and no makeup to go with the clothes, but he was staring at her like she was everything.

Why does his stare not make me feel as gross as Adam's did? Quinn frowned slightly at the conundrum. What was it about one man, one teacher, from another that did or didn't frighten her? Why did she welcome Michael's touch, but not Adam's?

Because Michael is kind, generous and true... Yes, he's attracted, but he puts you and your needs first. He doesn't use your looks as a way to further his own agenda.

Just like that, the old, logical Quinn stepped in and her fears disappeared. Each time they came out, she found them leaving faster and faster and she felt much more like her old self. Michael's support and kindness had been everything Quinn didn't know she needed.

"Hi," she said softly, then laughed when Michael's eyes snapped from her feet up to meet hers.

"Hi," he replied, his tone husky.

Quinn held up her bag. "I brushed my teeth," she teased.

Michael's face turned pink under his short beard and Quinn saw the tips of his ears flush.

Her grin couldn't have been contained if her life had depended on it. Her eyes landed on the two bowls at the table. "Did you wait for me?"

Michael shrugged. "It seemed the polite thing to do."

Quinn walked over and kissed his stubbly cheek. "You didn't need to do that, but thank you."

He smirked and Quinn could have sworn that his chest puffed up just a little. "I hate to make you endure my company when you're looking like that, but if you don't mind slumming it today, it's hot and ready to go."

Quinn let him seat her at the table. Her neck and back were still aching, but she was grateful that her legs and arms were starting to relax a little. Mostly her head was the source of her problems, but a couple of pills would hopefully help that. "I'm hardly slumming it," she said as they started to eat. "You're the best company I've had in months."

"At the rate we're going, I'll be the only company you have for months," he quipped.

Quinn laughed as intended. "I suppose there are worse things." She scrunched her nose. "Though, I would prefer a hot shower once in a while if it was going to be that long."

Michael leaned back, stretching his back a touch. "I'm not sure my students would handle it if I were gone that long. Especially if I came home looking like a homeless man." He scratched at his beard.

"Yeah…" Quinn squinted at his chin. "I've been noticing that your beard isn't the same color as your hair." She tapped his cheek. "Does that mean you dye your hair? Hiding grays, Mr. Dunlap?"

He scowled playfully at her. "My dad used to joke that I got Mom's hair on top and his on my face."

Quinn smiled as she took her last bite of soup and dropped the spoon in the bowl. The sound ricocheted through her head and she fought the urge to wince. Where was that headache medicine?

Not seeing it immediately, she stood and took her bowl and his. "If you want to shower, I'll get these washed."

"I can do that," Michael said quickly, rising to his feet.

Quinn stepped back, keeping the dishes from his reach. "Nope. You've been taking care of me the whole time we've been here."

Michael gave her a look. "It's been all of two days, Quinn. It's not like I've been slaving my whole life."

"Still." She waved an elbow toward the hallway. "Go shower and I'll wash this time."

"Are you trying to tell me I stink?" he joked as he grabbed his bag off the table.

Quinn smiled a little too sweetly. "I would never."

He chuckled and walked away. "Just for that, I'm not going to brush my teeth!"

"Your choices, your cavities!" she hollered.

His laughter continued until he shut the bathroom door.

Quinn smiled at the exchange. Why was that man so easy to talk to? She loved their flirting and teasing and loved how he treated her like such a princess. Quinn's attraction to Michael was soaring through the roof, yet Michael had utterly been a man of his word. He hadn't touched her or pushed any boundaries that she hadn't been willing to cross.

I trust him.

She paused at the words. The truth of them rang through her. She did trust him and for her...that was huge. Quinn hadn't been sure she'd ever trust a man again, especially one who reminded her of Adam.

And you're falling for him.

She froze. "What?" she asked out loud. She'd been welcoming that voice. The one that was most like the woman she used to be. Nurturing and supporting it to help rid herself of the terrible fear she'd been struggling with, but...Quinn gripped the edge of the sink. Was she falling for Michael?

She was attracted to him, that was for sure. She saw less and less of Adam in him and that helped. She felt like there were few men like him left on the Earth, but was she truly so far gone in only two days that she was falling in love with him?

Quinn stared at the window, noting that the frost looked thicker than it had when she'd first woken up, but not truly registering what that could mean, because something else had caught her eye.

The question of whether or not she loved Michael had no bearing on the fact that she was positive something dark was behind the frost...and it was moving.

Quinn's heart rate immediately skyrocketed and her knees tried to buckle, but she held herself up with the sharp edge of the counter. The wind was too loud for her to hear anything clearly, but Quinn's ears were sure she was hearing the squeak of the deck outside.

Her eyes darted around until they landed on a knife block. Grabbing the biggest one, she forced her limbs into motion and slid along the floor to keep from making any noise. Ever so slowly she came up to the window, barely registering that the white she'd been seeing wasn't frost, but a blizzard.

The dark shape to the side shifted again and a thud sounded against the house, causing Quinn to shriek and run back to the kitchen where she slid to the floor, gripping the knife tightly against her chest. "Michael," she whispered, unable to speak louder. "Please...help me."

* * *

MICHAEL WAS in the process of brushing his teeth when he heard a cry from out in the cabin and he paused. It was short, and over the sound of the wind hitting the vent in the roof, he wasn't quite sure it was Quinn.

Still, his gut said something was wrong. Quickly, he finished his brushing and rinsed his mouth out. If Quinn had been desperate, she could have shouted his name or knocked on the door. One small sound wasn't that big of a deal…right?

His movements belied his worries as he yanked open the door and ran out. "Quinn?" he shouted. "Quinn?" She wasn't immediately visible, but whimpering caught his attention and Michael spun to look in the kitchen area, then froze. "Quinn?" he asked, this time much softer.

She was curled into the corner, her back against the cabinets and knees to her chest. It would have been clear she was terrified even if she hadn't been holding a knife in her hands and crying.

Michael looked around, but didn't see anything that should have upset her. Very slowly, realizing she was once again not quite herself, he got down on her level. "Quinn?"

Her eyes went to his and widened. "Michael," she rasped. "You came." Dropping the knife, she scrambled across the uneven floorboards and flung herself into his arms.

This is better than her thinking I'm Adam, he thought wryly as he wrapped his arms around her. "Sweetheart, what happened?" he asked, rubbing her trembling back.

"There was something outside," she whispered thickly, burying her face in his neck. "I saw a shadow and it moved, then I heard a thud against the house."

Michael's head jerked toward the front door. "Where was it?"

Quinn's answer was to tighten her hold on him.

Michael climbed to his feet, the movement far from graceful as he had a human monkey clinging to him. Shifting his hold, he swung Quinn into his arms and walked over to the couch where he carefully set her down. "Sit tight," he said after detangling himself. "I'm going to go check it out."

"Don't leave," she begged. "He always comes when no one can see."

Michael hated this. He hated how much Adam had messed with Quinn and he hated that he needed to leave her in order to protect her. Cupping her face, he brought their foreheads together. "I won't let him near you," he promised. "But I have to go see what's out there. It's the only way to protect you."

Quinn bit her bottom lip and Michael was afraid she would bite right through it, the movement was so tension filled.

He tugged on her chin until the lip was loose. "Better," he teased. "I just finished brushing my teeth and have grand plans for those lips. Don't you dare ruin them."

She softened just a touch, but the fear didn't leave her eyes.

"Okay, I'll be right back." He stood and took his time walking away, making sure she was calm enough for him to go. He got to the door. "You'll be able to see me through the window, okay?"

Quinn's nod was jerky, but at least she was now responding.

Taking a deep breath, Michael unlocked the door and stepped outside. He had yet to notice it had been snowing and he hissed when his feet landed on a couple inches of white powder.

And I was worried about hypothermia before. He snorted. Slowly, he looked around. The wind was blowing the snow in a way that made it almost a full white-out. They were definitely stuck here for a bit longer. Hopefully, since it was mid spring, the storm would blow itself out quickly and Michael could get them to a phone signal.

"Or someone could just, you know, notice two cars on the side of the road," he grumbled to himself. A snapping branch caught his attention and Michael jerked toward it, but he relaxed when he realized it was simply snapping back from being dumped on by snow.

Shutting the door carefully and trying to ignore his frozen feet, Michael walked all the way around the cabin, being sure to look inside and notify Quinn of his whereabouts each time he hit a window.

He couldn't believe how scared she was. There had to be more to the Adam story than she was sharing, or maybe Quinn wasn't quite… right. Something seemed off with her level of fear and the story she'd told.

Not that Adam's behavior had been okay. It was sick. But if he hadn't actually touched her, then why did she act as if her very life were in danger if Adam arrived? It just seemed extreme in Michael's perception.

"The question is…does it matter?" he muttered to himself as he rounded the final corner of their primitive dwelling. "Does it change how you feel about her?" He waved through the last window, not seeing anything out of the ordinary, then headed for the front door. But before going inside, he shivered in the cold and let his mind mull over the answer.

He thought of her beauty, the first thing to catch his eye. He thought of her rejection and the cold reception she'd given him. He thought of her determination of moving as a single woman across the country and her courage in facing Michael when he reminded her of her stalker.

He thought of her laughter and smiles and kindness, all the pieces he'd been discovering in the last couple of days that were buried a little beneath a tough exterior.

No… It didn't matter. Michael's feelings weren't budging as he thought of all her attributes. Some were good, some were things she was fixing and others were quirks, but they all added up to what she was.

Michael knew he wasn't perfect either. He stumbled over his words, he was too quiet sometimes, he had old fashioned ideals in a modern world. Many would say he wasn't tough or manly enough since his nose was often in a book, but this was who Michael was.

Trying to learn to be bolder in public or speak up when necessary might be things he could grow and change through, but he liked himself as a bookworm. He didn't see that as a weakness even while others did.

Which all boiled down to, if Quinn liked what she saw despite his imperfectness, then he couldn't do any less.

Maybe his role right now was to help her feel safe enough to get past the nightmares she'd just been through. And if he was blessed enough to get more than that? Then he'd simply count himself the luckiest man alive.

CHAPTER 18

Where was he? Quinn couldn't seem to stop shaking. Michael had worked his way around the entire cabin—she'd seen him at the windows and he'd waved every time—and didn't look the least bit worried, which meant that she was probably going crazy.

Except that Michael hadn't come back inside.

Where…?

The door creaked open and her heart leapt to her throat until she saw that familiar head of blond hair. Michael stopped in the open door, leaning his head out to shake the snow out of it before coming fully inside.

Her heart relaxed when he locked the door and came in her direction. His nose and cheeks were bright pink and Quinn realized he was only in socks. "Michael." She gasped. "You're freezing."

He grinned and crouched in front of her. "That's what happens when you're dumb enough to walk outside during a blizzard." Snowflakes on his skin were melting and wetting the top of his T-shirt and the side of his face and neck.

Quinn jumped to her feet and ran back to the bathroom. She'd only found a single towel when she'd been showering, but it would be better than nothing. Grabbing it, she ran back to his side.

Michael was sitting in front of the fire, his feet out in front of him, and Quinn knelt next to him. "You're all wet," she scolded. "Why didn't you put on some shoes?" When those blue eyes met her and he didn't speak, guilt threatened to choke her. Her vision grew misty and her hands and the towel fell to her lap. "I'm so sorry," she pushed out. "I...I don't know what's wrong with me." She pulled back, ignoring the pain of the hardwood hitting her tailbone. "I think I'm going crazy," she said, her voice cracking.

"Hey, hey, hey," Michael scolded softly. He took the towel from her and then took her hands, pulling her closer until eventually settling her in his lap. "None of that now," he said. His warm hand tucked her forehead into the crook of his neck and he rocked her back and forth. "You're not going crazy."

"Something is *wrong* with me," she insisted. "It's not normal to keep thinking you're seeing a stalker who lives across the country out in the middle of a crazy storm."

Michael didn't respond right away and Quinn felt her sadness deepen. She really, *really,* liked this guy. Her inner voice that said she was falling was probably a little too accurate. She could name half a dozen men of her acquaintance who wouldn't have handled her hallucinations with such tenderness and care, or even been willing to still be her friend.

But Michael was here, and it wasn't just because they were stuck together. He seemed to genuinely care about her and stayed with her because he wanted to. He could have simply kept an eye on her and left her to her own devices, but instead every action he took was to ensure her health, her safety and her comfort.

She'd never find another one like him and instead of showing him how grateful she was, she was having a nervous breakdown.

"Did you see what caused the movement?" she asked, letting her body sink into his.

"Not for sure," he said as he rubbed her back. "But while I was out there, there was a loud sound when a branch dumped all the snow off of it. It's coming down fast and we're definitely stuck here for at least another twenty-four hours."

"I suppose if I have to have a breakdown, out here in the woods is better than at home," she said, trying to lighten the mood. The tension in the air after her words, however, let her know her joke had fallen flat.

Michael leaned back a little so they were facing each other. His face was hard and determined as he stared into her eyes. "You're not having a breakdown," he said with a steely tone. "You're under a lot of pressure, you were in an accident only two days ago, you're still recovering from not only a concussion but a traumatic experience in your past and maybe being cooped up in a cabin in the middle of nowhere is bringing it all to a head. I don't know, but Quinn... you're not crazy." He shook his head adamantly. "You're. Not. Crazy."

Nothing could have stopped Quinn from leaning in and kissing him. Absolutely nothing. Other than her grandfather, she'd never had someone so adamantly in her corner and so willing to fight for her... except her feelings for Michael were anything but familial. If she couldn't stop herself from acting weird, the least she could do is thank Michael for his support and this might be the only way she had to do it.

Wrapping her arms around his neck, she pulled herself as close as humanly possible and he responded with the exact same fervor. Just yesterday, she'd been sure that nothing could have been better than their first kiss. It had shaken her very foundation and made Quinn question everything she'd been planning since moving to Seagull Cove.

But this...this was full of angst, longing, desperation and relief. There was nothing gentle or exploratory about it, but a crash of once carefully controlled emotions that were too much for them to keep contained.

Quinn didn't even register the pain in her head or the way his hold was hurting her bruises. They were like flies in the background as she concentrated on giving and receiving everything she could.

Their ardor took a long time to calm down and Quinn was exhausted by the time their frenzied movements slowed.

Quinn's lips felt bruised and swollen, but she was thrumming with contentment and pleasure. Michael rested his forehead against hers, their heavy breathing combining between them and brushing over her skin.

"I'm glad I brushed my teeth," he whispered.

Quinn snorted a small laugh. "I'm grateful you got our stuff out of the truck."

He smirked. "It was worth the hike for sure." He shifted his weight and groaned. "I hate to say it, but I think my backside is completely numb."

Quinn laughed and climbed off of him. "I'm sorry. I shouldn't have attacked you like that. This hardwood isn't exactly sitting-friendly."

"I've never enjoyed an attack more," he teased back.

Quinn glanced sideways at him and caught her breath at the intensity of his gaze. He really was one of a kind. How his sisters found him so boring was beyond her. Quinn had yet to find him boring and she'd spent a solid forty-eight hours with him at this point.

Feeling the desire to go back and start kissing again, she cleared her throat and stood, walking toward the window. Maybe the cold air leaking through would cool her desire a little bit. They were seriously playing with fire if they gave into their attraction too much.

"Tell me about your work," she said as she stared outside. She could see Michael walking up behind her in the paned glass and leaned into his chest when his arms came around her waist.

"I work with a bunch of hormonal and bored teenagers," he said softly in her ear before kissing the edge of it.

She laughed shakily, her knees growing slightly weak at his attention. "But you love it."

He stilled for just a split second before nodding against the side of her head. "Yes. I love it."

* * *

Michael really did enjoy his job, but her use of the word *love* had caught him off guard. His skin was still hot and his pulse still trying to calm down after their time in front of the fire. He'd never had an experience like that with a woman and Michael was positive that he never would again.

Unless it's with Quinn.

His arms tightened around her just slightly. He probably needed to talk to her about what happened when they got back. He was falling deeper and deeper and knew that giving her up wasn't going to be an option. Somehow, he needed to convince her that these feelings weren't just because they were stuck together in the middle of Oregon's weirdest storm.

He watched the snow blowing outside. He could count on one hand how many times it had snowed like this during his almost thirty years in Seagull Cove. What were the odds that one would keep him and Quinn tucked away in the middle of nowhere?

"Quinn?"

"Hmm?"

"Do you remember what road we were on when you hit the deer?"

Quinn's eyes fluttered open and she looked at him in the window. "Not really. Why?"

Michael twisted his lips, his thoughts racing. "I'm just curious. I didn't have my GPS on, I knew we were headed south and assumed you knew where you were going. But it's been bugging me that no one has seen the cars and that I didn't see any tire tracks on the road when I went back to the truck last night."

Quinn looked away from him, her eyes slightly unfocused as she concentrated. "I...I had the GPS on, since I've never been to Gold Beach. But it was cutting in and out and I was trying to see in the rain..." She groaned. "Did I take a wrong turn somewhere?"

He pulled her in a little closer. "I think it's possible. But I won't know for sure until we can spend a little more time back at the truck. I need the road sign and I need a signal." He sighed. "I just find it odd that there's no service anywhere and traffic is so low."

"But animal sightings are high," she grumbled. "Oh man. I really put us in it."

Michael kissed the side of her head. "It's fine," he said. "I'm just glad you weren't alone." An irrational shock of fear hit his chest at the idea that she more than likely would have died from exposure by this point if she'd been driving alone.

Quinn spun in his arms and rested her hands on his chest. "If I had to be stuck with someone, I'm glad it was you," she said with a sweet smile.

Michael smiled back, but his thoughts kept going and it fell away. "I have another question."

"Oooh...sounds ominous," she teased.

He debated...and debated...and debated...but he just felt like he needed to know.

"Go ahead," she said, her tone soft. "It's something about Adam, isn't it?"

Michael's eyebrows shot up.

Quinn gave him a sad smile and stepped away from him, walking back around to the couch. "You get this look on your face every time his name comes up."

Michael wanted to shut up and go sit by her and cuddle the freezing day away, but this was important. "There's more to the story...isn't there? More than you've told me."

Quinn sighed and leaned back her head, closing her eyes. "Yes."

Michael's fists clenched. "Will you tell me?"

"Are you sure you want to know?" she asked, her voice hesitant. She sat up and twisted around, waving her hand between them. "It might change all this."

Michael nodded firmly. "If things change between us, it won't be because of what happened with Adam. It'll be because you changed your mind about me."

Her eyes flared for a split second and Michael bit his tongue, realizing just how much of his feelings he had given away. *Too late now.*

Quinn cleared her throat, a sure sign that she was slightly unsure, but she held his gaze, determination settling into her jaw. "He didn't touch me," she said bluntly.

Michael's breath whooshed from his lungs. He didn't realize how much he needed to hear those words before he could relax.

"He messed with me in a...more psychological way, I guess you could say." Quinn twisted around and faced the fire again.

Michael had to walk closer to hear her words.

"I know I mentioned that he used to come by after work and I found him staring at me a lot," she said. "But he did more than that." She pushed both hands into her hair, resting her hands on top of her hair. "I would find things moved in my classroom. Or missing." Quinn's troubled eyes, so beautiful, wide and gray, turned to him. "I thought I was crazy," she whispered.

No wonder she was having such a hard time with the weird things going on outside.

"It happened so much that I ended up having a psych evaluation."

Michael's chin fell to his chest and he closed his eyes.

"Adam also spoke to me," she continued. "On those times when I would find him on my porch or when he'd be waiting at my car, he'd say things about my looks, about how I belonged to him." Quinn wiped at her eyes. "One time he held up a book and I recognized it from my classroom, which was how I realized he was the one messing with my things."

It was all making sense now. That protective side of Michael that had been growing ever since spending time with Quinn came roaring into his chest like an angry lion. That Adam guy was even sicker than Michael had ever thought.

"I have...habits..." She said, her voice dropping. "Ever since getting away, I find myself compulsively checking my locks and going through routines to help me sleep at night."

Michael stalked over and sat down, wrapping his arms around her. He was going to hold her and never let her go. How had Quinn survived such an ordeal? "I'm so sorry," he said huskily. "But I can't figure out how no one caught him. No one is perfect. Adam had to have slipped up at some point."

Quinn relaxed into his chest. "I should have put up cameras." She sniffed. "Or something to catch him in the act. But I felt so alone and was always looking over my shoulder, and he was very careful about where he was seen." She sighed harshly. "It was always my word against his and my story seemed too fantastic."

Michael growled. "I think I need to have a word with your principal."

"No." Quinn sat up, wiping at her face. "I'm ready to let it go. I'm sorry I freaked out. It just felt like it was all happening all over again," she admitted. "The weird noises, the shadows, the flat tire…"

Michael cupped her cheek and used his thumb to wipe under her eye. "He shouldn't get away with it."

"Maybe not," Quinn said. "But I don't want anything to do with him or them. I'm here. I'm over it. I'm determined to get my old self back again and move on."

Michael couldn't help but feel swollen with pride at her determination. "Well, this time," he assured her, "you're not alone." *Not ever again.*

CHAPTER 19

Quinn was so tired. Her head was still killing her and she probably should take another nap to keep recovering from the crash, but she couldn't seem to stop watching the window. She felt ready to sleep, but also restless and insanely bored.

Her legs twitched with the need to move, but her eyes screamed to be shut so they would stop burning.

She closed them for a moment and rubbed her eyes with her fists. When she opened them, the snow still remained. How in the world did it snow mid spring? Especially in a place that rarely saw snow at all?

"Weird, isn't it?" Michael said from the kitchen.

Quinn nodded, her eyes still glued on the window. "Why hasn't it stopped?" she muttered.

"It will soon," he assured her. "Don't worry."

Quinn shook her head and jumped to her feet. She paused when she swayed, her hand going to her forehead.

"Quinn?"

She could hear Michael's footsteps coming across the floor. "I'm fine," she snapped, then sighed. "Sorry."

"Your head hurts," he said. It wasn't a question.

Quinn nodded and winced again. "Yeah."

"Did you take anything this morning?"

Quinn blew out a breath, trying to keep her tone under control this time. "No." She opened her eyes. "I don't know what's wrong with me."

Michael smiled kindly. "Cabin fever."

"We've only been here a couple of days."

He chuckled.

"How are you so calm?" she asked. "Why don't you have cabin fever?"

"Who says I don't?"

Quinn waved an arm in his direction. "I don't see you staring at the windows and moving around like you can't sit still."

Michael stuffed his hands in his pockets and shrugged. "I'm used to being in a classroom with two dozen antsy and exhaustive teenagers for eight hours a day. I've learned how to keep it under wraps."

Quinn huffed and began to walk around, being careful not to upset her head too much.

"Would you like a couple of pills?"

Quinn shook her head, then rubbed her forehead.

"Why not?" he pressed.

"I don't know."

Michael's eyebrows rose up. "So you're the type who gets hangry?"

Quinn put her hands on her hips. "We ate lunch."

He shrugged again. "But we've had the same thing at every meal. You're hangry."

Quinn pursed her lips. She wanted to stick her tongue out, but she was holding herself back…barely. She really was in a bad mood. Watching the snow should have been soothing, but when she was stuck in the middle of nowhere, her business was in jeopardy, she kept having flashbacks of her ex…well…

Michael dragged a chair across the floor, ripping Quinn from her thoughts. He took it to the side of the cabin and sat down, then leaned it against the wall with the two front legs off the floor, looking completely at ease.

It ticked her off even more.

Stalking over to the window, she pressed her hands against it, feeling the bite of the cold against her skin. "I'm grumpy," she corrected him. "There's a difference."

"My bad."

Quinn glanced over her shoulder. "You're driving me crazy."

He grinned and winked. "Ditto."

Quinn rolled her eyes. "That's not what I meant."

His grin remained. When she didn't turn away, he held out the bottle of pills and gave it a shake.

Quinn's shoulders fell and she walked over and took the bottle. "Thanks," she grunted. Heading back to the kitchen, she used her water bottle to swallow the pills. *Relief is only thirty minutes away,* she thought sarcastically. "But being rescued might be days," she grumbled.

"What was that?"

Quinn waved him off. "Just more grumpiness. It might be best to leave me alone for a bit."

He chuckled. "I don't know. This is the best entertainment I've had in days."

Quinn gave him a less than impressed look.

"Unless of course you count what we did to counteract the boredom earlier."

Quinn's cheeks and neck were immediately burning. Why were guys always so at ease talking about things like kissing? Sharing a moment like that with her best friend was one thing, but just blurting out that she'd been making out with a man wasn't how Quinn tended to operate.

She narrowed her eyes. *Is that how Michael usually acts? Has he been lying this whole time? Are we going to get back and he's going to brag to everyone about how he got me to kiss him while we were here?*

She closed her eyes and rubbed her temples. That couldn't be it. Quinn got absolutely no red flags from Michael at all, that had to stand for something…unless the part of her brain that could spot lies was severely broken. Which…she had to admit was definitely a possibility.

"You're thinking too hard," Michael said, his tone more serious than before.

Quinn slowly shook her head from side to side. "I can't seem to help it. I just…"

"As soon as you have a little time on your hands, you question everything you did in the spur of the moment," he supplied. "Motive, actions, how to read others, how others read you…"

Quinn looked up at him, her jaw slack. "How did you know that?"

He gave her a small smile. "Anyone who's had their trust broken as badly as you will end up reacting by going the complete opposite direction. If someone can be as horrible as Adam, then you've probably misjudged every other person you've had contact with your whole life."

Quinn deflated and shuffled to the couch. Her legs were still feeling weak even though she wanted to move. "I hate it," she whispered.

"I don't blame you," he responded.

"How do I get rid of it?" Her eyes were swimming now. She was getting whiplash in something other than her neck at the moment as her emotions swung from one extreme to another. One moment she'd been ready to wring Michael's neck, now she was ready to curl up in a ball and cry.

He sucked in a long breath, causing his chest to rise and then slowly move down. He really was quite fit for a teacher and Quinn was too human to not notice. "I don't know if it's something we completely get over or not," he mused, not truly directing his comments her direction. "Once something so precious is broken, I think there's always a scar." His eyes made their way to hers. "But even broken vases can be mended and are often stronger than before. I think we learn, make new choices and try to move on. What else can we do?"

* * *

HE COULD SEE her mulling over his words. Michael wasn't sure how helpful they were. He wasn't really offering her a solution, but honestly, any woman who had been treated so terribly by a man was going to struggle to trust other men. It was the law of nature.

Quinn might struggle for a while, especially since the trauma was so recent, but over time, he had no doubt she'd end up stronger than before, just like he was talking about with the broken vase.

The metaphor had been one he'd read about in an historical book, though he'd felt kinda dumb parroting it back. *Women like that kind of thing, right?* he questioned internally. He hoped they did. He was far from a counselor or psychiatrist and had no idea what to do to help her.

Quinn stared for a moment, then dropped her eyes to her lap. "That was really sweet. Thank you." She glanced up from under her lashes, making Michael's heart flutter.

Sheesh. I'm starting to think I'm the girly one here.

He couldn't seem to stop his physical reaction to this woman, and truthfully, he didn't want to. But he needed her to know that he liked more than just her pretty face. She'd made it clear from the very beginning that finding her beautiful was a complete turn-off. But how could he help it? She was Michael's fantasy come to life.

Those eyes got him every time and he wanted his fingers tangled in her curls at all hours of the day.

He smiled in response to her gratitude. "What number is that?"

She laughed, the tension in the room breaking down with the sound. "I lost count. Maybe three hundred and seventy-nine?"

"Sounds plausible," he teased.

Quinn's laughter subsided and she leaned back into the couch. "What are we gonna do, Michael?" She paused and lifted her head slightly. "Do you always go by Michael? Does anyone call you Mike?"

Michael rolled his eyes. "Only people who don't know me well or are trying to annoy me. Mainly my cousins, or sometimes Gavin and the gang."

Quinn relaxed her head again, a smile spread across her face. "I suppose with a big family, you're bound to get more teasing than the rest of us." She closed her eyes. "At least it's done in love, right?" She yawned and Michael frowned.

Did she need another nap? It's not like their days had been rigorous, but maybe she was still recovering from the wreck? She still moved stiffly and her head was still bothering her. "I suppose so," he murmured, keeping his response soft. He watched, waiting to see if she would fall asleep. He didn't like seeing her in pain and if sleep, combined with the headache medicine, would make her feel better, then he was all for it.

She cracked one eye open.

Apparently, not yet.

"I've never experienced sibling teasing, but watching you with Aspen and her sisters makes me think I might have had a love/hate relationship with it."

He chuckled and rubbed the back of his neck. "That's probably a good way to put it. I love my cousins, but they can be a bit much sometimes. And the problem with growing up together is that they know everything about me. They knew when I had a crush on a girl. They knew when I got in trouble at home."

Both of Quinn's eyes were open now and Michael wanted to smack himself. This wasn't helping her get better.

"How did they know all that? I'll bet you didn't tell them, and they didn't live with you."

Michael raised his eyebrows in response and waited for her to come to the conclusion on her own.

"Ooooh..." Quinn's perfect mouth made a perfect "O." "Your sisters."

"Bingo." He tapped the side of his nose. "I'm Estelle's age. And my mom had a little trouble getting pregnant after me, so my sisters are a little younger than Maeve."

Quinn nodded slightly, closing her eyes again. "Makes sense."

The silence in the room grew. Quinn hadn't asked a question, so

Michael waited…and waited…until he saw her breathing slow and her body relax, then his own followed suit.

Carefully, he brought his chair down and stood up, walking across the room. He didn't want to wake her, but he also wanted her in a position to sleep for as long as she needed to and sleeping with her neck cranked back like that was probably not it.

"Quinn," he whispered, cupping her cheek.

Her eyes fluttered and she nuzzled into his touch. "Hmm?"

"How about you lay down?" He kept his tone low and soothing.

She huffed. "Fine."

Michael helped her settle on her side, her head on a sweatshirt for a makeshift pillow. He knelt at the front of the couch, pulling a blanket up over her body and trying to fight the urge to touch her. His need won out and he lifted a spiral of hair from her face, laying it back out of her way.

"Thank you," she murmured. "For the three hundred and eightieth time."

Michael smiled and kept his laughter quiet. "Always," he whispered, leaning in for the lightest of touches against her cheek. Her contented sigh and relaxing of her body told him it was the right move.

For a couple of minutes, until his knees began to protest, Michael stayed there, watching her sleep. The lines of stress and worry were gone and he couldn't understand how one woman could be so beautiful.

But his favorite part was missing when she slept and he finally stood, stretching quietly. It was always better when he could see her eyes.

He looked around the cabin. Now what? He could use a nap as well, but maybe he should use this time to try and find a way to get them out of there. Walking toward the window, Michael stared outside. The snow was still blowing, but was it his imagination or was the snow starting to thin?

His heart thudded in anticipation. Maybe he should walk around outside and just double check that no one was there. Quinn had been so sure she'd seen something and though Michael had no proof, he hated that she felt like she was going crazy.

Probably better safe than sorry, he thought. *Besides, it'll give me a chance to get more firewood.* He glanced over his shoulder. *Which we sorely need.*

When they'd first arrived, he'd been confident they would have enough, but now they were staying a couple more days than he'd planned and the pile was low. Not quite dangerously low, but with the drop in temperature, they needed to make sure they were keeping the cabin as warm as possible.

Grabbing his sneakers and jacket, Michael tucked his neck down as much as he could, braced himself for the wind and slipped outside, praying fervently he didn't wake his sleeping beauty.

He paused just outside the door, but didn't hear anything unusual and he blew out a breath of relief, creating a puff of white smoke in the air. He rubbed his arms and began a quick walk around the cabin. If someone had been there, Michael was sure that he'd be able to see tracks in the snow.

But the going was much slower than he thought. The boards on the front porch were noisy and Michael was worried about waking Quinn, so he finally stepped off and began slogging his way a little farther from the house.

Everything was white. Solid white. It was no wonder people got lost in the woods during a storm. He'd read about it many times, but Michael had never truly experienced anything quite like it.

His eyes were glued to the ground as he carefully lifted his feet and placed them in the shallowest places he could find. It wasn't until he was about three quarters of the way around the cabin that he paused, his eyes caught on something that definitely wasn't white.

Glancing uncertainly at the cabin, Michael risked walking to the edge of the clearing where there was a pile of something black. The walk took him almost a full minute and the closer he got, the more Michael's stomach churned. He stopped, glancing at the cabin again, but there were no windows facing this direction, so it was no wonder they hadn't noticed anything.

Truthfully, without all the snow, Michael wouldn't have noticed it either. It only stood out because of the color. But he was standing, quite definitely, in front of the remains of a fire. And if Michael wasn't mistaken, the small wisps of white coming from the ashes indicated that the person who had been there hadn't been gone long.

CHAPTER 20

Quinn's eyes fluttered open and she realized the cabin was quiet. Too quiet. Sitting up, she looked around, but Michael wasn't there. "Michael?" Quinn stood, stretching her back and legs. She was so ready for the soreness to go away. Feeling eighty when she was a woman in her mid-twenties stunk.

She shuffled to the bedroom and peeked inside. "Michael?" It was empty, as was the bathroom, and Quinn's pulse sped up. "Why would he leave me?" she murmured, coming back out to the gathering area.

"Maybe because he knew you were already taken."

Quinn gasped so loudly she was sure it could be heard three counties over. She grabbed at her heart which had stopped beating completely and spun, stumbling away from the man standing only a few feet behind her. "H-how did you get in here?" Quinn stammered.

Adam smiled at her. It would have looked kind to anyone else, but Quinn knew better. The man was deranged. He hid it well beneath a peaceful veneer, but underneath was only darkness. Darkness Quinn had been sure she'd left behind.

"How did you find me?" she rasped.

Adam's eyebrows went up and he began to walk toward her, causing Quinn to walk backward more quickly. "Which question do you want me to answer?" he asked calmly. "I won't have time for them all right now, but perhaps on the drive back home we can get through a few more." His eyes darted to the window. "But right now we need to hurry."

Quinn turned and raced to the other side of the couch. "I'm not going anywhere with you," she said, her voice trembling and giving away her fear. She hated how scared she was of this man. He was only an inch or two taller than her and his physique was maybe half the size of Michael's, but he still terrified Quinn. *Michael...* "Did you hurt him?" she cried. "Where's Michael? Where is he?"

Adam had stopped walking and put his hands in the air. "Easy, beautiful."

Oh, how she hated that nickname.

"Your delivery driver is fine. He's out looking for firewood. But somehow I don't think he'll appreciate you deciding to come home with me, so we need to leave now."

"I already told you, I'm not going," Quinn argued, though she felt a heavy swoop of relief that Michael was supposedly safe.

Adam gave her the same look parents gave dramatic children. "Quinn...darling...it's been long enough. It took me a long time to find you and this tantrum is unbecoming. Now, let's go home and we can get started on our lives the way we're supposed to." He held out a hand, waving her to him.

The man was certifiable. How in the world did he truly think that Quinn would just go with him, leaving Michael high and dry, and why would Adam think Quinn was interested in playing along in his delusion?

"I am home," Quinn declared. "Now leave."

Adam dropped his arm and tilted his head. "Quinn, I don't want to force your hand, but I will. I've spent a lot of time and money chasing you down and you owe it to me to come nicely." His smile widened. "We're both in our upper twenties. It's the perfect time to get married and start a family."

She was going to throw up. The idea of letting Adam touch her or kiss her made Quinn physically ill. "Adam...I don't know how to make this any more plain than I already have. I'm not marrying you. I'm not going back. I'm staying here. I have a new life now and I'm not interested in you…at all." Where was Michael? Why hadn't he come back? If she screamed, would he come running? Could he hear her? Had Adam been lying about Michael's whereabouts?

The questions shooting through her brain were only making Quinn more unsettled and when Adam's face started to harden, her fear became almost uncontrollable.

"We've already been through this, Quinn," he said, his voice dropping to a dangerous tone. "I've already decided."

"Well, I haven't," she shot back. How did a person get a madman to leave them alone? Oh heavens, she should have headed toward the kitchen. Maybe she could find that knife or something else dangerous. She had nothing to protect herself with and the fire was starting to get really hot on her legs and back.

Sweat trickled down her spine and Quinn regretted wearing her blouse and slacks. If she needed to run outside, they wouldn't be any help against the weather.

"You still haven't answered my questions," she said shakily as her brain tried to come up with any way for her to escape. "How did you find me?"

Adam rolled his eyes. "It wasn't *that* hard," he said. "After the school stopped watching my every move, I began searching the internet for Quinn Peters." He smirked. "You should have changed your name if you wanted to stay anonymous."

Quinn jolted at the sound of his chuckle.

"Plus, you mentioned at our first dinner how you've always wanted to open an antique shop." Adam snorted. "I'm fairly capable of putting two and two together." He paused his slow approach. "I can see why you ran," he said, his voice calming down again. "You wanted to chase a dream and I can't fault you for that. I can even forgive your little liaison with the delivery driver, but I really must insist we leave. We need to get out before he comes back."

Quinn swallowed convulsively. "I'm not going," she said, though her voice was only a whisper. She thought she'd been so careful, not telling anyone her plans, but it turned out she was terrible at espionage. One little line about an antique shop and Adam knew how to find her. It probably only took a few minutes of searching her name in the business databases for him to pinpoint her location.

At least the school took something seriously, she thought, though the realization didn't give her any peace. After she was gone, they'd finally taken a look at Adam, but it hadn't mattered. He'd obviously been on his best behavior while she was gone and now he was after her again.

Adam was at the back of the couch now, his hands gripping the fabric. "Now, Quinn. You can open your shop back home again. I won't demand that you teach, though being in the same school would certainly bring us closer together."

Quinn shook her head. "No."

Adam's face turned red and he leapt over the couch, catching Quinn completely off guard. She would never have guessed he had that level of athleticism. Before she could react, he had her caged up against the fire and the mantel.

She screamed and pushed against him. "Let me go!"

Adam held her in place. "It doesn't have to be like this, Quinn," he said in a low tone, his face up against hers.

Quinn groaned. "The fire," she panted. "Too hot."

"Then agree to come with me."

She could feel the flames licking at her calves. The heat was becoming unbearable. She knew if she stepped back at all, she'd risk having her pants catch fire, which left her bent backwards slightly and off balance, making it more difficult for her to get away. "LET ME GO!" she screamed.

Adam reared back and slapped her. "SHUT UP!" he shouted, spit flying onto her cheeks.

But Quinn barely noticed. Between the concussion, her headache and the hit, she was seeing stars...literally. Her head snapped backward at the force and smacked on the mantel, adding to her agony. "Michael," she whispered. "Where are you?"

* * *

MICHAEL CREPT UP THE STEPS. He'd heard Quinn scream and everything in him wanted to rush in and take out Adam like a super-hero capturing a bank robber, but Michael knew better...sort of.

He'd never gotten in a fight, unless a person counted wrestling with Jayden when they were little. But Michael knew enough to understand that rushing into a situation he didn't know could get himself or Quinn killed, and that wasn't going to happen today.

He shifted to the window, clenching his jaw when he heard her scream again. The wind was whistling through his left ear as Michael heard what sounded like a slap come through his right. He saw red. Quinn's screaming had stopped, telling Michael his hearing had been spot on.

Risking being seen, he stepped up to the window for half a second, and stormed the door. He'd seen enough to realize they were at the fireplace, but between the slap and Quinn's head falling back onto the hardwood mantel, Michael wasn't sure if he could keep himself from killing Adam.

He rushed the guy before he had a chance to move and grabbed Adam by the back of his coat, throwing him onto the coffee table, which broke under the weight of the man's body. Without a second thought, Micheal stepped closer and punched Adam twice in the face. Behind him, Quinn's limp body hit the floor and Michael was torn. He hesitated just long enough that Adam scrambled to his feet and limp-ran out the door.

Praying she was alright, Michael took the few precious seconds to lock the door before slamming to his knees at Quinn's side.

"Quinn, honey, come on..." Michael gently gathered her body, cradling her against his chest, and shifted them away from the fire. Her back was so hot it was uncomfortable to touch and he turned her just enough to make sure her clothes weren't burnt before looking at her face again. "Quinn, sweetheart, please...please say you're alright."

Quinn's eyes were slits and her head rolled into his chest. "You're here," she whispered.

Did grown men cry? Would Quinn hate him if he did? There was no denying that his vision was a bit blurry as he looked down at her pale face. A bright red mark on her cheekbone told the story and Michael knew he needed to get her to a hospital. He was absolutely positive she'd already had a concussion, and now Adam had hit her… hard…and she'd also whacked her head on the edge of the mantel.

"I'm here," he assured her, leaving a tender kiss on her forehead. Hopefully it didn't hurt there. "I'm here, sweetheart. And we're going to get you out of here. We're gonna get you to the hospital."

"Adam…" She moaned. "He's here."

"I know," Michael bit out. "I'm sorry I didn't see the signs before. I don't know how I missed him."

"He's been…" she took a couple of labored breaths, "watching us."

Michael felt lower than dirt. Quinn had seen Adam. She'd. Seen. Adam. And Michael had talked her out of it, just like all the idiots back at her old school. Instead of believing her, he'd risked her life by saying there was no evidence, that logically Adam wouldn't have traced her across the country, and now Quinn had paid the price.

I don't deserve her, he thought in despair. *But I'm going to save her first.*

Gathering her close, he climbed to his feet and settled Quinn on the couch. "Quinn, honey, we're going to go get help, okay?" Michael looked at the window. Adam was out there. The storm was out there. But the hospital was also out there. He looked back down and barely had time to jump back before Quinn threw up over the side of the couch.

"I'm dying." She moaned after she was done. Her body was curled into a ball and Michael had never been more worried or hurting in his life.

He'd also never been as angry as when he'd seen Adam hit Quinn, but seeing her like this was a completely new emotion. "No," Michael whispered, carefully smoothing her hair from her face. "But we have to go." He stood and ran to their small pile of clothes. "We need to put all these on," he told her.

It took all his energy to help her get dressed without cursing. She was hurting so much, the pain sat in every line of her face and in her lethargy. It was killing Michael to see her like this. Before dressing her, he grabbed their keys and wallets and stuffed everything in the pocket of his jacket, then helped Quinn get dressed.

After getting the jackets and sweatshirts layered on her, Michael wrapped her in the blanket and then lifted her like an extra large burrito. It was awkward and he wasn't sure just how he was going to do it, but he had to get her help.

"You," she whispered hoarsely. "It's cold."

Michael looked down at his own sweatshirt. "I'll be moving," he said. "I'm fine." A prayer went heavenward that his words were true. He set down her feet for a moment to open the door, then barged outside and headed in the direction of the road.

With every step, Michael felt his muscles growing cold and stiff. The snow was deeper than he'd remembered. But every time Quinn groaned, he pushed past his own discomfort and kept going.

The wind was whining through the trees, but Michael did his best to keep his ears and eyes peeled for any movement. In this weather, odds were the animals would be hunkered down, so anything off the norm would more than likely be Adam.

"Hopefully he's holed up somewhere like the coward he is, nursing a broken neck," Michael muttered.

"I don't understand," Quinn whispered.

Michael shook his head, dislodging some snow from his hair. "Nothing, sweetheart. Just rest. I have you."

Her eyes finished closing before his words ended.

She had to be alright. She *had* to be alright. Michael knew after failing her this badly, he couldn't have her, but someone, some guy in the future, had to know and appreciate just how magnificent this woman was.

The idea of her belonging to someone else made Michael's skin flush with anger and he let the idea percolate to keep his body temperature in a more comfortable place. He'd have to move after all. He wouldn't be able to watch her fall in love with another guy and live her happy ever after. But he also couldn't admit that he'd fallen in love with her over the course of three days and that he'd failed her to the point of almost killing her.

What woman would welcome a man like that into their life?

Least the girls can't say I'm boring anymore, he thought without humor. *Now I'm just a failure.*

A break in the trees caught his eye and Michael blew out his breath with a puff of smoke. Heaven was watching at least a little bit because they'd found the road.

CHAPTER 21

Someone was trying to break into Quinn's skull. She was sure of it. The pain was so intense that her stomach churned from it. She had a vague memory of losing what little lunch had been in her system, but the way she was being jostled at the moment was causing her to think she wasn't quite as empty as she thought.

Her eyes fluttered, but bright whiteness caused her to squeeze them shut and groan.

"Hang on, sweetheart," a voice panted. "We're going to get you help."

Slowly, memories came back. How many times had Quinn been hit in the head at this point? *Too many,* came the sarcastic reply. She'd only just been recovering from one concussion when Adam..."

ADAM!" she shouted, though the sound wasn't as loud as the urgency felt.

"Shhh…" the voice said again.

Quinn relaxed when she realized it was Michael. "Michael," she whispered. "You came. You saved me."

"I'm working on it," was his heavy reply.

Quinn paid attention to the feel of his hold and the way her body felt thick and unable to move. "Why…?" She forced her eyes open and ignored the shot of pain straight to the middle of her forehead. It was snowing and they were outside. She was bundled in what felt like ten layers of blankets and sweatshirts, while Michael appeared to be wearing only a hoodie.

His breathing was heavy, his face red. She could practically feel the strain in his muscles, but the determined clench of his jaw said any help she offered wouldn't be accepted. "Did he hurt you?" she whispered.

Michael's blue eyes glanced down before going back to his path. "No."

"Where is he?" Quinn had a sudden fleeting picture of Adam lying broken and bleeding and possibly dead back at the cabin. Her mind was too fuzzy to remember exactly what had happened. "I can't…remember…"

Michael blew out a raspy breath. "I came running when you screamed," he managed, though his voice told her how angry he was. "I pulled him off you, but not before the—" He clamped his jaw shut.

Quinn had an irrational urge to giggle at the fact that he was holding back a curse word in this instance. She wasn't one to say those words, but right now? They somehow felt appropriate.

"Not before he hit you," Michael said miserably. "You have a bruise on your cheek, but it also knocked your head back into the mantel and I'm pretty sure any healing we accomplished in the last couple of days is completely gone."

"I got sick."

He nodded jerkily. "You did." Michael did curse quietly when they stumbled for just a moment before he found his footing.

Quinn tried to look over the side of the blanket, but not only was her view obstructed, but moving her head felt like a herculean effort. No wonder Michael was carrying her. If she couldn't lift her head, she probably couldn't lift her feet either. "I'm sorry."

His head jerked toward her. "What?"

"I'm sorry," she said again. Tears stung. How many times would she cry over this? How many times would thoughts of Adam and his craziness bring her to her knees? How many times would she cower in fear before he either killed her or was finally caught himself?

And just when I finally found the guy I actually want to spend my life with.

The words were bitter on her tongue. Quinn had been watching herself fall for her protector a little more each hour as he cared for her and showed her what it was like when a man was the same inside as he showed on the outside. And now that she was finally ready to fully give in to him, Adam was not only back, but she and Michael were outside in the elements and there was a very real possibility that one or both of them would be in very serious condition by the time they arrived at the hospital…if they arrived at the hospital.

"Where are we?" she murmured.

Michael shook his head and a shiver ran through him, shaking Quinn. "I'm not sure. I think we were right. You took a wrong turn in the dark. This isn't highway one-oh-one."

This time it was Quinn who cursed.

Michael snorted a laugh. "Never would have thought I'd hear that from you."

Quinn was struggling to keep her eyes open at the moment. "It felt good."

He made a face. "Indeed." His feet crunched in the snow and Quinn studied his eyelashes, which were currently frozen.

If they didn't do something soon, they wouldn't make it.

"We've been walking for about twenty minutes," he said through chattering teeth. "There has to be something soon."

Quinn swallowed hard. They needed a miracle. And they needed it now. A single tear slipped down the side of her face and into her hair.

It's not fair.

The thought brought with it a weight that robbed Quinn of her breath. It felt as if an elephant was standing on her chest, while someone else beat her head with a crowbar at regular intervals. What was she supposed to do? She was useless, literally a burden for Michael to carry.

"You have to leave me." She moaned.

Michael's eyes widened and drips of water ran down the side of his face. "What are you talking about?"

She almost couldn't get the words out, but Quinn knew it was the only way. "You have to leave me," she said, trying to be stronger. "You can't make it with me like this. Set me down and go on by yourself."

"You really think…?" Michael's jaw clenched again and he looked forward as if he was gathering himself. "Quinn, I want you to listen, okay?"

It wasn't like she had a choice.

"The only reason I'm out in this blizzard is to save you," he said, enunciating each word carefully through his frozen lips. "Why? Because I'm in love with you."

Quinn's breath left in a whoosh again, only this time, it wasn't because of despair. Had she ever heard such beautiful words? Or at least they were beautiful when they came from the right guy.

"And I will *not* sit back in that cabin and let you continue to suffer. Not from Adam. Not from your injuries, not if I have any strength left in me to help." He turned his head and coughed, his skin even redder than before. "I don't care if it takes all day, and all night, but I *will* get you somewhere safe and get you the medical help you need." He took several shuddering breaths. "There's no other option."

Quinn had no idea how to reply to that declaration. She wanted to offer him the same kind of hope and determination in return, but she was fading again. The pounding in her head was taking over and she was struggling to focus on anything else.

Even Michael's declaration of love wasn't enough to overshadow her injuries and she began to drift in and out, her body shivering despite the multilayers cocooning her.

"Hang on," Michael said, and Quinn felt his pace pick up. "Hang on, Quinn. We're not done yet."

What seemed only moments later, but Quinn knew she wasn't in a position to judge time, she heard the *whoop* of a siren.

Once.

Twice.

And then she was being handed over to another set of arms.

"Careful with her," Michael slurred. "Please…be careful with her."

"We've got her, buddy," a deep voice said, one that Quinn was sure she had heard before. "But you need to get in here too."

"No!" Michael shouted. "Take care of her. That guy…he…"

Quinn felt her back hit something semi-firm and she cried out in pain.

"Careful!"

"We've got her!" the deep voice said again.

Slowly, the voices faded and Quinn was barely able to acknowledge the movement of several individuals around her before she knew no more.

* * *

"Hey!" Gavin shouted, right in Michael's face. His large hands were on Michael's shoulders, holding him back from the back of the ambulance. "Get yourself together, man," Gavin growled. "You're going to die from hypothermia if we don't get you taken care of, so let us handle Quinn and think about yourself for a moment."

Michael relaxed only slightly. It wasn't like he had the strength to fight his enormous friend anyway. He tried to bring his gaze up high enough to see inside the ambulance, but the move brought with it a wave of vertigo and Michael's knees buckled.

"Okay," Gavin ground out, his arms around Michael as he kept him from hitting the ground. "Stevie! Winslow! Someone get over here!"

Michael was barely awake as he felt several hands land on his body and lift him into the air. He was shaking uncontrollably and no matter how he clenched his muscles, he couldn't seem to stop. It seemed as if his teeth would break and his bones would rattle right out of his body at the severity of the movement.

Gavin muttered under his breath. "You, my man, are in worse shape than her."

Michael tried to shake his head, but he couldn't seem to get his muscles to answer the call. His limbs clenched in erratic patterns and he felt his consciousness go in and out. *NO!* He couldn't black out. He needed to stay awake, to stay strong. When Quinn was taken care of, then he could sleep. He could sleep forever if it came down to it, but not until Quinn was taken care of.

He began to struggle again and Gavin's cursing grew louder. "Michael, you idiot, if you don't stop it right now, we won't be able to get either of you to the hospital and Quinn will only suffer longer."

Michael had never heeded words so quickly in his life.

"Better," Gavin grunted. "Okay. Up we go."

It wasn't a careful shift, but Michael felt his body land on what felt like a vehicle seat.

"We can only fit one gurney in the ambulance," Gavin explained as he reached around Michael and grabbed a seatbelt. "I'm going to follow them in the truck anyway, so I'll take you with me."

Michael's head fell back as his body spasmed again.

"Get me that blanket!" Gavin shouted.

Michael felt something being tucked around him. It was loud in his ears and far from the soft bed he wanted at the moment.

"Hang on, buddy," Gavin said, the slightest bit of worry in his tone. "Hang on."

A door slammed and Michael saw only black for a few moments, his head lolling around uncontrollably. A few moments later, a door across from him opened and the truck shifted as, presumably, Gavin got inside. His hunch was affirmed when Gavin spoke.

"Just hold on, Michael," Gavin said. "We're only twenty minutes from the hospital. We'll have you fixed up in no time." There was a grinding sound before the truck lurched into motion.

Michael moaned. He wanted to ask about Quinn, but he couldn't seem to get his mouth to work properly. Did they know she had a concussion? Had they seen the wreck? Was there anything they could do about the scar on her forehead? Or what about all the cuts on her hands that were still healing?

And where was Adam? Was he still lurking in the woods? Had Michael hurt him enough for Adam to go home with his tail between his legs? Or was the coward simply biding his time?

The presence ceased to exist as Michael's mind spun further and further down the rabbit hole of fear, worries and outright desperation for Quinn's safety. He barely noticed the movement of the truck at all, or the loud sirens blasting through the winter storm. And when his door opened and arms reached around him, lifting him from the truck and laying him on a gurney, his heart jolted, but his body lay limp.

The shivering had ceased and Michael was actually starting to feel slightly warm. He sighed, the relaxation of his muscles much better than the jaw-shattering shaking from before.

"No, no, no!" Gavin bellowed. "GET SOMEONE OVER HERE NOW!"

Cold hands landed on Michael's body and he wanted to pull away from them, but he couldn't seem to move. Then, as his body continued to heat, the hands felt good. Were Quinn's hands cool? Would she put her hand on his forehead? He felt as if he were starting to overheat and a dampness inside his sweatshirt made Michael want to take it off.

He began to shift. "Hot," he muttered. "Too hot…"

"Stay down," a voice ordered. It wasn't Gavin this time. In fact, Michael had no idea who it was.

He couldn't get his eyes to open, but someone else was doing it for him and something bright flashed across his vision.

"I want an IV in *now!*" the voice shouted. "And warm oxygen. Who's got his temperature?"

The noise and voices began to blend together and Michael found he couldn't differentiate one from the other. The room grew fuzzy and the sounds muted.

His eyelids, which were already closed, felt heavier than normal and he wanted nothing more than to sleep…for a very long time. "Quinn…" he moaned. He needed to know she was alright.

"She's fine, man," Gavin's voice said, right in Michael's ear. "They're taking care of her. Now I want you to focus on you. No one else is gonna shout *Moby Dick* at me during basketball games if you don't focus on yourself, so quit worrying about Quinn and focus!"

"Love…her…" Michael slurred as sleep began to tug him down. Gavin wouldn't lie to him. Michael trusted that Quinn was alright, and that let him relax just enough to slip away.

"Wait…what?"

But Gavin's reply was too late and Michael's head fell to the side.

CHAPTER 22

"Where's Michael?" Quinn asked her nurse for what seemed the thousandth time.

The woman gave her the side eye, but didn't reply.

Quinn pinched her lips together. "The man that came in with me. Please…I need to know he's alright."

Now the nurse was flat out ignoring her.

"Why won't you tell me anything?" Quinn demanded. She'd only been there a couple of hours, but she already wanted to leave. Her entire body ached, the whiplash seemed to have returned in her neck and shoulders, and her head pain was only under control because of the heavy dose of meds they'd filled her with, but Quinn still wanted out.

Michael had been struggling. She'd seen it and she needed to know he was okay before she could relax. If this chick didn't say something soon, Quinn was going to get out of bed and risk falling flat on her face just to find out herself.

The nurse sighed, then glared. "You're not supposed to be doing anything that'll bring up your blood pressure."

Quinn raised her eyebrows. "I don't see how keeping secrets from me is going to help that." Okay…apparently, medication made her bold as well. She might have been mostly pain free, but she was also restless and worried and sick of being treated as fragile. "Please," she tried in a softer tone. "He risked his life to save me. I…" She trailed off before admitting to something that Michael needed to hear first. "I need to know he's alright."

Shaking her head, the nurse glanced at the door, then back. "I can't talk about other patients. I'm sorry." With those parting words, she scurried out.

That was it. Quinn started moving cords and tubes out of the way just as the door opened and she froze, exactly like the deer that had smashed through her windshield.

"What do you think you're doing?" Gavin demanded, his arms folding over his wide chest.

Quinn had always thought Gavin was an attractive man, though he was very large, but for the first time ever, she barely noticed. He wasn't Michael. And that was all that mattered at the moment.

"No one will tell me about Michael," she said, shifting toward the edge of the bed. "I need to find him."

"Hold up." Gavin came over and took her heels, guiding her legs back in bed. "You're in no shape to go traipsing around the hospital."

Quinn glared.

He chuckled and held up his hands before backing away. "It's the truth, Quinn. You and I both know it. So how about instead of you wandering out and smacking your head on the linoleum when you already have like three goose eggs, we handle this like adults?"

She huffed and folded her arms over her chest in a rare public show of stubbornness. *Please look angry instead of pouty.* She wasn't sure she pulled it off by the way Gavin was grinning. Quinn sighed and let her arms drop. "Is he okay?" she begged.

Gavin nodded, though his smile fell. "He will be."

Quinn blinked rapidly and looked down at her blanket. She was always so careful with her feelings in public, but today had been nothing like normal. She felt slightly out of control and wasn't sure how to get her footing. "Can you tell me anything more?"

Gavin walked to a chair and lifted it, pulling it closer to the bed.

"Lean back and relax," he said as he sat and crossed a foot over his knee. "I have a feeling we've both got stories to tell and Michael is still unconscious, so I can't beat it out of him."

Quinn tried to relax, but she couldn't. The story she had to share would sound insane and she wasn't sure how much information she should give Gavin. What if he didn't believe her about the stalking?

"Quinn."

She looked up.

Gavin gave her a small smile. "I know we're more acquaintances than friends, but everything you tell me here will be strictly confidential unless you say otherwise." He put up his hand. "I'm not an officer, but I work closely with several of them and can get you help if you need it, without alerting the whole gang back in Seagull Cove."

Her eyes widened. "How did you know I need help?"

His massive shoulders shrugged. "Michael's knuckles were bloody and bruised." Gavin raised an eyebrow. "That man has never fought with anything other than his brain his entire life."

Quinn sniffled and grabbed the box of tissues next to her bed. "It's long and complicated," she warned her visitor.

Gavin just nodded and leaned back.

Closing her eyes and letting the tears drip, Quinn told him everything. Once the story started, it was like she couldn't close the floodgates, as if her system needed to purge itself and Gavin had become her captive audience.

Michael had listened out of kindness, but Gavin's tight muscles and alert eyes said he was listening for other reasons and his attachment to the law told Quinn he was probably formulating a plan.

She blew out a breath and wiped her face when she finished. "And now we're here."

Gavin rubbed a hand over the top of his head. "You're right. That was pretty complicated."

Quinn nodded, her gaze on her blanket. "I know." She peeked sideways to see Gavin rubbing his chin.

"And the police didn't do anything to the guy?"

Quinn shook her head, then stopped and winced. Even under

heavy medication it wasn't a good idea to move too much, apparently. "They said I couldn't get a restraining order unless he'd done something to prove he was going to hurt me. And when no one at the school would back up my claims about him being unbalanced, they didn't have anything to go on."

Gavin growled. "Stupid rules," he muttered. His leg came down and he slapped his knees. "Guess I know why Michael was so protective of you when we finally found you."

"Speaking of…" Quinn hedged.

Gavin smirked. "You two were hard to track down," he admitted.

"I'm still wondering how you even knew to go after us at all," she said. "We were supposed to be gone for a couple of days, so why bother looking for us?"

Gavin huffed a laugh. "Your boytoy is the most reliable man I know."

Quinn flushed with heat, but didn't correct Gavin. She was still hoping their connection hadn't all been a dream. Once they were home, would things change? Or would they still be…sort of…together?

"Aspen put out a call when she couldn't get a hold of him. Michael *always* answers a call or at least returns a message if he can't get to the phone. *Always.* So when he went off the grid, every single one of us tried to call him for two days straight and no one could get through." Gavin shrugged. "With the storms coming through, I was the only one with equipment qualified to go out and track you two down."

"How long did it take you to find us?" Quinn whispered. She hated that she had caused this much trouble, but was exceedingly grateful Michael's reputation led to their rescue.

Gavin snorted. "Longer than it should have. They've been plowing the main highway since this whole mess blew through, but you…"

"But I took a wrong turn and we weren't on the main highway," Quinn finished for him. She rubbed her aching forehead. "I'm not quite sure where I went wrong, but it was so dark out, and with the rain…"

"It was totally understandable," Gavin assured her as he stood up. "I'm going to check on Michael and if you want, I'll report back."

"I'd appreciate it, thank you," Quinn replied. Fatigue was settling in, whether from the ordeal or the medications, she wasn't sure, but she needed to close her eyes soon.

"It's the least I can do," Gavin replied as he pulled open her door. "After all..." He leaned in with that smirk from earlier. "It's not every day I get to deliver messages between my best bud and the girl he loves."

* * *

MICHAEL'S EYELIDS WEIGHED A TON. Literally. He could hear noises and the squeaking of a chair being pulled across a tile floor made him want to cover his ears, but he was struggling to get any of his muscles to obey his commands.

Something warm was rushing through his body and he could feel his temperature starting to heat up with it. Along with the feeling of his limbs, he noticed his head was pounding. *This must have been what Quinn felt like after the crash,* he thought wryly.

Images of her soft curls and light eyes had him working harder to get his eyes opened. A flash of light caused him to moan and the room came to a halt.

"Michael?" The deep voice could belong to no one other than Gavin. "Dude...are you awake?"

Michael concentrated on nothing but his eyelids. They began to flutter, sending more bright flashes to his corneas, which protested by sending pain to every crevice of his brain, but Michael pushed on. He needed to check on Quinn. Had Adam followed them? Had he been taken in by the police? Had Michael accidentally killed the guy?

And the most important question of all...was Quinn safe?

"Come on, buddy," Gavin encouraged. "Let me know you're awake."

Michael finally managed more than a mere slit, and it was as if the weight had been smashed. His eyes flew all the way open, only to squeeze shut as if a branding iron had landed on his face. He cursed. "Turn off the light," he muttered, though he could have sworn it sounded a bit slurred.

There was a shuffling of footsteps and a click. "Try again," Gavin called out, sounding a little farther away than before.

Michael opened one eye and then the other and finally was able to see the hospital room he was being kept in. He tried to raise his hand, but fatigue kept him from rubbing the ache in his forehead. "Quinn?" he croaked. "Is she alright?"

Gavin chuckled and came back across the room, pulling up a chair close to the bed. "That's funny. I just stopped her from marching through the hospital to find the answer to that exact question…" He tilted his head to the side. "Except the subject matter was you…not her."

Michael relaxed onto his pillow, letting his eyes close again. A smile played on his lips. She was okay. That was all he needed to know. No…wait. His eyes were open again and he strained to sit up. "Adam. Did someone catch Adam? We have to stop him before he gets her again."

Gavin leaned forward and put his hands up. "Hold on, man. You're not in any shape to do anything."

"It isn't safe," Michael insisted.

Gavin nodded gravely. "I know. Quinn told me. I was just about to start calling some of my buddies in the department when you began to show signs of waking up."

Michael's head fell the couple of inches he'd managed to gain. "The department? You can get the police involved?"

Gavin nodded. "We've got two witnesses, and a physical injury. I think we can get a warrant out."

"Thank you," Michael managed, his anxiety finally ebbing. He sighed, feeling his entire body sink into the hard mattress. "How's she doing? Emotionally?"

"She's worried about you."

Michael nodded. He liked hearing that, but was still worried she would change her mind now that they were on their way back to the real world. Especially since he'd been so late in stopping Adam.

Gavin cleared his throat. "So...Quinn told me everything that happened, but I'm guessing a few pieces were left out."

Michael tilted his head in Gavin's direction. His friend was smirking like he was the cat who caught the canary.

"Like just how two people who barely knew each other fell in love in three days' time."

Michael raised an eyebrow in return. "Wouldn't you like to know?"

Gavin held out his hands. "I just said I did."

Michael closed his eyes and faced upward again. "I don't think you need the details."

"Okay...but do I need to start planning a shotgun wedding?"

Michael's glare was so fast, he barely realized his reaction before it was too late.

Gavin only chuckled. "It was a joke, Mike. If there was any man I'd trust my sister to be trapped with, it would be you. You're straighter than an arrow."

"I didn't know you had a sister."

Gavin grinned. "I don't. But the principle remains."

Michael huffed, but let it go. Gavin didn't tease as much as Jayden, but the man still enjoyed a little ribbing now and then.

"You do realize this is going to be all over the news," Gavin said gravely.

Michael began to nod, then he realized the implications. "He'll find her." He turned to Gavin, his panic returning.

Gavin nodded. "Yep."

"What can we do?"

Gavin held up his phone. "You...are going to rest. I'm...going to make some calls." He grinned. "*After* reporting back to Quinn that you're alive and well. She's just as deep in this as you are. Congratulations."

Michael frowned. "How did you know I loved her?"

Gavin laughed. "You said so. When they were saving your sorry hide, you kept talking about 'loving her.' There was only one person you could mean." Gavin pumped his eyebrows. "She's a looker. I'll give you that."

Michael scowled. "She's also taken…" His words trailed off as he thought of his promise to himself when he was walking them through the storm.

"Uh-oh." Gavin sat back. "Looks like I haven't quite heard the whole tale."

Michael glared. "You need to stop watching so many crime shows."

"Why?" Gavin grinned. "I seem to have become very good at reading people. Maybe I should take up a new hobby."

"Such as?"

"Private detective," Gavin shot back. "I'll just sit and watch people and tell whether they're guilty or not."

"You're an idiot."

Gavin shrugged, not the least bit perturbed. "What made you so upset?"

Michael blew out a breath and turned back to the ceiling. He wasn't sure he wanted to talk about it. He was usually the listener, not the speaker, but if there was anyone who would take this seriously, it was Gavin. He was Michael's best friend and he would understand where Michael was coming from. Gavin knew what it was like to walk away from someone for their own good.

"I promised myself that if I got her back safe…I would walk away," Michael muttered.

There seemed to be a lot of unsavory words slipping out of mouths recently, as showcased by Gavin's reaction. "Why would you do that?" he growled.

Michael's previous anger returned as he glared at his friend. "Because she deserves someone who can protect her!" he whisper-shouted. He might want to bellow to the heavens, but Michael forced himself to remember that he was in a public place. "She crashed because I wanted to leave for the trip the night before. She got hurt, Gav. Really hurt. All I had to offer was a truck cab." Michael snorted in disgust. "She was nearly sick with exposure by the time I got her to the cabin. And then I terrified her because I reminded her of that

Adam guy. Twice, I left her, trying to help and neither time worked out well. I'm lucky Adam hadn't killed her by the time I got back the second time." Michael shook his head, ignoring the bowling ball rolling around inside. "She's hurt because of me. Because I didn't protect her. Because I didn't take her worries seriously. And then I almost killed her trying to save her as I took us into the storm." He turned back to the ceiling. "She deserves more."

Gavin stood and walked over until he was towering over Michael. "I'm going to let you stew in that sludge of idiocy for a little bit while I make some calls." Gavin pointed down at Michael. "But I expect you to come to your senses by the time I come back." Shaking his head, he did exactly that, nearly slamming the door behind him.

CHAPTER 23

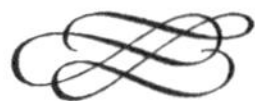

Quinn jerked toward the door when it opened, her mouth open and ready to riddle Gavin with questions, but it was a nurse instead.

The man didn't speak, just stayed by the door, keeping his face away from hers. He looked at his tablet, studying it for a moment, as he kept checking out the window in the door.

Quinn frowned. That hair...Her eyes widened. "Adam," she croaked.

He glared at her. "Be quiet."

Quinn felt a thrill go through her at the bruising on the side of Adam's face. *Good,* she thought. *At least Michael got in at least one good hit.*

Adam checked the hallway one more time, then marched toward her.

"Stay back," Quinn warned. "I'll scream."

Adam rolled his eyes. "If I'd known you were this dramatic, I wouldn't have come so far for you." He paused, watching her for a moment before slowly moving up to the bed. "Do you have any idea how much work it has been to come get you? All the months of waiting to get away from work, then sitting in my car for a week while I tried to figure out how to approach you without anyone else noticing?"

No matter how far Quinn leaned back, he simply followed until his fingers were brushing her cheek.

"I don't know if I could have stopped myself from coming," Adam mused. "I thought you taking a trip was the break I needed, but then that stupid storm hit and that idiot driver wouldn't leave your side." Adam snorted. "I thought I was going to freeze to death before I caught a break. It was a good thing I'd come prepared to sleep in the woods behind your house until I could take you with me." He shook his head and took his hand back. "We have to hurry before the new rotation gets itself settled." He pulled out a needle and went for Quinn's IV.

"NO!" she screamed, batting it out of his hand. Nausea churned in Quinn's stomach at his story. It had been so much worse than she'd thought, but she couldn't let him win now. Not now, not after everything that had happened.

The look of rage on Adam's face had her scrambling out of the bed, but all the tubes kept her from going far. She stubbed her toe on a nightstand and tripped with the pain. Before she could hit the floor, however, arms banded around her, but they were all wrong.

Instead of tenderness, they were like steel and they were choking the breath from her.

"You'll have the whole place down on our heads," Adam hissed, his eyes wide and crazed as he hauled her to her feet. He jerked her backward, the IV dragging along with them as he made his way back to the thrown needle. Still holding Quinn, he reached for it.

Quinn had never known fear as she did in that moment and she'd experienced several terrifying moments with Adam. But she knew that if Adam managed to get her with that drug, she might never see the light of day again.

DO SOMETHING! she screamed at herself. Someway, somehow, she had to push past her paralysis and save herself.

Using every bit of energy she had left in her body, she jabbed her elbow into Adam's side, causing him to lean and grunt, but he didn't fully stop. His fingers fumbled for the needle and Quinn reacted on instinct.

She brought her heel down on his hand, smashing it into the needle and the ground with every ounce of her weight.

Adam howled and threw Quinn away from him.

She crashed into the IV stand and her bed, gripping the railing to hold herself upright and keep from getting yet another concussion.

Adam began shouting obscenities, but Quinn's head was ringing from all that had happened, and she found her movements sluggish.

Just as hands landed on her back, the door banged open and bodies began to swarm the room.

Quinn found herself being yanked in multiple directions, but Adam's hands were pried off her hospital gown and she was wrapped up in large, warm arms. Not the right arms, but ones that made her feel safe nonetheless.

"Get him out of here!" Gavin bellowed, his hold on Quinn tightening.

Adam was screaming at the top of his lungs, but Quinn couldn't understand a word. She watched from her place at Gavin's side as security guards dragged the crazed man out of her room, wincing with every insult he threw her way, especially when they were followed with begging and screaming for her to come to him.

"Ignore him," Gavin said in a sharp tone. His hand went to her head and pressed it into his chest, covering her ears and helping muffle the noise of the situation.

A wheelchair came barreling through the door just as Adam was yanked out and Quinn's eyes widened. "Michael…" she breathed.

Michael tried to stand up, but the orderly pushing him shoved Michael back down. "Hang on, man. We'll bring her to you."

Quinn started to move and Gavin wrapped an arm around her waist, helping her walk until they made it to Michael's feet, where Quinn leaned forward, collapsing into his hold.

Michael's arms wrapped around her, pulling her onto his lap. "It should have been me taking him down," he growled, while burying his face in Quinn's hair.

Quinn's voice broke on a sob. "He's gone, for real, now. Right? He can't come back?"

Michael's hands framed her face and brought her up so they could see each other face to face.

"Dude…make it quick," the orderly whispered. "If my boss sees this, I'm toast."

"He's gone," Michael said decisively. "He's been caught. There are witnesses. He absolutely, unequivocally, cannot come back. Ever."

Quinn closed her eyes and let Michael bring their foreheads together. This was all she needed, though it would have been nice to have it without all the beeping and the shouts of people and equipment.

She could feel it though. Down to her bones. Everything was going to be alright. Adam was gone. Michael was here. Quinn had been brave enough to fight back… Now was finally the time to truly live her life.

She and Michael would return to Seagull Cove. She could save her shop. They would date and eventually…if all went as she hoped…she and Michael would live happily ever after.

"I'm sorry, ma'am," the orderly said. "But I have to take him back."

Quinn sat up and looked longingly at Michael. She smoothed his hair from his face. "I'll see you soon?"

He smiled at her, rubbing his thumb under her eye. "Just try and stop me."

Gavin helped Quinn to stand and she watched the man she loved be pulled from the room just before the security guards, armed with several doctors, filled the space Michael had just vacated.

"Better get you back down on the bed," Gavin whispered. "I have a feeling this is going to be a long night."

Quinn sighed, but let herself be guided back. When she was finally settled and her doctor had reset her IV and every other cord connected to her body, she turned to the waiting police. "It's a long story," she warned.

The officer snorted. "I think we have time."

Quinn nodded and once again told about a time in her life she'd rather forget, but this time, for the *first* time...it ended on a note of hope.

* * *

IT FELT as if someone was tearing his heart from his body as Michael was wheeled farther away from Quinn. She needed him. She'd just been attacked, *again*, by Adam and Michael had been brushed aside like a recalcitrant child.

His fists clenched as he was taken back to his room.

"They'll let you out soon," his volunteer said, "and then you can spend more time with her." The young man grinned. "Can't say I blame you. She was something else."

Michael grunted and stood up, his knees shaky, before transferring to the bed. He'd been ready to crawl on his hands and knees to get to Quinn, but the young man had been coming in to clean up and had convinced Michael the wheelchair would be faster.

It was, but it also meant Michael wasn't able to stay as long.

He bit back another curse. Never in his life had Michael spent so much time with those words running through his mind and out his mouth. His mom was going to wash his mouth out with soap if she ever figured it out.

Speaking of... He wondered if anyone had contacted his parents. He didn't want them traveling in the snowstorm, but he knew his mother well. There was no way she'd stay home if she knew what had happened.

"That was the best entertainment I've had in ages," Gavin boasted as he came through Michael's door.

"You left her?" Michael shouted, then clutched his head. Shoot, he needed to go back to being the Michael who thought before he spoke.

Gavin laughed and plopped himself in a chair. "You two are made for each other, you know that? Neither one cares about their own health, only the other one." His smile softened. "Have I said congrats yet?'

"I think you did," MIchael muttered, leaning back against his pillow.

"Well…I mean it. That's something worth celebrating."

Michael relaxed and smiled back. "It is, I suppose."

"And now you see why you can't leave her."

Michael froze. He hadn't even realized how his little foray into Quinn's room had sent that exact message.

Gavin was right. Selfish as it might be, Michael couldn't leave her. He'd never survive it. And from everything he saw, neither would Quinn.

"You suck."

Gavin's grin grew. "Being right only stinks to those who are wrong."

Michael huffed.

Gavin glanced at his watch and hummed. "I'm thinking it'll only be another fifteen minutes or so."

Michael raised his eyebrows. "For what?" One side of Gavin's smile rose higher than the other and Michael couldn't help but scowl. Just what was his friend up to?

Gavin shook his head, then laced his fingers behind him and leaned back. "I think I'll just watch your reaction."

A lightbulb dawned, clear as anything drawn in a cartoon. "They're coming, aren't they?"

"Like a swarm of locusts."

"All of them?" Michael asked, wincing as he waited for the answer.

Gavin's eyes went to the ceiling as he mentally seemed to count. His eyes came back to Michael's. "Near about."

Michael sighed and carefully rested his head against the pillow, closing his eyes. "Wake me when it's over."

Gavin's chuckle was nothing short of devious. If he was feeling better, Micheal would have punched his friend right in the face. The giant firefighter was enjoying this way too much.

His guess, however, was a few minutes off. It only took ten minutes for Michael to hear a dozen voices growing louder in the hallway as they headed toward his door.

"Courage," Gavin teased. "You're gonna need it." He leaned forward. "And just wait until your mother hears you're bringing a girl home."

"Shut up," Michael got out before the door flew open.

"Michael!" His mother gasped, her hands covering her mouth and tears gathering in her eyes. She rushed over and flung her arms around him, immediately breaking into tears.

"Easy, Hope," Michael's dad, Enoch, said. "You can't throw him around like that." He grinned at his son over his wife's head. "I'm betting you have a killer headache."

Michael nodded as best he could. "It's been better, that's for sure."

His dad chuckled.

Loud voices were still at the door and Michael realized his cousins had all come as well. Aspen and Maeve were arguing about a slice of cake that Aspen had been hiding in her coat, Ethan was standing to the side, wisely staying as far away from the fight as possible. Austin, however, walked confidently across the room and reached out a hand to Michael.

"Dude, you're a superhero!"

Michael grinned. "If only," he said, shifting his mother's hold a little. She was starting to get heavy.

"Come on, sweetheart," Michael's dad said soothingly, prying his wife off Michael's neck. "Let him breathe."

She sniffled and leaned into her husband's side. "I don't really understand what happened," she whispered thickly. "Why were you on that road? And why did you have to beat someone up?"

"I didn't know you even knew how to throw a punch!" Ethan added, coming up to join the conversation.

Estelle, who had been quiet until now, tsked her tongue. She eyed Gavin. "I'm guessing he had a teacher."

Gavin grinned and leaned onto the back two legs of his chair.

Michael's dad laughed, but his mom scowled.

"Here," Aspen said, plopping a Tupperware in his lap. She glared at Maeve, but turned back to smile at Michael. "This'll cure anything. Even hypothermia."

Michael gave her a tired smile. "Thanks." He fingered the container. He loved Aspen's cake, but right now he wasn't exactly hungry. Truth was, he was so tired he could sleep for a week, but there would be no sleeping in the foreseeable future.

"Do you need help?" his mom asked, darting forward. "Where's a fork? I can feed you."

"Mom," Michael said quickly, just as his dad also stepped in.

"Sweetheart, he's tired, not helpless." Michael's dad pulled his wife back. "He'll eat when he's hungry, I'm sure."

"But…"

Michael's dad shook his head and pulled her in even tighter. "Hon, he's going to be just fine. But he's going to take a couple of days to get his strength back. Just calm down."

Michael's mom scowled and poked at her husband's chest. "He's my only son!" she said fiercely. "Don't tell me what to do!"

"Way to go, Aunt Hope!" Aspen said with a laugh. "I didn't know you had it in you!"

Michael watched his mom blush from her jaw to the roots of her hair and she collapsed into her husband's side. He smiled. At least he knew where he got his protective nature from.

"I'm sorry," Michael's mom said softly. "I didn't really mean it."

Michael's dad just chuckled and rubbed his hand up and down his wife's arm. "Aunt Emory and Uncle Tony send their love," he said, relaying a message most likely from Emory herself.

Michael nodded. He knew why they couldn't come. There was no way Uncle Tony was traveling anywhere, especially in weather like this.

Michael's mom reached out and took his hand, giving it a light squeeze. "We'll get you home tomorrow and then you can rest," she said with a teary smile. "And hopefully you'll feel much better by the time the girls get home this weekend."

Michael's eyes widened. "Why are they coming home? School isn't out."

His mom frowned. "To check on you, of course."

Michael laid back on the pillow and closed his eyes. All this attention was already getting to be too much. And now his sisters were coming back? Geez, he didn't need to worry about not being enough for Quinn. She was going to spend five minutes with his family, all acting like crazies and bolt for the hills on her own.

"Hey, think of the silver lining," Maeve said with a teasing smile. "At least Delilah and Ruby can't tease you about being boring anymore."

CHAPTER 24

Quinn popped the prescribed pills into her mouth and swallowed them down. She hated taking medication, but the nurse had said she couldn't go home otherwise. "All done," Quinn said, feeling like an obedient dog.

The nurse gave her an understanding smile. "As soon as Dr. Mower gets here, we'll have him sign the paperwork and you can go home." She went back to her tablet. "You can probably go ahead and call whoever is picking you up."

Quinn froze. Who was picking her up? She hadn't even thought of that. "Uh…"

The nurse looked over. "Don't you have a family member or friend who can take you home?"

Quinn bit her bottom lip and shook her head. "Well…the man I came here with was sort of my ride. Michael Dunlap?"

The nurse frowned for a second, then it cleared and she looked sympathetic, which immediately put Quinn on edge. "He was released several hours ago. His family took him home."

If a dagger had landed in her heart, Quinn wasn't sure that it would have hurt worse than the news she'd just received. Michael had left her? He left with his family, but still…he just…left? He didn't stop by to talk to her or to set a time when they would see each other again?

Quinn fell back against the pillows.

"He wasn't driving," the nurse hurried to assure Quinn, as if that made a difference. "He's not allowed behind a wheel for a few days, so he wasn't the one planning his release." She raised her eyebrows expectantly. "Is there someone else you can contact?"

Quinn nodded. "I'll get it figured out…thanks."

The nurse must have understood that Quinn needed a little time to think, because she patted Quinn's knee and shuffled out of the room.

The beeping of the monitors was the only thing that was left, which was a good thing because Quinn wasn't sure that her heart could have kept time on its own anymore.

He left me.

The words floated through her head like a lost balloon, drifting and continuing on its way with nothing able to stop it. Yet unlike a balloon, which didn't bother anyone, the words were painful. They stung and the pain settled in her chest, making it difficult for Quinn to keep breathing.

"Call someone," she whispered to herself. She needed to hear the words out loud. Her brain wasn't functioning and Quinn had to have some kind of external stimulation if she was going to survive this.

Who could she call?

Her first thought was Aspen, but Quinn quickly tossed the idea away. Aspen was Michael's cousin. She was probably part of the very family that had taken Michael home and Quinn wasn't sure she could face the reminder at the moment.

Gavin.

Quinn closed her eyes and hung her head. He was the only other friend she had. Though Quinn had met several women since moving to Seagull Cove, she hadn't let herself get close to any of them. Her naturally quiet nature, mixed with the fear Adam had instilled in her, had caused Quinn to hold back from getting too close to anyone, women and men included.

Slowly, she shook her head. It was just another mark on the tally sheet of things that Adam had once taken from her.

Clenching her jaw, Quinn lifted her head. "Then take them back," she whispered harshly to herself. Adam wasn't here anymore. She wasn't still looking over her shoulder. Yes, some valuable lessons had been learned, but Quinn had also come to realize that she wasn't helpless.

She might not have been the one to give Adam a black eye, or to finally haul him off to jail, but she had fought back. She had done what she could and it had been enough to bring others running and to save her.

She pushed the hurt from Michael aside as well. If she chose to, she would muse on it later, but right now, she needed to take care of herself. Not Adam. Not Michael. Herself. And it started with finding someone willing to give her a ride home.

Since Gavin had already shown he was willing to go out of his way to help, she chose him. It took a few minutes for Quinn to finagle Gavin's number, but the guy at the fire department was finally willing to cooperate and she made the call with trembling fingers.

"Hello?"

"Gavin?"

"Quinn. I'm glad to hear that you're up and awake." He chuckled. "I was beginning to worry that you and Michael would never get your heads on straight after everything that went down."

Quinn tried to smile at his teasing, but she needed all her strength to beg a favor instead. "Yeah…it's been a bit bizarre." She cleared her throat. "But I'm afraid I have another favor to ask."

"Go ahead."

She relaxed a little at how easy-going he was. "I'm sort of stranded at the hospital," Quinn admitted. "Would it be possible for you to come pick me up? I know it's out of your way, but I'm happy to pay for gas and more for your time." She mentally calculated what that was going to do to her bank account, but it wasn't like she really had a choice.

"Quinn, I'm more than happy to come get you, but why isn't Michael taking you home?"

Nope. Not crying. I'm strong. I survived much worse than this. "He's already gone," Quinn said. She was unable to stop the slight quiver in her voice, but was proud that was as far as it went. Hopefully Gavin hadn't heard that particular piece of weakness.

"Gone?"

"Yes. The nurse said his family took him home."

A few choice words were muttered on the other end of the line, but Quinn only managed to catch some colorful descriptions of the words *idiot* and *bozo* before Gavin came back. "I'll be there in an hour."

Quinn stared at the receiver, the line having gone dead as soon as Gavin said his piece. "Men," she muttered. With a huff, Quinn hung up and laid back in bed. Now she just had to hope that the doctor got there quickly and got the papers signed. Sometimes places like this took forever and Quinn wanted nothing more than to go home and lick her wounds in private.

Where she could get a cup of tea, turn on her favorite movie and ignore the world for a day or two.

She rubbed at the scab on her forehead. She would have to take a minute to call Mrs. McCain and let her know that she hadn't been able to make it to the auction. "And, of course, there's your car to consider," Quinn murmured to herself.

With a sigh, she let her head hang back. Relaxing at home was overrated. Maybe working and getting back on her feet would be exactly what Quinn needed to move on from her brief whirlwind relationship and small shot at saving her business.

"Who cares," she said to the ceiling. "If the shop fails, that only gives me another opportunity to try somewhere else. Away from Adam *and* Michael."

* * *

MICHAEL WAS ABOUT to punch something. He knew it was ungentlemanly and he knew it was more like a toddler than an adult, but if someone didn't start to listen to his protests soon, he would have to take matters into his own hands.

"Are you comfortable?" his mother asked as she tried to fluff his pillow.

Michael closed his eyes and prayed for patience. She was doing the best she could, but his mom was seriously smothering him at the moment. "I'm fine, Mom," he said, forcing a calm tone. "But I need to go back to the hospital."

She must have realized he was being serious, because for the first time since they'd broken him out of the hospital, his mom frowned, then stood back and put her hands on her hips. "What did you forget? I'll send your father."

Michael shook his head. He wasn't ready to tell them about Quinn. His mom would go crazy and his sisters would jump down Quinn's throat and generally make a nuisance of themselves. He needed to speak to Quinn by himself and prepare her for what was coming.

As Michael thought back on how much Quinn had struggled with just meeting *him*, he knew she wouldn't handle an entire household of individuals at once. She needed time to adjust, to accept him now that they were away from the cabin and then he would introduce her to his family.

But not yet.

"I can't tell you."

His mom's eyes narrowed. "Is this about the girl who was with you?"

Michael swallowed, trying to look unaffected. "I need to go back."

His mom threw up his hands. "I'm sure her family is taking care of her," she argued. "If she needs anything, surely she'll call."

Michael groaned and threw his head back against his pillow. "Mooom." How could he tell her that Quinn didn't have any family? That he wanted to be her family? That Quinn needed a gentle touch while she recovered from the trauma she'd been dealt?

The door opened and Delilah stepped in. She held out her phone. "It's Gavin," she huffed. "Said it was important."

Michael grabbed the phone like a lifeline. "Gav?"

His mom smiled and slipped out, taking Delilah with her.

Thank goodness.

"You're the biggest jerk I've ever known."

Michael blinked. "Excuse me?"

"So, what was it?" Gavin demanded. "All just an act at the hospital? All that nearly killing yourself to get to her and threatening to take out anyone who touched her, even though you've never fought a day in your life?"

"What are you talking about?" Michael shouted back.

"Okay, look," Gavin said, calming his voice down. "We've been friends a long time, Mike. And this is definitely not something I ever thought I would accuse you of, but...did you play that girl?"

Michael felt the blood drain in his head and his mouth flopped open like a gaping fish. "I...what...?"

A long sigh came through the line. "When was the last time you spoke to Quinn?"

"Two days ago, when Adam went crazy," Michael offered. "They wouldn't let me go see her after that."

"And where are you now?"

"At home," Michael snapped, his newfound anger starting to build. "My mom and siblings dragged me out of the hospital kicking and screaming and refusing to listen to any of my protests."

Gavin chuckled, but the sound was dark and lacked humor. "Oh, man...you really stepped in it."

"Would you just tell me what happened?" Michael demanded.

"Have you told anyone about Quinn?"

Michael clenched his jaw. "No," he said tightly. "I need to speak to her myself before I let my family at her. You should know that. My sisters will eat her alive. But no one will let me near her. The hospital nurses stopped every attempt to get out of bed, I'm under orders not to drive and they actually threatened to sedate me for the ride home if I didn't calm down." Michael pushed his hair out of his face. "My mom's convinced I sustained some kind of brain damage because she's never seen me so upset."

This time the laughter was more genuine. "Man, this'll be a great one for the grandkids someday." Gavin blew out a breath. "Quinn called. She's stranded and didn't have anyone else to call."

"What!" Michael bellowed. "Why didn't she call *me?*"

"Because you left."

Michael fell back against his pillow, the wind sucked from his lungs. "No." He knew...he *knew* what that would mean to Quinn. She would think he abandoned her. After their time at the cabin, the real world had intruded and Quinn would think he'd left her behind, like it had all been pretend.

He'd thought he'd have more time. That she wasn't going to be released for another day or two, but he'd been wrong. No wonder his conscience was kicking his backside right now.

"Come swing by and get me," Michael demanded, throwing off his covers. He swayed slightly when he stood up, but sheer stubbornness had him keeping his feet.

"Are you sure that's a good idea?" Gavin asked. "She might not be too thrilled to see you."

"I need to set the record straight," Michael said. He stumbled to the suitcase his mom had packed and began throwing on the first clothing items he saw. "I'll be out back."

"Sneaking out, are we?" Gavin laughed. "Oh, this is gonna be fun."

"Shut up and just get here," Michael growled.

Gavin's laughter only grew. "Someday, we'll teach you how to threaten like a man," he said. "But today, we have a damsel to rescue. Be there in five."

Michael threw his sister's cell on the bed, then leaned against the post as he put on his clothes. He was done with this. He was done trying to save people's feelings and setting aside his own in the process. If he'd had any idea how quickly Quinn would be released, Michael would have chained himself to the hospital bed if necessary, but no one, not his well-meaning mother, not his overly calm father, not his crazy but lovable sisters, were going to keep him from Quinn.

Quinn would have to adjust to his family quickly, because the stunt that Michael was about to pull would let the cat out of the bag.

There'd be no way to hide his feelings for Quinn after this and very little time to prepare her for what was to come.

But that was alright. Quinn was stronger than she gave herself credit for and they would survive this…together. Exactly the way they were supposed to.

CHAPTER 25

Quinn sat on the edge of her bed. Her legs were antsy and she wanted to walk around, but she still tired easily. "Maybe tired is better than cabin fever," she whispered. She'd been cleared by the doctor, the check out folder was in the plastic bag of things they were sending home with her, and all she needed now was her ride. Which wouldn't be there for…Quinn checked the wall clock. "Fifteen minutes," she grumbled.

So much for resting. She stood and began to pace the room. She couldn't help it. She needed to move even though every muscle in her body screamed for her to lie down. This called for an ice cream coma and a nap this evening.

A curl fell in her face and she tucked it behind her ear, only to have it pop out again. *Stupid hair.*

She paused, her foot skidding just a touch as she remembered how much Michael had said he liked her hair. His hands were always in it. Her curls didn't let him run his fingers through it, but Michael hadn't seemed to care. He had tugged on the ends and looked thoroughly amused as it bounced back.

Quinn had never had someone so fascinated with it before. Her curls had always been a love/hate relationship, but for just a few short days, she had loved them, simply because of the look on Michael's face.

Quinn scowled, rubbing where the movement pulled on her scab. The doctor said she would more than likely have a scar, just like Michael predicted. Luckily, it wouldn't be large, but it would forever be a reminder of her experience surviving a record breaking storm system…and unfortunately, her time with Michael.

Quinn stopped and closed her eyes. Scar or no scar, she wasn't sure she would ever forget what that man had done to her. How he'd pulled down her walls and been sweet enough to help her trust again.

"At least until he showed his true colors," Quinn whispered thickly. This talking to herself was starting to get out of hand. It was just another reminder of just how alone she was in this world. Maybe she needed to get a pet? Riley would be thrilled if Quinn relieved the shelter of a little kitten or puppy.

"Maybe you better figure out if you have enough of a job to feed it," Quinn told herself. She sighed. That was going to be a long road. But she would make it. She wasn't leaving herself any other choice.

A knock on her door had her spinning and she began to smile when she saw Gavin's huge frame come through. It quickly fell, however, when she saw who was behind him.

Gavin stood to the side, holding the door as Michael stayed on the threshold. His skin was pale and he looked ready to fall over, but Quinn wouldn't let herself feel any sympathy for him.

He made his choice.

"Hello, beautiful," Michael said, his voice slightly hoarse.

Quinn held back her wince, even as her heart lurched. She turned to Gavin. "Are you ready to go? My papers have already been signed."

Gavin gave her a small smile. "I'll meet you two in the lobby when you're done."

"Don't you dare," she warned him, but Gavin just waved and left.

Quinn glared at Michael so hard, she kept imagining lasers striking him down, but unfortunately, he never seemed to feel the heat. "What do you want?" she asked.

Michael pushed his hair out of his face. "To explain."

"I think I know enough."

Michael shook his head and shuffled forward "You don't know what happened."

"You left me," Quinn said in clipped tones. "I think I know what happened."

Michael stepped even closer. She watched him straighten his shoulders and slowly rise to his full height. Even though Michael wasn't as big as Gavin, his presence affected Quinn much stronger and she felt herself shrink at the man before her.

How was she ever going to survive without him?

It's not that I can't...it's that I don't want to. And that was the problem. She wanted him. She wanted him in her life. And she wanted him to want her.

"Quinn..." he said softly. His eyes were full of sorrow. "I'm so sorry. I didn't mean to leave you behind." He huffed and stuffed his hands in his pockets. "I want to tell you it was all my family's fault, but it's not fair to blame it all on them." He tilted his head and smiled softly. "Would it help if I told you that the nurses threatened to sedate me if I didn't calm down when they were releasing me?"

Quinn's eyes about popped out of her head and her jaw scraped the ground. "What?" she breathed.

Michael chuckled and the sound warmed her from the ground up. "My mom was intent on getting me home, my sisters wouldn't stop talking, the hospital wouldn't let me visit you and I..." His shoulders dropped and he stepped back, taking all the heat with him. "I never told my family about you, so they didn't know that I wanted to see you."

How many daggers would it take until Quinn's heart just stopped beating altogether?

Michael held up his hands. "But it's not what you think!" he hurried to say. "I..." He shook his head. "My family...they're a lot," he said carefully. "I've told you a little about them. My mom is sweet and quiet, but you mess with her babies and suddenly she's a major mama bear."

Quinn couldn't help the snorting laugh that broke through her lips. She could see the family resemblance. Michael was exactly the same. Quinn hadn't seen any kind of anger or protectiveness in him at all, until it came to…her.

Michael smiled at her response. "And my sisters? Geez." He rubbed the back of his neck. "I'm a little afraid you'll be so scared of them that you'll run for the hills and I'll never see you again."

Quinn's lips were still quirked up as she shook her head. "Oh, ye of little faith."

His laugh was shaky. "That's probably about right." He dropped his hand, and his face grew serious. "Quinn…I really wasn't trying to leave you behind. I wasn't happy about going home, but since the hospital wouldn't let us see each other anyway, I assumed I had a couple of days to figure out how to get back here. I had no idea they'd release you so soon."

Quinn sniffled, her emotions flipping a one-eighty. "You could have called," she said.

"With what?" Micheal held up his hands. "I still don't have a phone. I had to borrow my sister's for Gavin to chew me out and let me know what was going on."

"And just what was going on?" she asked him. She wanted him to say it. *Needed* him to say those words.

He stepped up until they were toe to toe and ran his knuckles along her jawline. "What's going on is that the woman I love is being released from the hospital and I'm trying to come rescue her."

"Rescue?" Quinn hiccuped.

Michael nodded. "I've been fumbling my rescues for days now and nearly got her killed in the process, but I've discovered something." He raised his eyebrows. "Life doesn't have to be perfect for us to find what we need. In fact, sometimes the most unusual circumstances are exactly what will wake us up from the status quo and show us what life is all about."

Quinn had no words. Once again, her wordsmith had stunned her.

He leaned in a little. "Isn't this where you should say you love me back?"

Quinn's shoulders shook as she silently laughed. "I think you took the words out of my mouth." She raised up on her tiptoes, ignoring the pain in her muscles, and wrapped her arms around his neck. With as weak as they both were, Quinn was fully aware they might end up in an ungainly heap on the floor, but she didn't care. "Oh, and one more thing…"

"What's that?" His bright blue eyes were glued to her lips.

"For the five hundred and thirty second time…" Quinn left the briefest kiss on his lips. "Thank you."

* * *

MICHAEL MIGHT HAVE BEEN ACTING like an idiot when he pandered to his family's smothering, but right here, right now, he wasn't about to lose an opportunity this good. His arms wrapped around Quinn's waist and he pulled her in, pressing their mouths back together.

How was it that she seemed so perfectly made for him? He loved how tall she was and that he didn't have to crane his neck to reach her. He loved how she snuggled in so close, trusting him to hold them upright. He loved how she so easily forgave him, even though he hadn't truly said those words.

Shoot.

He pulled back. "I was supposed to say I'm sorry," he panted.

Quinn closed her eyes and rested her forehead against his cheek. "Forgiven," she said softly. Pulling back, she stared at him. "Always."

Michael relaxed and hugged her close. "You're amazing."

"You're going to fall over," she teased.

Michael knew he was swaying slightly. Dang that hypothermia. It had totally zapped his strength and he was struggling to get it and his appetite back.

"Come on," Quinn said, taking his hand. "Let's find Gavin and get out of here."

"I like the second half of that sentence," Michael said as he pulled the door open for her.

Quinn grinned. "Between my concussion and you about to hit the floor, I think it's a good thing we're not driving."

"Miss Peters? Wait!"

They paused as a nurse hurried their way with a wheelchair. "You're not supposed to walk," the woman scolded. "You were supposed to let me know when your ride was here."

Quinn stepped closer to Michael. "I'm fine," she replied. "I can walk."

The nurse raised an eyebrow "Hospital policy." She eyed Michael. "Do I need two of them?"

Michael stiffened his knees. "No," he said firmly. "I'm fine." He looked at Quinn. "Go ahead and sit down. Arguing is futile." He rolled his eyes. "I should know."

Quinn kissed his jaw, then did as she asked and they walked down several hallways until they reached the front of the hospital.

Michael rolled his eyes again as they walked in on Gavin's smirk and the stance he used when he was showing off his muscle. The fire-fighter's arms were folded over his chest, causing his biceps to bulge, and from the glances of the nurses nearby, it was absolutely doing its job.

"Show off," he muttered as they got closer.

Quinn snorted, but bit back her laugh.

Gavin's smirk grew more devious. "Michael, why don't we put you in the back and allow the lady up front?"

"Over my dead body," Michael growled.

The nurse tsked her tongue. "Are you sure you want to go home with these two?" the older woman said, eyeing both Michael and Gavin. "They're a shifty lot."

Quinn's eyes remained glued to Michael's and were dancing with humor. "I trust them with my life," she said easily.

Michael's posturing relaxed.

"And that's exactly why you're riding up front," Gavin huffed. "If you think I'm chauffeuring while you two make googly eyes at each other the whole way home…"

Michael smacked Gavin on the back, ignoring the pain in his arm. "Thank you for your sacrifice." Laughter came from the front desk area and Michael smiled at Gavin's scowl.

Grumbling under his breath, Gavin led the way out to his waiting SUV. Michael headed for the back. Much as he hated to admit it, Gavin's suggestion was good. Quinn would be more comfortable up front.

A clearing of a throat caught his attention.

Michael turned to see Quinn giving him a look. "Forget something?" she asked sweetly. "Again?"

"You don't want the front?" Michael teased, moving to that door. "Awesome! I'll take it."

Quinn squeaked in outrage and Michael laughed. Coming back, he held out his hand to her. "Sweetheart, I will never forget you. I honestly thought you would want to rest in the front seat."

"I think I've discovered just what we need to work on in our relationship," she grumbled at him as she climbed into her seat.

Michael took the opportunity to reach over and buckle her in. Anything to stay close for a few more moments. "And what's that?" he asked cheerily.

She narrowed her eyes. "Our communication."

Michael paused with his face close to hers. "Good thing we have plenty of time to work it out," he said softly.

Quinn's face relaxed and she began to lean into his invitation when Gavin growled.

"Don't even think about it," the firefighter said.

"Too late," Michael replied, winking at Quinn. He finished buckling her and closed the door, walking around to the other side to get into his own seat. Passing Gavin, he gave his friend a smirk. "Jealous?"

"Actually…yes," Gavin shot back.

Michael paused. He'd been teasing, but it seemed like Gavin was serious. "You were interested in Quinn?" he asked quietly.

Gavin shook his head. "Nah…ignore me. I'm being stupid." He climbed in his seat and slammed the driver's side door.

Michael made a mental note to speak to his friend later. Gavin had always been so easy-going, it had never occurred to Michael that his friend might be feeling as restless as Michael had before this whole incident began.

Michael got in his seat and buckled up. *There are a lot of benefits to a small town,* he mused as he took Quinn's hand and rested it on his thigh. *But maybe finding a significant other isn't one of them.*

The problem was…they all knew each other. And yeah, people like Ethan and Maeve had fallen in love back when they were teenagers, but for the most part, the kids Michael knew from growing up were like family to him. Riley, Harper, Brielle…they were younger sisters to Michael. He didn't look at them and want to hold their hands or kiss their mouths. He had taken Brielle to prom when they were in high school, but it had only been as friends.

But Michael had been too caught up in his own worries to realize that others might be feeling just as stifled. He panicked for a brief moment thinking that Gavin might choose to move, the same way Michael had been planning, but then forced himself to relax. If it came to that, Michael would want what was best for his friend. And if Seagull Cove wasn't it…then he'd support that.

Meanwhile…he looked over and smiled at Quinn's closed eyes. She must have still been tired. Unbuckling, Michael slid to the middle and got himself situated, then brought Quinn into his shoulder.

"Thank you," she murmured as she snuggled into his shoulder.

"Always," Michael replied.

"For the five hundred and thirty third time," she murmured before slipping into sleep once more.

Michael caught Gavin's eye in the rearview mirror and smiled.

Gavin shook his head, but was grinning. "Lucky jerk."

Michael nodded. "I know," he said softly, turning to look out at the passing scenery. "I know."

CHAPTER 26

Quinn fussed with yet another curl that wouldn't lay down right. She growled. Michael had managed to hold off his family for two days to let Quinn recover and "prepare" as he put it, to handle the craziness they would bring.

"So why, today of all days, is my hair being so stubborn!" she muttered to her reflection.

Her heart had been pounding hard all morning and Quinn was positive her blood pressure was higher than was safe. Michael was such a sweet, down to earth guy, it worried her a little that he kept talking about needing to be ready for his family.

From his stories, Quinn was sure that the sisters were a handful, but surely his parents were good, calm people? Michael had to have gotten his instincts and behavior from somewhere!

But his unrelenting insistence had Quinn walking on tiptoe. She blew out a breath, causing the curl in question to shift and float in the small breeze, but it still refused to lay down with the rest of its family.

"I give up." Quinn threw her hands in the air and stalked out of the bathroom. The Dunlaps could hate her if they wanted, but today was simply *not* going to be a good hair day.

A knock came at the door, a signal that Quinn recognized as

Michael's and she ran over, throwing the door open. With a cry of greeting, she threw herself into his arms, wrapping herself around his torso.

"Wow," Michael breathed into her neck. "If I'd known taking you to dinner with my family was going to bring this kind of reaction, I'd have let the lions loose a long time ago."

Quinn laughed softly and pulled back. "They can't be that bad," she insisted, though they'd been over this argument many times.

Michael made a face and pushed his hair back. He still hadn't cut it in the couple of days since they'd gotten home, but Quinn wasn't sure she wanted him to. His hair was thick and soft and she enjoyed running her fingers through it. Having a little extra length might be a good idea.

Apparently, we're both obsessed with each other's hair, she thought wryly.

"They're good people," he said, bringing up the exact same words he'd used yesterday. "But they're...a lot." He smiled. "My mom is so excited to meet you she can barely talk straight."

Quinn closed her eyes and shook her head. "I'm sure it's all going to be fine. I get along with Aspen and Maeve and Estelle."

"True," Michael murmured. "But you haven't met my sisters yet."

There went that rapid heartbeat again. His sisters. The ones who always called Michael boring and had made him feel inadequate through all his growing up. Quinn kind of wanted to hide from them, and she kind of wanted to slap them silly.

How could they treat someone so wonderful as if he were nothing?

Swallowing down her doubt, Quinn ran her fingers through his hair. After all, Michael had already messed it up. She was just putting it back into place, right? "I'm sure it'll be fine," she said again. "I can handle a couple of young women."

Michael snorted. "Well...I'll be there anyway, so between the two of us, hopefully we can manage to keep them at bay."

"You handled Adam," Quinn said as Michael helped her put on her coat. "This should be a piece of cake."

"*You* handled Adam," Michael corrected her. "I'm still amazed at how well you did at holding him off even though you were hooked up to an IV and stuff."

Quinn squeezed. "I'm just glad he finally got desperate enough that he showed his hand in a way that gave us witnesses."

Michael nodded, a frown on his face. "I hate that it happened at all," he said softly.

Quinn gave him a sad smile. "Me too." She raised her eyebrows at him. "But at least it brought me to you."

Michael smiled and leaned down to give her a slow, sweet kiss. Goodness, Quinn couldn't get enough of those. She loved how soft and tender he was with her. Even after she had pushed him away for nothing more than having blonde hair and blue eyes, he stayed steady and kind and those were some of her favorite pieces of his personality.

"Quit distracting me," he said as he pulled back. "I'm supposed to bring you to the house on consequence of family banishment."

"After all your warnings the last few days, I'm surprised that's a worthy consequence for you," Quinn teased. She locked the door behind them, only stuttering a little with the desire to double and triple check it. Michael's calm presence and Adam's imprisonment were already helping her heal.

"And lose my mom's cinnamon rolls? Are you crazy?" Michael asked. He grinned as he helped her into the passenger side of his truck. The truck that now had brand new tires and had been brought back just last night.

Quinn's car, on the other hand, was going to take a lot more work. She'd been afraid to look at it when it had been towed into town yesterday, but Michael had been with her. He'd gotten a week off from work in order to recover and they found that they were using much of their time to fix all the details from the ordeal, such as cars, getting a hold of the cabin owner, and filling out insurance claims.

The process had only begun and Quinn was already thoroughly sick of it, but Michael had sat by her the whole time and working together had made it all much more endurable.

The drive to his family's inn was only about ten minutes long, but it was enough to allow Quinn's anxiety to come rushing to the front again. Why, oh why, couldn't she at least have had confidence in her hair tonight? If a woman was going to be facing the eager family of the man she loved, the least fate could do was let her be confident in her looks.

"Hang on, beautiful," he said as he slipped out his door. "I'll get your door."

Quinn sat still, wringing her hands. It didn't even faze her anymore when Micheal called her beautiful. He'd proven himself time and time again that when he said the words, it wasn't because he was obsessed with her looks. He was always very clear that her beauty was inside and out and he loved her for it.

He opened her door and held out a hand. "Ready to tackle yet another challenge?"

Quinn shook her head. "Nope. I changed my mind."

He smiled and leaned in, caging her in the seat. "I know I made a big deal out of this all week, but they're going to love you." He kissed the tip of her nose. "The same way I do." He gave her a smirk. "No one can help it."

She gave him a light push. "That's not true."

"It is." He unbuckled her belt and helped her climb down. "You're stunning, you're smart, and you're the bravest person I know. Falling in love with you was inevitable."

Quinn leaned her head on his shoulder. "You really should be a writer, you know."

He turned and kissed the top of her head. "No point," he whispered against her curls. "My words are for you and you alone."

* * *

MICHAEL KISSED the top of her head one more time, then reached for the doorknob. He wanted to take Quinn's hand and run her back to his apartment, not let his sisters at her.

They were fun, but ruthless at times. Michael knew his mom might overreact at first, but Quinn would eventually love his mother the same way Michael did. His dad would stay easy through the whole situation. But his sisters? Yeah…they had no filter and both of them relished it. Michael might not care about how they treated him, but he already could feel his protective instincts flaring at the thought of them hurting Quinn.

Taking a fortifying breath, he stepped inside, bracing himself for impact. "They'll be in the kitchen," he said. "We only have two guests at the inn at the moment and they ate an hour ago so that we could hold this dinner for you."

He could hear the voices coming from the other side of the house and wondered if he should warn Quinn that his close family weren't the only ones there tonight. Michael had noticed a lot of cars in the parking lot and knew that Aspen, Austin, Maeve, Ethan and probably Estelle were all there tonight as well. He figured Aunt Emory and Uncle Tony were still at home since Uncle Tony rarely left the house, but otherwise, they were going to be bombarded tonight.

"Quinn!"

Too late.

Aspen walked briskly into the entryway and threw her arms around Quinn. "I'm so glad you're okay," Michael's cousin said in a thick tone. She was sniffling as she pulled back and wiped at her eyes.

Quinn smiled, then stepped back and took Michael's hand again. "Thanks. Me too."

Aspen laughed through her tears. "No one told me you were at the hospital," she said, giving an accusing glare to Michael. "If I'd known, I would have snuck you cake as well."

"You got cake?" Quinn said aghast, looking at Michael. "And you didn't share?"

Michael shrugged. "It was already contraband stuff. I was afraid it would get taken away if I smuggled any to you."

Not to mention, they refused to let me get up and see you. He was still ticked about that one. The hospital staff kept telling him that they didn't want her over-stimulated and that he had to heal himself, so they kept him from visiting. But it had simply been cruel and unusual punishment in his mind.

Quinn dug her elbow playfully into his side. "Just for that, I'm expecting you to treat me to a slice another time."

"Deal."

"Don't worry," Aspen said with a wide smile. "Did you really think we would have a family dinner and I not bring dessert?"

Quinn blanched. "Family dinner?" she asked softly. "As in...*all* of you are here?"

Yep. He definitely should have warned her when he saw the cars.

Michael squeezed her hand. "Sorry. I didn't know they were all coming."

Quinn leaned into him. "It's okay," she wheezed.

"Quinn!" Aspen cried. "You're not scared of us, are you?" She tugged on Quinn's free hand, yanking her from Michael's grasp. "You've already been a friend, now you're just taking another step to be part of the family. Come on. They'll love you!"

Michael hurried after them, knowing there would be no stopping the Aspen train now. She was almost as forceful as his sisters, though Aspen had grown up enough to not be quite as...harsh...about how she dealt with things.

"She's here!" Aspen announced as they entered the gathering room.

The extra large room was filled to the brim and Michael had to stop himself from backing out. This was his family and it was already too much. He searched the mob as they stared at Quinn and forced himself to step forward. *Man up, idiot,* he told himself. "Everyone...this is Quinn." He smiled down at her, not missing the terrified look in her eyes. "She's the most perfect woman I know." He glanced up. "Sorry, Mom."

The crowd chuckled.

"But I'm bringing her to meet everyone because I trust you all to be nice..." He raised an eyebrow at his sisters. They smiled innocently. "And because when she finally does join this family, officially, she'll know exactly what she's getting into."

Quinn gasped up at him at the exact same time the rest of the family did. That might have been a little bit more information than he'd offered previously.

"What?" she breathed.

Michael smiled down at her. "Did you really think I would let go after getting to know you?" He leaned a little closer. "Unless you want me to let go, of course."

Her light eyes were wide with wonder. "It's just…so fast."

He shrugged. "This isn't a proposal. Just a warning." He made a pointed look sideways. "To them." He came back to her. "And to you. Eventually, when the time is right. We'll make this official. Until then, we're just a couple of people, dating and enjoying getting to know each other on a deeper level with each passing day."

Quinn's smile was slow, but bright. "I'm going to start writing down everything you say. Who would have thought I'd find such a poet in Seagull Cove, Oregon, of all places?"

He kissed her forehead. "As long as you don't go running for the hills, I don't care."

"Quinn?"

Michael leaned back, recognizing his mother's voice.

Hope Dunlap was a beautiful woman. Soft spoken, and elegant in her poise and dress. Michael had no doubt his dad had been completely smitten when he'd met her for the second time.

Right now, her eyes were pleading as she held out her hand. "It's so good to meet you. I've always prayed that Michael would bring home someone just like you."

Quinn smiled. "It's good to meet you too. Thank you for sharing your son with me."

Michael's mom made a little cry and lunged, hugging Quinn tightly.

MIchael panicked until he noticed Quinn squeezing his mother just as hard as his mother was squeezing Quinn.

"Thank you," his mom whispered. "And I'm so sorry for everything you went through." She pulled back, cupping Quinn's face. "But he's gone and you're here and you're not alone anymore."

Quinn's bottom lip trembled and the women hugged again, both of them with tears streaming down their cheeks. .

Michael felt a small trickle of guilt. *She needs this,* he realized. He should have recognized just how much Quinn needed the strong support of a family. She had no parents, no mentors, no siblings...and Michael brought so much family, it was kind of obnoxious, to the table.

"My turn," a deep, gruff voice interrupted. Michael's dad, Enoch, gently disentangled his wife and reached out to offer a firm hug to Quinn as well. "We're glad to have you here," he said, offering his usual steady strength.

Quinn wiped at her eyes. "Thank you," she said with a small laugh. "I'm sorry I'm such a mess."

"Well, who wouldn't be?" a voice said, coming up behind Michael's parents.

Michael stiffened. *And, here we go.* "Delilah," he warned.

His sister held up her hand. "Easy, bro. We got this." She smiled at Quinn, then gave her a fierce hug. "Welcome. We're so excited to meet you." Stepping back, Delilah wrapped her arm through Quinn's and began to walk. "Have we got some stories for you!"

Michael shook his head as Ruby trailed after them, laughing with mischievous glee. Every embarrassing moment he'd ever had was about to be rehashed and he couldn't find it in himself to care. Let them talk.

He'd meant it when he said Quinn was going to be part of their family...unless she decided otherwise. His heart and mind were made up and he couldn't imagine his life without her. When he was sure she felt the same, then he would make his move. But until then, he'd let his family smother her with love and affection. It seemed to be just what the doctor ordered.

CHAPTER 27

Quinn had never felt so claustrophobic…and so wonderful. The only thing that surpassed it was spending alone time with Michael. Her small family growing up had done nothing to prepare her for a family like this one.

But despite the anxiety still thrumming through her system, she couldn't seem to stop the smile that was sitting on her face. It had become a permanent fixture, even with Michael's sisters, who were indeed a handful.

After showering her with stories of Michael as an awkward teen and threatening to pull out naked baby pictures, the girls left her in Michael's care, which was tender despite the scowl on his face.

"Doing okay?" Michael whispered, leaning over against her ear.

Quinn's mouth was full of food, so she simply turned and smiled at him. After swallowing, she managed to respond, "They're great. A lot. But great."

He rolled his eyes. "They are good people, I suppose." His eyes roamed the large table, which was so full that elbows were whacking every time someone took a bite.

"I can't imagine what it was like to grow up with this," Quinn said as she put another bite in her mouth. "Mmm…" She closed her eyes. "And your Aunt Emory can cook like a professional."

Michael chuckled. "She was. She went to culinary school and learned to bake. Her husband, Uncle Tony, was a chocolate sculptor. Sorry if I forgot to mention that."

Quinn nodded. "You didn't. It came up once at the cabin, I think. Funny enough, I've heard of him." She paused, hesitating.

"Go ahead," Michael said. "Ask away."

Quinn squished her lips to the side. "I can see he's sick."

Michael nodded.

"Is it okay to ask what he has?"

Michael wiped his mouth on a napkin. "Yeah. Of course." He leaned his arms on the table, getting a little closer to her. "He's got Parkinson's disease."

"Ah." Quinn nodded. "I wondered, because of the shaking."

"Yeah…it's pretty noticeable, huh?"

Quinn gave him a sad smile.

"I actually am surprised to see them here," Michael said in an even softer tone. "Uncle Tony doesn't get out of the house much, so I assumed you would have to meet him later."

Quinn looked over to see Michael's Aunt Emory feed her husband another bite of food and the way they looked at each other nearly broke Quinn's heart. She wanted a love like that. Michael's fingertips grazed her cheek and Quinn's eyes jerked to meet his.

I might already have it.

She blinked, but the look didn't go away. Michael was absolutely looking at her like she was the most precious gift in the world and instead of being freaked out, Quinn wanted to lean in and hold on for all she was worth.

"You're gonna burn the inn down if you don't knock it off," a voice shout-whispered, breaking hers and Michael's moment.

"Shut up, Jay," Michael muttered, the tips of his ears turning red. He leaned back from Quinn and put his focus back on the food.

Michael's cousin leaned around Michael to grin at Quinn. She knew Jayden a little. He seemed like the class clown type and they'd crossed paths when Quinn had joined in on friend activities with Aspen and Maeve.

"Hey, Quinn. I haven't had a chance to speak to you tonight."

Quinn smiled. Annoying as the interruption was, nobody could be upset around Jayden. His goofiness was fun rather than obnoxious. "Hello, Jayden. How have you been?"

"Good, good." He nodded, then tilted his head toward Michael. "You know…I have some information about this dork that you might want to hear."

Michael pushed against the table, leaning back in his seat and rolling his eyes to the ceiling. "Here we go."

Jace snickered. "Dude…someone has to warn her."

"Warn me about what?" Quinn asked, though she had a good idea. Michael's parents might be quieter, but there was no mistaking the fact that mischief ran in the family. Michael's sisters and Jayden all seemed to get an abundance of it.

"Jayden Gordon," a female voice snapped. "Don't you dare try to run that girl off."

Quinn pinched her lips together to try and keep from laughing. Isabella Henry, Jayden's mom, was probably the actual root of all those troublesome genetics. The woman was a little loud, definitely opinionated, but somehow…completely endearing.

Michael had mentioned that Mrs. Gordon had been a reporter before she got married, so it made sense that she was a little more forward than everyone else.

"Aw, Mom…you know me better than that," Jayden said with a charming grin. He rocked his chair back on two legs.

"Four on the floor," Mr. Gordon said with a raised eyebrow.

"Gonna arrest me?" Jayden teased.

His dad snorted, but Michael's sisters squealed in delight. "Do it, Uncle Hank!"

"On what charges?" Jayden argued.

"For acting like a two year old," Uncle Tony piped up in his shaky tone.

The table broke out in laughter and the ribbing continued.

Quinn could barely keep up. It was like a tennis match, except there were a dozen people on the court instead of two. Her whiplash was going to last forever if she kept having to try to follow the shouts and teasing.

"Ready to run yet?" Michael whispered, his arm slung on the back of her chair.

"Not yet," Quinn whispered back, resting her hand on his knee. "I have to see who wins."

Michael laughed. He kissed her temple. "You're amazing."

"Me? You grew up with this much chaos and still managed to turn out as good as you did?" Quinn tsked her tongue and shook her head. "You're the amazing one."

Michael's chuckle continued. Quinn loved the sound. His family was fun and she was completely serious about how wonderful it was, but she was also thrilled that Michael wasn't the center of the action.

She understood better than ever why he'd wanted to prepare her for this. Her quiet upbringing could never have her imagining just what a scene like this would entail, and it was great, but Quinn would also be very happy to go back to her quiet evenings with Michael, curled up with a book or in front of a movie.

He took her hand and kissed the back of it. "Come on," he whispered. "We can go get some fresh air while they're all busy."

Quinn's smile couldn't be contained as she and Michael snuck away from the playful squabbling going on. She tripped happily behind Michael as he led her into the kitchen, then down a hallway and finally into a laundry room.

"Why are we in the laundry room?" Quinn asked, glancing around. The smell of detergent was pleasing but pungent and there was a long line of clothes hanging against one wall. Was this the only place in the house that they could get a little peace? It seemed an odd spot for a man to bring a woman.

Michael grinned and pumped his eyebrows. "Because of this." With a little work, he pushed open a door in the wall, causing Quinn to gasp.

"What?" she breathed, stepping forward. "A secret passage?"

Michael nodded and tilted his head. "It's a little stuffy, but go on in and I'll show you around."

Quinn wrinkled her nose. "It's dark."

He reached behind him and grabbed a flashlight, turning it on. "Ready for a little adventure?"

Quinn laughed. "With you? Always."

* * *

MICHAEL HELD onto Quinn's hand and carefully guided her up the stairs and through the skinny hallways until they reached the secret room in the attic. He sighed as they got inside, enjoying the sight of one of his favorite places in the whole house.

Everyone in his family knew about the secret room and as children, he and all his cousins had spent endless hours playing between the walls.

But eventually, the novelty wore off and Michael had been given permission to make it his own. So as a teenager, he'd maneuvered a couple of chairs, a coffee table, a mini fridge, and three very large bookcases through the walls of the house until he'd created his own private nook.

Since moving into the apartment above the shop, he didn't spend as much time here as he used to. It had been a gift when escaping from his little sisters, but during the last couple of days, Michael had cleaned it out, stocked the fridge and brought in a few soft touches.

A basket full of soft blankets now sat in the corner and a couple of candles waited to be lit on the coffee table. His mom had helped him pick out a rug to put under the couch, so the floor was soft and inviting, and Michael watched with amusement as Quinn took off her shoes and flexed her toes in the shag carpet.

"This place is amazing," she whispered.

Michael came up behind her and wrapped his arms around her waist. "It's a little nicer than the cabin, isn't it?"

Quinn leaned into his chest and laughed. "That's an understatement. But there's something to be said for a fireplace on a cool winter night."

Michael let go of her and went over to the candles, getting them lit. "Close enough?" he asked.

Quinn grinned. "Close enough." She walked toward him and Michael held open his arms, welcoming her inside.

It was like she was made for that exact spot. Never had a woman so fully filled his arms in such a satisfying way and once again Michael wondered that he'd ever survived without her.

"Thank you," he said into her hair, nuzzling against the soft curls. The minty smell of her shampoo made him want to stay there forever. He'd never known he had such a thing for hair until he met Quinn… but he wasn't complaining.

"Did you just smell my hair?" she asked, laughter in her voice.

"I plead the fifth."

Quinn spun in his arms. "You're ridiculous."

He smiled.

"So…tell me the story about this room."

Michael's eye wandered around the space. "Well, it all starts with a foster runaway and my mom being accused of theft."

Quinn's eyes widened. "You're joking."

Michael shook his head, smirking. "Nope."

Quinn pulled out of his arms and yanked him toward the couch, where she burrowed into his chest. "Okay. Go ahead. I'm ready."

He laughed, causing her to bounce slightly. "Are you sure? Do you want a blanket first?"

"You'll keep me warm," she said confidently. "Go for it."

Michael leaned his head back, fully relaxing in their slouched position, and proceeded to share the story of how his parents met, which ultimately was his aunts' and uncles' love stories as well.

The tales had been passed down to the kids like legends and was the main reason they were all so close. Technically, Emory and Belle were his mom's cousins, making them cousins of Michael as well, which meant Aspen, Jayden and everyone else were his second cousins, but the adventure that led to all of the couples getting married brought them closer than siblings and they'd all stayed in Seagull Cove, raising their families together.

"Wow," Quinn breathed when Michael finished. "That's quite a tale." She paused. "And this space became yours?"

"We all played here when we were little," he explained. "But it became my sanctuary as we started getting older."

"A place to escape the twins?"

"Bingo."

Quinn sighed and Michael felt her melt into him. "I could get used to this place."

He hesitated, but ultimately couldn't hold it back. "We could decorate a space in our home like this someday." He held his breath, eager but terrified of her response. They hadn't had a chance to talk about his announcement earlier, though Quinn's acceptance of his family had encouraged Michael to believe she wasn't completely opposed to the idea.

"Unless I'm very much mistaken, Mr. Wordsmith," Quinn said in a flirty tone, "you have yet to propose to me."

Michael picked up a curl and twisted it around his finger. "If I was sure you'd say yes, I'd ask right now."

She stiffened, then slowly sat up, and the curl popped off his finger with the movement. "We've only known each other a couple of weeks," she said breathlessly.

Michael nodded. "And I'll stand by my words, that I would never rush or force you. If this very second you told me you were done with me, I'd let you go, though it would break me to do it."

Quinn's jaw dropped.

"But I also know myself," Michael continued. "I've never felt like this for anyone before and I'm positive that I'll never find anything quite so perfect ever again." He ran his knuckles along her jaw, loving the softness of her skin. "I've waited a long time for someone like you, Quinn Peters, and I'll continue to wait as long as I have to until you say you feel the same."

Quinn blinked several times and her eyes grew glassy. "Was that the proposal?" she whispered.

"Do you want it to be?"

She chewed on her bottom lip, then gave a short jerky nod.

Fire exploded in Michael's chest and his body leapt into awareness. She wanted him to propose? She was ready to move ahead? It was mind blowing. He'd been prepared to wait months, possibly even a year before asking for her hand, but if she wanted to take the next step, he wasn't about to stop her.

Working hard to control his anticipation and eagerness, Michael sat up straight, then slid off the couch. "Quinn Peters," he said, his tone husky. "My beautiful, brave, intelligent companion. I know it's fast. I know we were thrown together in a way that many people will never understand and I know that some might think we're crazy, but, besides the obvious, there are a few things I've discovered in the last couple of weeks." He swallowed hard, praying that his word skills wouldn't fail him in this moment.

"I've discovered that being patient brings great dividends," Michael said with a teasing smile. "I've discovered that beautiful, wonderful things can come from frightening, horrific situations." He tucked a curl behind her ear. "I've discovered that snow in the off season can be a blessing—"

Quinn snorted a short laugh.

"And that bad weather provides the best cuddling opportunities." He wrinkled his nose. "I've also discovered that I hate beef stew."

Her laughter was the best incentive to keep going.

"And most of all, I've discovered that while the perfect woman doesn't exist...the perfect woman *for me* does."

Her bottom lip began to tremble.

"And while I cannot guarantee to never be boring or to always say the right thing, I can guarantee I will always...*always*... put you first. Your safety, your health, your success, it means so much more to me to see you rise above than I ever got out of my own work. And if you would deign to let me continue to watch you conquer the world, one antique sale at a time, I'd consider myself the luckiest man alive." Michael cleared his throat. "Quinn...will you marry me?"

Quinn wiped at her face. "I think I'd keep you around, just to hear you speak," she teased. "I've never felt so loved, so protected and so *seen* as when I'm with you."

"You realize I'm jumping the gun," Michael hedged. "I don't have a ring."

Quinn shook her head and cupped his face. "I don't need the ring. I just need you to know that while I've spent the last couple years of my life trying to hide, I'll never not be grateful that you brought me back to life." She gave him a soft kiss, smiling when he made a protesting sound at her retreat. "Yes, Michael. I'll marry you. Because I've also discovered a couple of things."

He raised his eyebrows, waiting for her to continue. His muscles were bunched and ready to celebrate as soon as she was done responding.

Quinn brushed his hair away from his forehead. "I've discovered that family support is amazing." She grinned when he rolled his eyes. "I've discovered that being seen by the right person makes all the difference." She leaned in close, letting them share air for just a moment, which made Michael's heart rate triple. "And I've discovered that while I'm strong enough to take care of myself...I'm happiest when we take care of each other."

Michael was done waiting. If she had more to say, it would have to wait because if he didn't kiss her right now, he was going to keel over.

Leaning up, he pressed his lips to hers, banding his arms around her and showing her with every part of him just how much he loved her and was grateful she had agreed to be his.

When their lips broke for the slightest second, Quinn sighed and Michael took the opportunity to join her on the couch where he could hold her better and take complete advantage of the fact that they were alone. Over and over again, he kept his words to himself and used his actions to celebrate their upcoming life together.

"Knock, knock! I brought cake!"

Michael jerked back from Quinn, his chest heaving as his cousin opened the door on them.

"Oh my gosh," Aspen said with an embarrassed laugh.

"Pay up," Austin said from behind her.

Aspen shot a look over her shoulder and when Michael stood up, he realized his cousins were all standing out in the hallway. He looked down at Quinn, with her swollen lips and mussed hair and slowly shook his head. "Sorry," he mouthed.

Quinn covered her face, laughing into her hands.

"Are we going in or not?" Maeve demanded.

"Um…" Aspen made a face.

Michael closed his eyes and waved them in. "Come on," he said, then cleared his throat when his tone gave away what he'd just been caught doing.

Aspen moved in and her husband, followed by her siblings, plus Ethan and Jayden, filed through the small doorway. The room was suddenly packed. Michael sat down on the couch, making himself as big as possible. They might be coming in, but they could all pull up floor space for all he cared.

Quinn tucked into his side, her face bright red.

Aspen gave them a sheepish grin.

"I said pay up!" Austin said again.

"Austin!" Aspen scolded.

Ethan rolled his eyes and grabbed his wallet out of his back pocket before slapping some money in Austin's hand. "Michael…all these years I thought you were so straight laced." Ethan shook his head, then grinned and winked. "I'm glad to know I was wrong."

"Oh my word, stop." Estelle moaned as she plunked down on the floor. "Aspen, serve that cake before Quinn dies of embarrassment. You guys are all a bunch of crazies."

Michael tightened his hold on Quinn. "You sure you want to be a part of this?"

Quinn snuggled closer. "If it means being with you? Always."

EPILOGUE

Gavin tried not to fidget. His best friend was getting married and it was not a good time to act like a restless two year old. Especially since Gavin was standing at the front of the church as the best man.

"I now pronounce you man and wife," the preacher said with a smile.

Despite the whoops and hollers that followed the couple kissing, all Gavin could feel was relief. His tie was choking him, he was sweating like a pig in his suit, the air in the church apparently hadn't moved in twenty years, and the lovey-dovey scene going on in front of him was making him slightly nauseous.

You're jealous.

Much as he would like to, Gavin had no argument for the stupid voice in his head. It was right.

He *was* jealous.

That was supposed to have been him. Not that Gavin was in love with Quinn or begrudged Michael his happy ending. It was simply *having* a happy ending that was the struggle.

A hand slapped his back and Gavin glared at Jayden's grinning face.

"You're supposed to look like you want to be here," Jayden said out of the corner of his mouth. "Stop being such a sourpuss and pretend like this is your favorite thing ever."

Gavin rolled his eyes. "I'm not that bad," he muttered.

Jayden gave him a look as they made their way down from the front stand in the church. "Dude, you look like someone poured lemon juice in your breakfast cereal."

Gavin gave Jayden a small push with his elbow. "Watch it, or I'll take you out back."

"Geez," Jayden whined, rubbing his shoulder. "What are you bench pressing now? Semi trucks?"

Gavin smirked. It was true. He'd gotten quite a bit bigger in the last year. *Yeah...because you have nothing else to do but lift weights,* that sarcastic voice shot out again.

"If you didn't waste your time running around taking pictures of butterflies, you might be able to impress the ladies as well."

Jayden scoffed. "If it was actually my goal to get female attention, believe you me, friend, I wouldn't have any trouble."

Gavin chuckled and shook his head. "And yet here you are...a single pringle...*friend.*"

"Single pringle?" Jayden made a face. "What are you? Twelve?"

Gavin gave Jayden another push.

"Why do you feel the need to solve everything with violence?" Jayden groaned.

"Gentlemen," Mrs. Dunlap scolded, coming up beside them. "We're trying to gather for pictures?" It might have been phrased as a question, but there was no denying the expectation behind the words.

Gavin gave Michael's mom his best smile. "I couldn't exactly walk over there unless I had the most beautiful woman in the room on my arm, now could I?"

Mrs. Dunlap blushed and laughed before shaking her finger at Gavin. "Little Gavin, if I didn't know you so well, I'd say you were quite a charmer." She was one of the few people who still got away with calling Gavin by his childhood nickname.

Jayden snorted.

Mrs. Dunlap rolled her eyes. "I *do* know you, Jayden. And I think maybe you should take lessons from Gavin."

Jayden gaped and blustered, but Gavin could only laugh. He loved Michael's family. Gavin's family had moved away from the Oregon Coast during his college years and were determined to never come back, which suited Gavin just fine. They had originally moved to the area when he was little because of his father's work.

They had left because the small town life had felt stifling.

Gavin completely disagreed...most of the time. He loved their town. He loved it enough that after school he'd come back and joined their district as a volunteer firefighter until he was able to get through the academy and be hired officially, despite the disdain of his family who hated that he was wasting the education they'd provided him with.

But lately? Lately he'd understood their need for more.

At one point in time, Gavin had had the world at his fingertips. He'd been top of his class, following in his father's footsteps to become a financial advisor, the job offers were pouring in and the most beautiful woman in his college was hanging on his arm.

But right before graduation, just as Gavin had been ready to celebrate a proposal and a graduation...well...

He shook his head and offered his arm to Mrs. Dunlap. "Shall we?" he asked.

Michael's mom put her hand on his elbow and tapped his forearm. "Little Gavin...I think perhaps we need to make sure you're next."

Gavin shook his head. "Nice as that thought is," he said while navigating the crowd, "I don't think being settled down is for me."

"What about me?" Jayden asked from behind them.

"You need to grow up a bit more," Mrs. Dunlap told her nephew.

Jayden grumbled and while Gavin enjoyed the familial ribbing, he focused on simply putting one foot in front of the other.

Several years ago, he would have agreed with Mrs. Dunlap. The woman who was like a mother to him. He'd wanted a wife and a family and to be just like his best friend Michael, who had more family than he knew what to do with.

But life hadn't been kind and despite the jealousy coursing through Gavin's system, he had no desire to open himself up to the heartache he was certain would follow if he tried again.

Once was definitely enough.

"Give it time," Mrs. Dunlap said softly, glancing up at him and continuing their conversation. "It heals all wounds."

Gavin gave her a smile, but there was no hope or humor in it. He came from stock that prized money and power over family and he seemed destined to be affected by it…no matter how much he wanted otherwise.

"You know, usually we're waiting on the bride and groom," Michael said, sauntering over as the small group emerged from the church. He gave his cousin a look. "Not the photographer."

Gavin looked at Jayden, who smirked. "Some things are worth waiting for," Jayden shot back before walking toward his pile of equipment.

Mrs. Dunlap let go of Gavin and walked away with her son, leaving Gavin by himself, in the middle of a large crowd. *Some things might be worth waiting for,* his inner voice grumbled. *But some are also worth avoiding. Good thing I know the difference.*

Don't miss Gavin's story next in "The Sweetest Season"